ANTIQUES HUNTER'S Death on the Red Sea

C. L. Miller started working life in publishing as an editorial assistant for her mother, Judith Miller, on the *Miller's Antiques Price Guide* and as a researcher for the *Antiques Hunter's Guide to Europe*, and then went into hospitality and events. After she had children, she decided to follow her long-held dream of becoming an author and began writing full time. She was an Undiscovered Voices 2022 winner and showcased in the UV 2022 anthology.

C. L. lives in a medieval cottage in Dedham Vale, Suffolk, with her family.

Also in this series

The Antique Hunter's Guide to Murder

THE ANTIQUE HUNTER'S Death on the Red Sea

C. L. MILLER

PAN BOOKS

First published 2025 by Macmillan

This paperback edition first published 2025 by Pan Books
an imprint of Pan Macmillan
The Smithson, 6 Briset Street, London EC1M 5NR
EU representative: Macmillan Publishers Ireland Ltd, 1st Floor,
The Liffey Trust Centre, 117–126 Sheriff Street Upper,
Dublin 1 D01 YC43
Associated companies throughout the world

ISBN 978-1-0350-2177-2

1 3 5 7 9 8 6 4 2

A CIP catalogue record for this book is available from the British Library.

Illustrations © Adobe Stock 201953939 Rawpixel.com

Typeset in Janson Text LT Std by Six Red Marbles UK, Thetford, Norfolk
Printed and bound in the UK using 100% Renewable Electricity by CPI Group (UK) Ltd

MIX
Paper | Supporting
responsible forestry
FSC
www.fsc.org   FSC® C116313

Visit **www.panmacmillan.com** to read more about
all our books and to buy them.

*For anyone who seeks the courage to try
a different path in life.*

'Truth is rarely pure and never simple'

Oscar Wilde

Prologue

Phil

One year earlier, The Embankment, London

Arthur Crockleford sat on a bench overlooking the murky waters of the Thames as it swept under the Hungerford Bridge and lapped against the Embankment. Heavy grey clouds darkened the sky above him, and the damp wind picked up an old chocolate bar wrapper and bounced it down the pavement. His arm was stretched over the back of the bench in a casual pose, but his jaw was clenched.

Phil had been studying Arthur from a distance, searching for clues as to why he had demanded a meeting out of the blue. With Arthur everything was methodical and precise; nothing was a coincidence.

'Everything all right?' Phil asked as he approached. His friend had bags under his eyes and was thinner than the last time they'd met.

Arthur pulled his arm back and tugged nervously at his cuff while he scanned a group of tourists who had stopped to take a photo overlooking the river. 'I've heard there is to be a succession . . . The Collector is stepping down and a new one will be chosen.'

The Collector?

Phil froze.

The last time he had heard the name was at a meeting with Interpol five months before; a Shakespearean First Folio printed in 1623 – one of only eighty-three known in existence – had been stolen from a private collector in New York. One of the younger agents, Sloane, stated that she'd heard the Folio had been trafficked to the United Kingdom on the same day. The theft was meticulously planned, and the only lead they had was CCTV recording of a white van leaving the scene. When the van was discovered days later, it had been torched. All that they discovered, a few paces from the wreck, was a broken key chain of a serpent eating its own tail.

'I'm sorry, I . . .' Phil ran a hand over his face, trying to clear his thoughts, and slumped on the bench next to Arthur. 'Let me get this straight. You're implying you believe The Collector is real? Like, one man is responsible for all those million-dollar thefts spanning hundreds of years!' He shook his head and searched Arthur's face for answers. 'Most believe that he's a myth . . . a legend of the black market . . .'

'Most do, but *you* don't.' Arthur gave Phil a knowing look.

Phil ignored the statement – he wasn't going to discuss his old partner, Ed, the folder tucked away at the bottom of Ed's desk drawer, or his decades-old theories. Theories that had always been laughed off. 'Keep talking.'

'Straight to the point, as always.' When Phil glared at him, Arthur sighed. 'Very well. Remember the Ming Dynasty vase stolen from a Greek museum back in 2001? The one I was employed to track down?' Phil blinked slowly. How could he have forgotten? Arthur continued, 'I ended up in Jordan, where

I believed a sale was to take place at sea. The vase was so rare I still wonder what sum they had placed on it. Definitely in the millions. Throughout my investigation The Collector's name came up repeatedly until it was hard to dismiss the idea that there might be some truth to the stories of the legendary antique thief.

'My main contact back then was Chris Prince – I saw him as a low-level thug for hire with no real interest in antiques or antiquities. Although, with all the information he provided, I suspected that he worked for The Collector – or people associated with him – and was on the boat transporting the vase. When it was destroyed in a fire, I believed he was one of the four men who perished.'

Phil wove his fingers together and tried to shut down the memories – but decades couldn't take away the overpowering smell of gas and burning wood. Or the nauseating panic as he tried to get his small fishing boat close enough to search for survivors and smoke hit the back of his throat.

'Phil?' Arthur reached out and patted his hand, bringing his attention back to the Embankment. 'I know Ed . . .'

He shook his head at Arthur, not willing to discuss Ed. 'Chris Prince . . .'

'Right, of course. A few days later, I found Chris, miraculously alive, waiting in my hotel room. He was skittish and pale, gripping a box to his chest and begging me to hide it. I believed him when he said that he would be killed if he was found with it. Chris and the vase had not been on the boat that morning. He said I was the only one who knew.'

'Chris was *alive* and had the vase all along?' Phil locked down the rage, but his next question was laced with venom. 'Why did

3

you keep this from me? I could have tracked him . . . gotten answers.' He would have had retribution by now.

'In hindsight, dear sir, I should have. I should've handed the vase over to the authorities immediately – but please understand that I wasn't willing to put a man's life at risk for an object.' Arthur sighed. 'You were raw with grief . . . livid . . . I didn't trust—'

'That I wouldn't have gone in and torn everything down to get . . .' *revenge* – it was what Phil would've done back then, perhaps even now, even after all this time.

'That you wouldn't have done the wise thing.' Arthur's gaze rested on Phil's clenched fists, which were now the only crack in his calm, professional mask. 'But Chris didn't stop there. He also played on my desire to bring down the black market and convinced me that we could use the vase to bait The Collector out into the open. He said The Collector coveted the vase more than anything else, as if they were emotionally connected to it. We struck a deal and then Chris disappeared. I began to believe he'd told me a pack of lies and that he had come to a bad end.

'Until he sauntered up to me bold as day at a party last winter and demanded to know where the vase was. He was a different person to the one I'd known. He'd always been confident, but there was more to him now – he was troubled. His light had darkened. I wanted to know why the vase was now so important to him decades later. We struck another deal.'

Phil flexed his fingers then raked a hand through his hair. 'The FBI . . . We . . . I won't like this, will I?'

'I told Chris the vase was in a museum and that someone I trusted could retrieve it. But the clue to where it's hidden will only mean something to the right person.'

'You went too far with your secrets this time, old man. Too far.'

'I'm here to make it right.'

'Tell me where this vase is, and we'll set the trap. Tell me how to find Chris.' Arthur shook his head, and Phil's impulses took over – he reached out and grabbed Arthur's forearm. 'Arthur! You've made me wait *decades*.'

'Not now.' Arthur pulled back and straightened his jacket. 'I'm told there's to be a *special* antiques cruise next autumn – where a new Collector will take up the position. There will be one meeting when the outgoing and incoming Collectors will be together. Get on that cruise and identify them once and for all. It's the only way to stop it. To stop all the death that goes hand in hand with their operation.'

A pigeon pecked around their feet and Arthur adjusted his trilby hat as he rose from the bench. 'I understand how deeply you want this.' He looked down at Phil with a furrowed brow. 'All those years ago, at the funeral, I promised you that I'd help you get justice for Ed's death, and I meant it. I'm asking you to wait a little longer. I need to make sure everything is in order.' He reached out and placed a hand on Phil's shoulder and squeezed. 'You will have one chance, my friend.' Arthur started walking away.

'What about you?' Phil called after him. 'You'll be there too, won't you?'

But Arthur didn't reply.

DEDHAM VALE NEWS

Murdered Thief and Priceless Hoard of Antiquities Found in Suffolk Mansion

A manhunt is underway to find the murderer of art-and-antiques thief Giles Metcalf. It is believed he had accumulated a vast collection of stolen antiquities and hidden them in secret vaults beneath his family seat, Copthorn Manor.

Scotland Yard Art and Antiques Unit, the FBI Art Crime Team and local antique hunter Freya Lockwood have been praised for their part in the recovery of the priceless hoard of Middle Eastern artefacts.

Ms Lockwood, 47, declined to comment when approached by the Dedham Vale News. It is known that she and her aunt, Carole Lockwood, recently inherited Crockleford Antiques, Little Meddington, from the late Arthur Crockleford.

Local business owner Agatha Craven of the Teapot Tearooms commented: 'I knew Arthur very, very well. He used to hunt down and recover stolen antiques, returning them to museums and the like. He was the kindest man. He donated a painting to Lowestoft Maritime Museum, just to fill a space on their wall! How lovely was that?'

Freya Lockwood is part of a rapidly growing fine arts sector working to return stolen works to their rightful owners and items of cultural significance to their country of origin. Over the past few decades, stately homes across the UK have been targeted by specialist art thieves who, many believe, steal to order for unscrupulous collectors.

The black-market trade in art, antiques and antiquities has an estimated global value of £40 billion, and the market continues to expand. From the British Empire's looting of artefacts during the imperial era to the pillaging of ancient sites during recent Middle Eastern conflicts and art theft from war-torn Ukraine – the ruthless plundering of our cultural heritage shows no sign of slowing down . . .

Chapter One

Freya

Crockleford Antiques was deathly quiet. I sat at Arthur's old partners desk, gazing out the window as four schoolchildren hurried past, huddled under a striped golf umbrella, all gripping the handle to keep their shelter braced against the wind. One of the boys shrieked as a particularly strong gust swept down the high street and threatened to bowl them over; for a moment their laughter drowned out the drumming of the rain.

I turned away and sighed – the shop seemed darker than normal. There was a small desk lamp within reach, so I switched it on and picked up the first of three glass snuff bottles I had retrieved from the cabinet by the window. It fitted neatly into my cloth-covered palm. When I brought it closer to my eye, I saw a small flea bite or nick in the bottom of the glass. A customer might not notice, but that wasn't how I did business. I pulled off the original £550 price sticker. It was still a very pretty piece – Chinese, from the late nineteenth century, reverse-painted crystal – and I hoped that someone would see its charm in spite of its damage and purchase it. Just as with people, damage didn't equal worthlessness. Dust clung to its graceful shoulders and furred the top of its red stopper. I gently brushed one corner of the cloth over the bottle, and the Chinese characters painted beneath the surface came to life once more.

After my parents' death in a fire when I was twelve, I had spent my teenage years working for Arthur in this shop and later had joined him in his antique-hunting escapades. He was no longer at his rightful place behind his desk, but his presence was etched into the worn arms of his chair and the sweet, musky scent of polish that still filled the air. Having been estranged from Arthur for decades, I was now back where I belonged.

I picked up the next snuff bottle: Chinese Qianlong pewter with an engraved chilong dragon design and a green stopper. My fingertips brushed over the cool metal, and I removed the stopper to see the tiny spoon attached to the inside, used to measure a pinch of snuff.

A fresh shower of rain pelted against the shop's windows and wind whistled through the cracks in the warped door, making the poster stuck to the inside of it flutter. I checked the Georgian longcase clock to my left as the hand reached three and the gentle chimes rang.

Sky's late. Strange.

Sky Stevens was a twenty-five-year-old who had started working as a shop assistant a few weeks back. She was smart, reliable and responsible. She'd quickly become indispensable because no matter how much I loved my aunt, punctuality was not one of her many talents. Sky had also begun an online presence for the shop by making us a website and putting items up for sale there and on specific antiques sites – she was quite the computer genius – and it had increased our profits substantially.

I breathed deeply and scanned the empty shop. Not for the first time I found myself wondering if antiques were more reliable than humans. People could fade gradually out of your life, drawn to new places and new friends – or, worse, leave without warning. If inanimate objects were lost or stolen, there was always the possibility they could be found and returned. In my twenties, with Arthur, I had done just that: tracked down stolen antiques across the globe and returned them to their rightful owners. There was nothing quite like the thrill of the hunt, carefully piecing together information until the location of an item was laid bare. But if I wanted to reignite that life, first I needed a client to commission a new search. That was where I was currently out of luck.

I looked back to the clock. Was Sky to be one more person that faded away?

The rose snuff bottle could wait. I replaced all three safely in their cabinet and wiped a grey streak of dust from my elbow. I sat down and pulled out my phone to call her, hoping my fears were wrong.

The shop door flew open and crashed against the wall. I leapt to my feet to see my sprightly aunt Carole standing in the doorway. Cold, damp October air rushed in behind her, along with a wave of her signature scent, Chanel N°5. The late-October day might have been overcast before her arrival, but Carole always brought a special kind of sunshine with her.

'No Sky?' she asked, struggling to manoeuvre her wide-brimmed hat and an armful of shopping bags through the doorway. She almost toppled over then, and I ran to help her.

Carole resorted to shimmying sideways, her enormous, slightly wilted sun hat brushing against the door frame. *Sun hat?*

'I was in Bury and the end-of-summer sales were on,' she explained. 'You know I never miss a sale.' I took some of the bags from her. 'Thank you, darling. I got a few bits and bobs for you too. I'm absolutely gasping for tea after all that excitement.'

I hung up her raincoat with my free hand. 'I'll pop the kettle on.' As I placed her shopping bags on the floor by the desk, I noticed a beach towel peeking out. 'You do remember that the antiques cruise cancelled my appearance, don't you? Or have you decided to go on holiday anyway? I really am fine on my own here if you want to travel like you used to . . .' My voice trailed off. I wanted Carole to live life to the full and had spent the past few weeks insisting she should travel again. I promised that I definitely wouldn't be lonely if she went. I had been on my own for a long time. 'I'll get some biscuits too,' I said, ducking under the dark, thick medieval beams in the corridor and heading for the kitchen.

A month ago, I'd received an invitation to be an onboard expert on an antiques-themed cruise to Jordan. With it came the possibility of new customers and the ability to network with antiques specialists. I had assumed this was a job that Arthur had usually been asked to do and that I was being invited in his place. I was over the moon at the idea of following in his footsteps, and Carole and I celebrated with prosecco in the Crown that evening. But a week later a man from the cruise line emailed stating that I was no longer needed.

After that disappointment, I had eagerly reached out to all the contacts I remembered from when I'd worked with Arthur over twenty years ago. Most were no longer in the art-, antique- and antiquity-hunting business, and the ones who were sounded wary of me. One especially tactless man commented that it was strange to be starting up a private art investigation business 'later in life' and could not get me off the phone fast enough.

I had also searched through every bit of paper Arthur had left in the shop – there was a detailed log of the antiques on sale and their provenance, but I couldn't find any mention of people he had worked with. It was as if Arthur had destroyed all that information before his murder or else someone had removed it after his death. I had literally no contacts in the industry apart perhaps from Bella – the art thief I had encountered a few months ago on the Copthorn Manor case. But I couldn't start an antique-hunting agency with someone who was very much on the wrong side of the law. Plus, if I did want her help, I didn't have her contact details.

When I re-entered the shop carrying mugs of tea, Carole was settling her sodden new hat on a Victorian wig stand. Seeing me, she rummaged inside one of the shopping bags she had flung down next to the desk. 'Look what I have for you!' Her brow creased as she ran her eyes over me. 'You look a little gaunt. Is trying to sort out the shop and setting up your' – she scanned the customer-free area and leaned closer – 'top-secret antique-hunting agency too much stress for you? When the cruise line wrote to say they were cancelling, I decided I'd still go shopping and book us both a summer holiday – have a grand adventure – meet new friends.'

I winced. 'Is this like your plan last month to hold puppy yoga in the village hall?' That had turned into a close encounter with a smelly old sheep and three pensioners having tea. It was actually quite fun, but I wasn't going to let on I'd enjoyed myself or it would encourage even more outlandish schemes.

'Everyone loved Edna, and you did make three new friends.'

Carole pulled a slip of red polka-dot material out of a bag and held it up.

My mouth dropped open. 'That's a bikini.' I hadn't worn one since before I gave birth to Jade over twenty years ago.

'I know! You're gobsmacked because it's fabulous, and you love me so much for finding it for you at half price.' She flapped the flimsy material in my face, but the gaze she fixed on me was full of warmth. 'You were so excited when the invitation came through . . . and now . . .'

I hardened against the twist of disappointment. 'And now I will find another way to get the business going.' I reached out for the thin strings of the bikini and changed the subject. 'I'm too old for this.' I shook my head in disbelief. 'You kept the receipt, didn't you?'

'You're never too old for a jolly good—'

The bell above the door tinkled.

'I'm so sorry.' Sky came hurrying in, her tall, slender frame hunched over a wheelie suitcase. When she straightened up, we saw that her hazel eyes were full of tears. 'Sorry,' she said again, tucking the case away next to the mahogany hat stand. 'I'm . . .' A tear tracked down her cheek.

I rushed towards her and pulled her into a large hug, relieved she had arrived and worried for her at the same time. 'What's happened?' I stepped back, still holding her shoulders, and tried to meet her eye. Sky looked away and brushed raindrops from the knee-length, bright pink cardigan she wore instead of a traditional coat.

'Come and sit down,' I said, gently steering her to one of the Victorian balloon-back dining chairs on the other side of the desk. 'How can we help?'

'I've left Aaron and now . . .' Her eyes returned to the suitcase.

'And you need somewhere to stay?' I asked and she nodded. 'You can stay here.'

Tears flowed freely then. 'I'm sorry. I've nowhere . . .'

Carole handed her a tissue. 'I'll put the kettle back on.' She hurried towards the kitchen. 'And we have the chocolate-chip cookies I was saving for this very emergency.'

As Sky raised her hand to blow her nose, I saw red, raw bruising on her wrist. She noticed and pulled down her sleeve. 'It was a bad breakup. Aaron . . . he . . .'

'I can see that. We need to report it.'

Her eyes shone with fear. 'No. I can't.'

'How about we talk this through when you're settled? There's a bedroom upstairs that's yours for as long as you need.'

Carole stood in the hallway holding a cup of tea and watching us. Sky looked up at her, embarrassment flushing her cheeks. 'When I saw that newspaper article about you finding those stolen antiques, then looked you up and found out about this job,' she sniffed, 'I felt so lucky. And now I'm here, ruining it with my mess.' She reached out and took the mug of tea Carole handed to her.

'We're a team. And there's no mess! You're the tidiest twenty-five-year-old I've ever met.' I looked over at Carole, who smiled in agreement. 'You can do a lot better than Aaron.'

'I love this place,' said Sky, her expression lightening a little. 'It isn't just an antique shop. It has a bigger purpose and that makes me feel part of something. You both make me feel part of something.' She took a long, steady sip of her tea.

I'd had my suspicions about her boyfriend over the past few weeks but hadn't liked to pry. Now I wished that I had.

I remembered a comment about Aaron not liking her friends, so she didn't see them anymore, and that she had to have the flat 'clean and tidy' with 'dinner on the table' when he got home, like she was a fifties housewife. And then there were the bruises . . .

I was warmed by the connection she felt to the shop because I felt it too. 'We just need our first case and then the antique-hunting side of the business will really be off.'

Carole was nodding enthusiastically. 'And not only do we think you're utterly fabulous, but all your computer magic has been wonderfully helpful. You're an asset to the team. I'm sure once we get a case, then your fancy computer studies degree can help us with some hacking.'

I glared at her. 'Um, no. That's absolutely not what Sky'll be doing. We are going to remain on the right side of the law, remember?'

Carole hurried over to our new assistant and pulled her into a hug. 'It's going to be OK. Let me help you make up the bed.'

The phone rang. We all turned to stare at it.

The shop phone never rings.

Chapter Two

My aunt snatched the handset from the old-fashioned rotary-dial phone that Arthur had refused to replace. *Is this a run-of-the-mill stock enquiry or something far more exciting?*

'Crockleford Antiques,' said Carole.

A hush descended over the shop as Sky dried her tears and I concentrated on following the conversation.

'Yes, this was Arthur's shop, although I'm afraid he's no longer with us.' Carole's face clouded slightly when she said this. The caller continued to speak rapidly. 'A man's body?' Her sparkle had returned. '*And* a stolen painting? Then you called the right place, darling.'

I reached out to grab the receiver, but Carole shooed me away with a flick of her hand.

'And did he die of natural causes, or was he *murdered*?' she asked.

I raised an eyebrow at her and mouthed: 'Be sensitive.'

But I desperately wanted to know the answer too.

'I'm so sorry, darling. Of course, how remiss of me,' she was saying. 'Introductions first.' Her tone became clipped. 'I'm Carole Lockwood, Arthur was my best friend, and my niece Freya and I inherited his shop about five months back.

Now, how may we help with your murdered man and theft?' I squished in beside her and put my ear next to the phone.

'I found a dead man behind the museum and police say he was stabbed . . .' The woman's voice quivered. 'A small painting was stolen and no one is telling me anything.'

Carole gripped my arm in excitement. 'A museum theft. We're the women for the job' – I tried to take the handset again; by now I was desperate to talk to the caller. 'It will take us an hour and twenty minutes to get to you if I drive like the wind,' said Carole. She slammed down the receiver. 'Sky, will you be OK here on your own for a couple of hours?'

Sky nodded, clearly as fascinated as we were. She'd pulled off her cardigan coat to reveal a pencil skirt and striped polo-neck jumper. 'I'm fine to work.'

'You would say if you weren't? I could always go on my own,' I said.

Carole looked shocked at the mere suggestion of being left behind. 'If it's all too much, just lock up the shop.' She hurried to put on her raincoat. 'The caller, Betty Peters, is a volunteer at Lowestoft Maritime Museum. She says the police are concentrating on the murder and aren't talking to her about the painting. Betty doesn't like their attitude and thinks a specialist antique-hunting business is her best hope of finding out what happened to the painting.'

My heart skipped. *Our first case.*

Sky pulled out her phone while I grabbed my bag. 'Let's get some background on the place before you go.' After some rapid clicking and scrolling, she turned her phone towards us. 'Lowestoft Maritime Museum has occupied a converted

Victorian cottage in Sparrow's Nest Park, Lowestoft, since 1968. An extension was added in 1977 and another in 2008.'

'Probably as the museum's collection grew,' I said.

Another click and Sky continued. 'There are also a few press reports from three days ago saying an unidentified male – no fingerprints or dental record match – was found at the back of the museum behind the recycling bin but that there were no obvious signs the museum was broken into.' She scanned Carole's face and then mine. 'We are just looking into the painting, aren't we? Or do we now hunt for murderers as well?'

'No, we only track down stolen art, antiques and antiquities.' Though, truthfully, I think I would've hunted almost anything to get the agency up and running with its first case.

'The museum is run by volunteers, has extensive displays on the history of the local fishing community . . .' But Carole and I were already by the door. The thrill of the hunt had taken over.

'We will be back with our first case in hand,' called Carole as Sky took my place behind the desk.

I linked arms with my aunt. 'Who needs a cruise when we've got a maritime museum case to solve?'

* * *

Carole's vintage and – appropriately – nautical-blue Mercedes was parked, unlocked as usual, just outside the shop. She settled in behind the wheel, with the door still open, and started raking through her handbag for something. The keys probably. Then she yanked out her special driving headscarf and adjusted the rearview mirror so she could see herself properly while she tied it Grace Kelly-style over her long blonde hair, the loose ends crossed gracefully before her throat and knotted behind her neck.

'Shall we put the roof down?' she suggested hopefully. It was one of her favourite things.

'Um, it's October and still raining.' I stayed on the pavement, unsure if Carole's car was our best option. 'Is there petrol?'

'Of course there is,' she said indignantly.

I stuck my head inside to read the gauge – there was half a tank left.

She beamed at me. 'I'm very well organized, darling. Petrol for the car, bikini for our summer holiday.'

'I might mention that it was only last week we ended up being driven home in Simon's tractor because you thought we definitely had enough petrol to get to Hadleigh and back,' I replied.

'And wasn't it fun? You were all quiet until I took us on a tractor safari.' Carole revved the engine. 'As I've said before, you can't just sit around waiting for fun to find you – you have to seek it out.' She leaned towards me. 'There might be no specialist antiques cruise to be an expert on, but we can still have some grand adventures on our own. Come on, get in. We are off to Lowestoft!'

Of course, Carole was right. Now that we had our first case it was all going to be fine.

'The museum normally closes for winter at the end of October so we're lucky they broke in while it was still open or Betty may not have discovered the painting was missing until much later,' said Carole.

It was a good point. Why *would* someone break in while it was still open? Why not wait a couple of weeks when there would be a lot less chance of anyone noticing something was amiss? What exactly was so pressing?

At the time, as I watched the rolling farmlands of Suffolk speed by, I trusted that what we'd heard so far was the truth and all of the truth . . . and that was my first big mistake.

Chapter Three

It took exactly one hour and twenty-three minutes to drive to Lowestoft from Little Meddington – a hair-raising journey with Carole at the wheel. The coastal town had been battered down by the storms of time and was trying to get back on its feet – I admired its fighting spirit. Outside a row of Edwardian seaside homes was a rubbish bag being picked over by a squabble of seagulls.

Within minutes we had reached the golden sands of South Beach, where feeble rays of afternoon sunshine were lighting the murky North Sea. I longed to stop and savour the deserted, windswept beauty of the place. The area felt as if it was on the brink of something – the calm before the storm of artists and independent coffee-shop owners discovering its low-cost housing, uninterrupted stretches of sand and healing salty air.

Carole saw me leaning towards the window to get a better look. 'If we're quick, we might have time to grab a cuppa and some chips before we head home,' she told me.

I beamed at her. 'I'd love that.'

Lowestoft Maritime Museum was situated at the northern end of the town, near a holiday park and over the road from the sea. It was housed in a diminutive flint-faced Victorian cottage with an oversized flagpole flying a Union Jack. A huge letterbox-red WW2 mine – hopefully disarmed – loomed beside the path. In the window next to the front door was an Open sign, but the museum seemed abandoned.

'Hello?' called Carole as she crossed the threshold of the museum.

I hung back and studied my surroundings. The building didn't look like it had been broken into lately – there were no shattered windows, and the door was intact – but when I bent closer to the lock, I noticed a tiny hairline scratch on the weathered brass.

This lock has been picked recently.

A small gift shop through an open doorway to our left also doubled as the ticket office. A tall thin woman with perfectly curled white hair and a silk scarf draped around her neck stood up as we entered.

'Betty?' asked Carole.

'Carole? I'm thrilled you came.' She hurried towards us.

'I'm Freya from Lockwood Antique Hunter's Agency.' I smiled with pride and stuck out my hand. 'How may we help?'

Betty reached out both her hands and closed them around mine. 'I'm so grateful you came at such short notice. The police are focusing on the poor dead man found behind the recycling bin.' She threw her head backwards in the direction of the wall behind her. 'I gave them an in-depth account of all my suspicions, but no one is telling me anything.'

'It's always the not knowing that eats away at us, isn't it?' Carole squeezed her shoulder and then picked up a guide to the museum.

'Oh, it is, it is!' Betty spun and gripped Carole's hand instead. 'I can't do much to help that investigation, but when I saw the painting was gone, I knew Arthur would've been able to help with that, so I took a chance that you would too.' She looked Carole and me up and down, as if to check we were up to the job.

'The front lock looks like it has been picked recently. The scratch is bright against the antique brass,' I told her. 'Were there any other signs of a break-in?'

'A picked lock?' Betty's eyes widened. 'Oh, well, the police didn't tell me that.'

'How about you start from the beginning,' I suggested.

She straightened her skirt, tucked a handkerchief under her cardigan cuff, and gave a quick nod. 'Follow me, then. It all started two days ago when a youngish man came in while I was selling tickets . . . thirties, blond hair and too much of it. He arrived in an expensive car – I saw him park it outside. He was wearing a flashy suit, handmade shoes, gold serpent ring with green eyes. You know the sort of man – suited and booted.' She ushered us through a doorway to the right of the ticket desk, and down a small corridor with wooden floorboards that reminded me of a gangplank.

We entered a large room with model ships inside display cases. 'He walked straight up to the ticket office and asked if there was a grey vase on display – never mentioned a painting – said he was looking to borrow some items for a talk or something. Have you ever heard of such a thing?'

When Carole and I shook our heads, she continued. 'I said we didn't have a grey vase and nothing in the museum could be "borrowed"! What a thing to ask!' Betty searched my face for answers, but I didn't have any just yet. 'Well, then he went off and I locked up as usual at the end of the day. Then I came in the next morning and the painting Arthur donated was missing.'

Arthur? I was about to ask her to explain what Arthur's relationship was with the museum when Betty sniffed and pulled out her handkerchief. 'Then I started to tidy, as I always do . . . I was just putting out the rubbish around back . . . never expected to see a gloved hand . . . a body. I had to get Clive from the holiday park to help.' She wiped the end of her nose again. 'He called the police and I waited at the desk. Then they closed the museum.' Betty breathed in deeply. 'It's not the sort of thing that happens here. Our CCTV doesn't even work . . . it's just for show.' Her voice faltered and I stepped closer to her, resting my hand on her arm.

'We don't need to talk this through in any further detail if it's too painful for you.' I lowered my voice to try and calm her. 'I'm sure it was very distressing finding the victim like that. But perhaps you can tell us more about the painting Arthur donated? Do you have a photograph of it?'

Carole and I exchanged glances.

My curiosity had already been ignited and we had only been there a few minutes.

Betty placed her handkerchief back in her sleeve and met my eye. 'I'll show you where the painting was hung. Maybe you can find a clue as to what happened to it there.'

We strode through the first gallery, passing towering glass cases displaying model ships. Betty was now in full tour guide mode – it was clearly her favourite role in the museum. She pointed to each of the large models we passed, naming the man who had made and donated it. Soon we arrived at a reproduction wheelhouse covering a small corridor leading to the next exhibition area. Betty stroked her fingers up and down the wooden door frame. 'This came from a real ship.' Carole and I stepped into the area and stood next to the old-style wooden wheel. Above that, a computer screen showed the real-time location of all the boats currently off the coast around Lowestoft.

I watched Carole grab the wheel and give it a spin. 'I bet kids' – she whirled the wheel to left then right and back again – 'enjoy pretending to steer a ship when they're here.'

My daughter, Jade, would have loved that when she was a child. The thought surprised me and I pushed the ache of missing her away. Now twenty, Jade hadn't been back since moving to America last summer to attend university. The only thing her very wealthy father ever did for her was fund her university education. I was thrilled that she was so happy, but at the same time I was wistful for all the time we used to share.

Betty tapped Carole's arm to move her on, and when that didn't do the trick, she linked her arm through Carole's and practically dragged her away. 'Follow me. I arrived at eight in the morning and walked through the galleries, as I always do. When I arrived at this very spot . . .' She had guided us through almost the whole museum when she came to a stop at the far end opposite a wall with a nail sticking out.

'The painting was missing from there?' I pointed.

'Yes! Arthur told me it was a reproduction. Not worth much. Now, let me tell you some of my theories. I know I look like butter wouldn't melt, but I do like a good true-crime binge watch on the telly.' There was a glint in Betty's eye that told me she never missed a clue. 'I think there were two men here that night. Mr Suited and Booted returned to steal the painting with an accomplice and then . . .' She jabbed her finger to the ceiling as if she'd had a eureka moment. 'They argued and the accomplice was killed.'

'Did the police find proof of a fight or a murder *inside* the museum?' I tried to keep my smile steady, but I was quite confused by Betty's theory – it was honestly rather outlandish. Why would a thief kill his accomplice at the scene? However, I had learned years back that it was best to keep witnesses talking, as sometimes they held important information that they didn't realize they had.

'Hmm.' Betty frowned. 'Well, then, they took the fight outside – like pistols at dawn. Then Mr Suited and Booted stole the painting and hid the accomplice's body behind the bins. I've shared all this knowledge with the police, but they don't seem to be taking me seriously.'

'But the poor dead man was stabbed, darling,' said Carole. 'No pistols.'

Before I could pose another question, Carole grabbed Betty's hands and squeezed them. 'We will get to the bottom of this. A murderer stealing a painting is just our thing. Freya has a lifetime of experience.' When I opened my mouth to object, Carole nudged me. 'We are the very best women for the job!'

I beamed at Carole, because I actually believed that we were.

Chapter Four

The museum cooled as the autumn sun sank towards the horizon and daylight faded from the windows. But the empty space on the wall shone brightly at me.

'Do you have a photo of the painting?'

'Perhaps there is a photo. I'll have to ask Steven, the manager.' Betty frowned.

'Can you tell me what it depicted?' I pressed on.

'It showed a big old sailing ship with cannons along one side and huge sheets which had caught the wind. A captain at the helm . . . but half of the ship was engulfed in flames and sinking. The sea was black and stormy, and overhead there were rain clouds . . . Arthur said it was a nineteenth-century reproduction of an earlier work – decorative but nothing special.'

A painting of a burning ship?

A shudder rippled down my spine.

I stared at the single nail sticking out of the wall, but my mind whirled . . . I had remembered something. After his death last May, I had found seven of Arthur's journals hidden in the antiques shop, all of which contained lists of often-priceless stolen or missing art and antiques that had found their way onto the black market. Although he had been blackmailed into assisting at the illicit dealings in Copthorn Manor, Arthur had planned eventually to seize back as many of these antiques as he could and return them to their owners.

He had not lived long enough to achieve his ambition. He left the journals where he knew his heirs, Carole and I, would find them. We had then managed to help save the Copthorn Manor haul of Middle Eastern antiquities. One of these journals listed a large number of nautical art and antiques, and in the back was a photograph of a painting of a burning sailing ship. I couldn't remember if there was a captain depicted, but I knew Arthur had written something underneath. The sight of flames always brought up unwanted anxiety, so I hadn't dwelt on the photograph. But now I needed to see it again . . .

'It looks so bare,' sighed Betty, bringing me out of my thoughts.

'We'll try and get it back for you, but I just have a few more questions. If you don't mind? When exactly was the painting donated?' I asked.

'The fifteenth of May this year,' she said. Arthur had been murdered only a few days after that; his death had been made to look like an accidental fall. He had known the danger he was in and made elaborate preparations to tie up his personal affairs beforehand.

When I followed Arthur's clues in the Copthorn Manor investigation, he had shown me the scale of the illicit trade in art and antiques by organized crime, and the way in which artworks had become an alternative form of currency without the need for banking checks and procedures. All that was needed was an antiques verifier to confirm an object's value – work that Arthur had been forced to undertake for the Copthorn Manor gang of international forgers to save me from being framed for murder. Luckily, he'd kept his options open by secretly feeding information on their activities to the FBI. A small museum that concerned itself with seafaring and coastal fishing memorabilia seemed an unlikely hangout for international art thieves. But since the only thing to have gone missing was the painting Arthur had donated, that meant it had to be more significant than it appeared.

What were you up to, Arthur?

Carole returned from interacting with the exhibits and stepped ahead of us into the kitchen while I asked Betty if she could remember anything else Arthur had said about the painting.

'How did you know Arthur?' I asked.

'Oh, I've known him for donkey's years. My cousin, Agatha, runs the Teapot Tearooms in Little Meddington. Arthur was just the best, wasn't he? Always on hand to help. He was here when the Princess Royal opened the new kitchen extension over there.' We walked a little farther on, and Betty pointed to the museum guidebook in my hand. 'It's inside, see.' I opened the guide for the first time and saw a photograph of Arthur standing next to Princess Anne. In his hand he was holding a tiny teacup as if he were about to attend a dolls' tea party.

'And when was this guide designed?'

'It's quite new. Yet another thing Arthur volunteered to do.'

I smiled to see my old mentor again. I desperately wanted to ask him why he was so involved with the museum.

'And when Arthur redesigned the guidebook, did he also choose which photographs appeared in it?' I asked.

'Well . . . yes. Always very thoughtful was Arthur. He noticed that in that picture of him with the Princess Royal there was a bare patch of wall by the kitchen door and a few weeks later he turned up with the painting to fit it – even brought a hammer and nail to hang it as well.'

Did he?

'Do you know where Arthur got the painting?'

'Not really. He arrived one afternoon, said he'd picked it up in Norfolk and driven straight here. He hung it, like I said, and I told him it was very generous of him. He said there was no need for any fuss, it wasn't valuable.'

That jogged my memory about something I'd seen recently. 'But I read about Arthur donating that painting in the *Dedham Vale News*.' Betty's mouth dropped open and she shook her head in disbelief, a guilty expression creeping over her face. 'You did tell someone, didn't you? You told Agatha at the Teapot Tea-rooms in Little Meddington. She mentioned it when our local paper was writing about the Copthorn Manor case. Someone could have read about it and come here especially to steal it.'

She clamped her mouth shut and her eyes welled with tears. 'I might have . . . but she promised not to say anything! It was just . . . Agatha came in for a catch-up, and we were walking around together when she noticed it and asked about it straight off. None of the volunteers had paid any attention to it. But she's such a chatterbox!'

I touched her lightly on the arm. 'It's a small local newspaper. I'm sure it was of no importance.'

Betty sniffed and changed the subject. 'I do believe the victim and the painting are connected,' she said, pulling at her sleeve to find her handkerchief. 'Arthur always said to trust my instincts.'

'And Arthur was always right,' replied Carole.

I considered Betty. There was a good chance that she knew more about Mr Suited and Booted than she had told us. 'Did the suspicious visitor ask you about anything else? Think back if you can . . . There was a grey vase . . . the painting . . . and . . .'

The mention of a grey vase made me remember a case Arthur and I worked on decades ago when we were employed to track down a similar object that dated from the Ming Dynasty. But I pushed it from my mind – it couldn't be the same, because the vase was never recovered.

Betty's gaze drifted ceilingwards as she tried to remember. 'Well . . . oh, now you say that . . . he asked about a naval sword and when he saw my mug of tea by the ticket desk he rambled on about teacups in shipwrecks, if you can believe it. I told him we've never had anything like that round these parts.'

Betty had got the wrong end of the stick – there really were ship-wrecked teacups – so I decided that perhaps if I gave her a brief introduction to shipwreck ceramics, she might recognize one. 'Shipwreck ceramics are very collectable. For over a thousand years, ceramics were traded between Asia and Europe, merchant ships sailing between the two full of cargo, but they had to journey through perilous waters. Sometimes the ships went down with all their cargo.'

The idea of undisturbed items under the sea for hundreds of years, where barnacles, corals and shells grew over them, sometimes fusing together into 'sea sculptures', was as romantic as it was fascinating.

'Oh, now, that does sound wonderful, doesn't it?' said Carole, taking a few steps away down the corridor. 'I'll have a look for some.' It was clear that she wanted to keep exploring the museum's exhibits rather than stand around talking.

One of the things I loved most about shipwreck ceramics was that they could sometimes be traced all the way back to the potter's wheel where they originated and, because of captains' logs, to the precise date a ship sank. The Hatcher Collection and the Hôi An Hoard contained some of the best-known and documented discoveries. I found it somewhat charming to imagine divers discovering an underwater world frozen in time.

'It sounds mesmerizing all right, but we definitely don't have anything like that lurking in the North Sea, I don't think . . . Well, actually, there was that discovery, wasn't there?' said Betty.

'What discovery?'

'The wreck of HMS *Gloucester* was found near here some years ago and kept secret while the marine archaeologists were at work. Went down in 1682 with hundreds of souls lost at sea, though the Duke of York, the future King James II, survived. I do like a bit of local history, don't you? I suppose if there was a teacup found from that ship you could call it shipwrecked, couldn't you? I never heard of one here, though.'

I opened my mouth to ask more about the location of HMS *Gloucester*, but Betty checked her watch and said, 'I'm so sorry but we should be closing for the day soon.'

'Of course, there is one last thing. What was the talk Mr Suited and Booted wanted to borrow something from the museum for? Did you ask him?'

'He said he was leaving to be an expert on a specialist antiques cruise in a few days and needed some fine pieces to show at a talk he was giving – and if he had found what he was looking for, maybe we could've loaned it to him. I tried to search for the cruise on the library computer, but computers aren't really my thing.'

I smiled at Betty. 'We will look into it.' I reached for my phone and called the shop. Perhaps Sky might like a distraction. She could find out a thing or two about the other experts on the cruise as the Lockwood Agency's chief (and only) researcher.

'Sky, it's Freya. I'm wondering if you could help – is there a special interest cruise with antiques experts sailing this month? Perhaps the one I was meant to be on? I need a list and photos of all the experts involved.'

'I'm on it,' she replied, and hung up.

* * *

We had just pulled out of Lowestoft when a text message came through from her.

I read it out to Carole.

'Only one cruise featuring antiques is sailing this year and it departed yesterday. It's run by MVGoldstar. Has TV antiques experts and some others doing talks, mini-excursions, etc. It sails from Greece to Jordan.'

Carole took her eyes off the road. 'That was the one you were meant to be on!'

Another text came through shortly afterwards.

'It says there are "at least five onboard experts". But the only information they post is about their star expert – Mark Rush-well. I'll need to do more digging. The only other thing to note is that there's been a recent change to the cruise's advertised onboard exhibition. It's now featuring a private collection of antiques. Here is the updated info . . .'

The pictures on the MVGoldstar website made me gasp. In the background of the photo was a scabbard for a naval sword. I'd seen it before! I zoomed in on the background of another shot showing a large display cabinet. Inside was a collection of shipwreck ceramics. One was a distinctive sea sculpture that I recognized.

I reread Sky's message.

'It can't be a coincidence that Mr Suited and Booted might have been talking about the cruise I was meant to be an expert on. And an exhibition of nautical antiques . . . Arthur wrote about those in his second journal. I'll check it as soon as we get back.'

I needed to verify in person if the sword and scabbard, the shipwrecked ceramics, and the sea sculpture in Arthur's journal were the same ones in the onboard collection.

'We need to get on that cruise,' I said to Carole.

She beamed at me in reply.

Chapter Five

Crockleford Antiques was shrouded in autumn's darkness when we drove into the village, and my stomach tightened uneasily. *Where is Sky?*

'Do you think she went out?' asked Carole, clearly wondering the same thing I was.

I checked my watch. 'It's only five fifteen – maybe she closed up early and went upstairs.' We jumped out of the car. The shop keys were already in Carole's hand and she unlocked the door.

'Hello?' I called. The image of Sky's bruised wrist came crashing back to me. With the flick of a switch the shop was illuminated, and I headed towards the staircase leading up to the flat. 'Sky?' I called.

Carole was close behind me. 'Perhaps she had a change of heart,' she whispered. 'Decided to go to London after all.'

'Maybe . . . But I don't think so.' There was a dim glow creeping out from beneath one of the upstairs doors.

We found our Sky half-asleep on the sofa, noise-cancelling headphones on and a zombie apocalypse film playing on her laptop. A sigh of relief escaped me and I realized I'd been holding my breath.

I smiled at Carole, and we tiptoed back downstairs, happy that she was safe and looked at home.

'With Sky up there, can you keep a lookout here?' I said, pointing to the stairs.

'What don't you want her to see?' asked Carole.

I winked at her and turned to the Georgian mahogany bookcase that ran the length of the shop's back wall. 'I need the second journal,' I told her, and started pulling old catalogues and reference books from one of the shelves and placing them on the desk. 'It turns out Arthur had quite a few hiding places in this shop – you know what a whiz he was at carpentry – and over the past couple of months I've uncovered them.'

The shelf was now empty, and I reached towards the back of the bookcase.

'What on earth are you doing?' Carole pressed in next to me.

'Aren't you meant to be watching out for Sky?' When Carole didn't move, I tried to be quick as possible. 'I hid the journals in different places. So if someone does try to search for them, they'll only find one at a time.'

I pressed my fingertips against the back of the bookcase.

Click!

A hidden panel slid forward.

'Darling.' Carole's hand was quicker than mine. Her fingers closed around the journal I had hidden. 'I've found it.'

'How can you take credit for finding what I opened?'

Carole tutted. 'Pure semantics, darling. Don't be picky.'

She settled into the chair behind the desk and opened the journal.

After flicking through the first few pages she sighed and flopped back. 'There's nothing here that tells us who stole the painting.'

'Oh, sorry, I thought that as this was your discovery . . .'

I smiled at her and held out my hand, waiting for her to surrender the journal to me.

I flicked though the pages. 'I've been through all Arthur's journals over the past few months. None of the items in this book are on the Art Loss Register, so I assumed they were not stolen, unlike the first journal, which related to the Copthorn Manor case.' I flicked back to the first page. 'Last time, Arthur left us a letter and guided us towards the manor by booking us in there. At first I didn't understand why he didn't leave a letter in each journal. But letters are risky, they can easily fall into the wrong hands . . . Ah yes, this is what I remembered seeing.'

PART 1: THE COLLECTION

A fine nautical collection containing many items of shipwreck ceramics from the Hôi An Hoard (Vietnamese c. 1450–1500) and the Hatcher Cargo (Chinese c. 1643) – the finest-quality items from both wrecks. These well-painted pieces were designed to appeal to the wealthy upper classes of the time. All with the auction-house stickers showing and clear provenance.

'Why is it called the Hôi An Hoard?' asked Carole.

'I don't think they ever found the name of the ship, so they named the collection after the nearest town, Hôi An in Vietnam.' I studied the photographs and descriptions of the shipwreck ceramics, taken from auction catalogues. I retrieved my phone and opened the photographs of the cruise exhibition that Sky had sent me earlier. 'The ceramics in the onboard exhibition look very similar to the ones in Arthur's entry, but hundreds of pieces were found in each wreck. We need to look for something more easily identifiable.'

Further into 'Part 1' were lists of paintings with maritime subjects and many other notable nautical antiques. This was a huge collection.

'There!' I pointed to a photograph of a naval bronze sword. 'I knew I recognized it.'

Next to the photograph in the journal was a newspaper clipping which read:

> *A rare sword over 200 years old, presented to a captain for his bravery at the Battle of Trafalgar and valued at around £200,000, was stolen from the Rushwell family seat late on Saturday evening.*

I checked the date. 'This was over fifteen years ago.'

> *The pristine bronze 100 Guinea Sword was awarded to Captain James Rushwell of the 74-gun HMS Swiftsure for his role in helping the British to victory in 1805.*
>
> *Only twenty-three of them were awarded to captains from the world's most famous naval battle. This one remained in Rushwell's family for over 200 years before being stolen.*

'The one in the photo and this one look exactly the same. We would need to investigate where the other twenty-two swords are and if this is the stolen one. I would like to see it in person.' I flicked through more pages in the journal. 'Maybe Arthur arranged for us to be invited onto the cruise, knowing that it would lead us to this collection of treasures . . .' I looked over at

Carole to get her advice, but she was lost in her own thoughts. 'I couldn't put the pieces together when I got the invitation because these items weren't advertised as being on the cruise.'

I turned to the back of the journal and started flicking through the pages . . . then stopped. There it was, on the very last page: a photograph showing an oil painting of a sailing ship in flames. A sky full of storm clouds and choppy black waters surrounded the vessel with the main mast already engulfed in flames. It was as if the artist were hovering just beyond the danger as they watched the ship go down. Scrawled under the painting in Arthur's hand was 'The Battle of Scheveningen, 10 August 1653.' And on a line below, 'What fire does not destroy, it hardens – Oscar Wilde.'

'Arthur told Betty it was a reproduction. We would need to have it seen by an expert to verify that.'

I took a photo of it and sent it to Betty – the reply was instant: *That's the painting.*

Carole was looking over my shoulder as the message came in. 'So, Arthur took a photo and put it in the journal before taking it to the Lowestoft Maritime Museum?'

'That would make sense, although Betty said he came from Norfolk to deliver the painting . . . so what was in Norfolk? The place it was stored, perhaps? If the painting is now on the ship, then . . .'

Carole nodded in agreement. 'Maybe we can convince them to let you on board. Let's call them.' She pulled out her phone and tapped in a number.

'Hello,' she said when someone answered. 'I know this is going to sound awfully daft and you're probably just about to close up for the day, but . . .'

'Hasn't that ship already sailed?' I whispered, hope building inside me despite my words of caution. 'How do we get onto a cruise when it's already at sea?'

Carole put a finger to her lips to silence me as she continued to explain there had been a misunderstanding. She listened for a moment, then whispered to me that the Head Office of MVGoldstar Cruises had been sent a letter stating that she and I wouldn't be able to attend. 'But darling, we received an email that purported to be from you, saying our place on the cruise was cancelled.' She lamented the terrible deception, and asked if there was a chance that we could still . . .

Carole's prodigious charm was in full flow. It was her super-power, the way she could bend almost anyone to her will.

I turned the journal towards Carole and pointed at the picture of the painting of the burning ship. Her eyes widened. 'What's that . . . ?' she asked, having let me distract her. 'Yes! We can make it to Cyprus tomorrow and join the ship before it enters the Suez Canal!' Carole grabbed me in excitement.

'Well done,' I mouthed, and started looking up flights.

Carole scribbled down some information and hung up.

'I'll see if I can buy the air tickets while you go and ask Sky if she'll be OK to look after the shop for the next couple of days.' I opened my laptop.

My aunt turned back to me when she was at the foot of the stairs. 'Now, aren't you glad I got you that bikini?'

'There'll be no time for sunbathing.' *Thank goodness!* 'We've a stolen painting to recover.'

Chapter Six

Bella

Ever since the events at Copthorn Manor five months ago, Bella had been living in Edinburgh and believed that the names Freya and Carole Lockwood would never cross her lips again. Or perhaps it was just blind hope . . .

In her silent tenement flat with its high ceiling and large windows, Bella picked up her phone. She found the number and called it. She got the same dead tone. It had been three days since she'd last seen Chris. She'd tried the location app – again – but the phone was still off. Was it possible that the trip to Suffolk had gone wrong? He wouldn't just abandon her, would he? Bella glugged down some wine to wash away the unusual feeling of hurt swelling inside her.

People don't leave me, I leave them.

She poured some more wine into her glass. 'Best for me to think of it as just a fling . . .' she told the glass. 'That's what everyone does in their twenties, isn't it?'

Maybe he had decided to cut and run after their last fight?

The wine was meant to relax her, but instead a memory sloshed around inside her – one that began to twist her stomach. Bella had stood in the doorway to prevent Chris from leaving. Her hand had gripped the door handle. Until a shuddering realization hit her. From the age of about five, every time her father left, she used to scream at her mother – 'You should've stopped him from leaving us.' But she was a hurt child back then . . . and in the years that followed she would grow to pray her father would never come back.

So Bella had made herself move aside for Chris.

'You can't just turn up there!' She'd cringed at the sound of desperation in her voice. 'That private detective – or whoever you paid for that file you have – could be wrong. It was just a stupid article in a local paper.' She was trying to backtrack, and it wasn't working. When her words failed to stop Chris putting on his suit jacket, she reached out and grabbed his arm. 'Please,' she whispered.

He shrugged her off, his face tight with annoyance. She knew he hated clingy women – he'd told her often enough. 'Arthur said the vase was "safe in a museum". And here he is in some museum guidebook together with the mention of him donating a painting to Lowestoft in the local news. It's not coincidence . . . it's confirmation.' He held up the file he had been given the day before. 'It's a lead worth checking out. If I can find the vase and present it on the antiques cruise, it will change everything for us – prove that I can find what's been lost.' He plucked his car keys out of the bowl. 'With money from that sale, we can do whatever we want. I'm doing this for us.'

His face softened momentarily. He pressed a warm palm to her cheek and stared deep into her eyes. 'I do love you, you know that, right?' And at that moment Bella had believed him. He was just like her: strong-willed and dedicated to the thrills and spoils of an underworld existence.

He left moments later.

Now, days later, she opened the fridge and threw all the remaining food into a bin bag – her oat milk and his protein drinks.

He wasn't coming back.

Reluctantly, she started her habitual cleanup routine – pulling on her yellow rubber gloves and retrieving the kitchen spray from under the sink. Once the flat was spotless, she went through the wardrobes. All his items went into one bin bag for the charity shop, and her clothes, the ones that would not serve the new life she was about to create, went with them.

Afterwards, Bella lay on the bed and stared at the ceiling.

Who will I have to become next?

It was tiring to inhabit a new persona multiple times a year. She had allowed herself to believe, just for a little while in Chris's arms, that it wasn't necessary anymore.

Bella breathed in deeply and focused on the things she could control, her own talents. She turned on the TV and flicked through the channels – it didn't take her long to find an actress to base her next incarnation on.

With her hair brushed smooth and tied in a tight bun, Bella checked every inch of the spick-and-span flat. It was important that she didn't get sloppy – if someone had dealt with her lover, then they could come after her next. And they would be professionals. Those types always checked the trap under the bathroom sink for a stray hair with a follicle or under the glass coffee table for fingerprints.

This didn't bother Bella one bit; she too was a professional, and quite soon there would be no trace that she had ever lived there.

She decided to reclean the countertop in the galley kitchen, especially the part where the top protruded. It was just the place to leave a thumbprint. The stench of bleach stung her eyes, but while her hands cleaned her mind wandered. Bella didn't like loose ends. She wanted to know for sure what had happened. That meant checking out the MVGoldstar antiques cruise. Chris was scheduled to attend . . . he was obsessed with that cruise, and she knew it had something to do with the legendary Collector.

Bella didn't believe that such a figure even existed – stories of The Collector's rapacious exploits had circulated for over two hundred years, and nobody lived that long. But if The Collector was real, perhaps they were behind the rumoured illegal archaeological dig in Egypt where a whole tomb was looted and the finds sold on the black market not long ago. It was so wild Bella hadn't believed it until Chris mentioned something about a meeting in Egypt to move some items from a secret dig. It got her thinking.

Perhaps she might use a strawberry-blonde wig undercover this time? Tinted contact lenses to disguise her brown eyes, a thick coat of pale foundation? The passport image of her with blonde hair was a triumph of the forger's art. Yes, she'd go with that.

The cruise itinerary – Greek islands, which she'd miss, then Cyprus, through the Suez Canal, ancient Egyptian sites, and culminating in a visit to Petra in Jordan – held no interest for Bella. She had seen it all before, many times over. But she needed to get onto that ship at Limassol in Cyprus. She needed to know if Chris was alive.

Bella scanned the flat one last time and prided herself on a job well done.

Goodbye, Susan Jones. Hello . . . ?

What would she call herself this time? Perhaps she could put her makeup skills to good use and become someone older once she was on board? No one ever paid close attention to the elderly.

Chapter Seven

Laura

Laura Scott, specialist events manager, sat at her desk on board the MVGoldstar cruise ship *Emperor of the Ocean* staring out at the port of Limassol as it shimmered in the hazy Cypriot sun. She hated her job. She was bone-tired of it all.

When she had first been offered the role five years ago, the idea of sea travel had excited her – it was a good way for her to save some money and see the world. But now . . . she'd had enough of the constant movement . . . of the same endless blue ocean . . . of looking over her shoulder.

She bit her lower lip at the sight of the passengers flowing back on board from the shore excursions. Probably three or four hundred of them, depending on how many had left the ship that morning. Within the hour the Premium passengers and the specialist antiques experts (the two that turned up) would be entering the private Library. Some would end up at her desk with the same petty grievances – not enough coat hangers, extortionate laundry costs or inadequate bottled water in their rooms.

Only four days and I'm out of here.

Laura's gaze tracked the length of the port, scanning for

signs of Chris Prince. When she'd heard rumours that he had been killed before they set sail, a wave of complicated emotions flooded her – relief and terror. If he was dead, then he couldn't track her down and force her to keep working with him. Like he had done once before. But her next thought was: What if someone had decided to take down everyone Chris worked with? Who knew what she did? Was she next? She had calmed herself with the idea that Chris was a cockroach – he could probably survive anything. She was going to stick to her plan.

Laura made another search of the passengers, and her eyes locked on two women standing at the customs desk. They looked familiar so she strode the length of the Library, pressed the exit button, and stepped onto the private deck – shielding her eyes and leaning over the balcony to get a better look.

Freya and Carole Lockwood – they weren't supposed to be here.

Laura's pulse picked up and she hurried back inside. She reached for her fourth coffee of the day and closed her eyes as the hot, sharp liquid hit her tongue. The smell of coffee always reminded her of home – Byron Bay, Australia. A smile touched her lips as she pictured her favourite cafe, next to her sleek new flat. She'd spent her teenage years watching the waves lick the golden sands . . . her two brothers striding towards her with surfboards tucked under their arms. She breathed deeply, trying to let her homesickness soothe her.

Only four days left. The countdown had become her mantra.

The flat she'd purchased three months ago under her real name was fully furnished and waiting. She would go home with all the money she needed and look after her mum as she recovered from chemo.

In four days I'll disappear.

From the moment she landed in the United Kingdom seven years ago, back when she was eighteen, she'd told everyone she was from Perth and had a mother, father and younger sister . . . which was of course true of the backpacker whose identity she had stolen. She had kept the truth hidden, but was it enough to keep her safe when she started her new life?

Laura scanned the Library and schooled herself; she would keep her act up one more time. Make sure no one suspected her. Deny she ever knew Chris if she entered a conversation where gossip was being thrown around.

From the other side of the door the murmur of voices and the rumble of laughter trickled through as her phone pinged.

'Freya Lockwood will now be attending as an antiques expert. Her guest is Carole Lockwood. Please make arrangements. Thanks. Dave.'

'Bit late, Davy,' said Laura to the empty room. 'They're already here!'

She reluctantly picked up her lanyard and placed a sign on her desk saying she would be back in ten minutes. Head Office had decided that on this trip Laura should have her desk in full view of the 'executive guests' – it was a terrible setup for her as it meant she was always on call. Dave in Head Office didn't know his ass from his elbow, but he had registered the complaints about Laura's frequent disappearing acts on the last antiques voyage. She never actually completely disappeared, of course; she was merely attending to the other *business* that Head Office or Davy the dickhead turned a blind eye to – presumably because someone had been offered a sizeable cash inducement.

Laura had boarded the MVGoldstar four days ago, a day

before the passengers embarked. It was her job to make sure that all the specialist cruises – from master classes with Michelin-star chefs and gastronomic excursions to talks from antiques experts and visits to ancient sites – went to plan. She ran the schedule of talks by the experts and organized the expert guided tours off ship when they docked in each port. But from the moment she started work on the arrangements for the sixth antiques cruise, nothing had gone to plan.

The problems started when Arthur Crockleford was murdered and therefore couldn't attend – which was unreliable of him, to say the least. Soon after, she received an email saying that his associate, Freya Lockwood, would take his place. And then another email stating that she wouldn't be able to attend either. When Laura had complained to Head Office that there weren't enough experts, they said they would sort it out . . . and Ben Wells would attend instead.

On the day they set sail, antiques expert Ben Wells didn't show up.

Neither did Chris.

Chris didn't answer her frantic calls or reply to her messages. Ben Wells didn't either. It was all very . . . strange.

Laura hurried down the stairs to meet the women on the welcome deck. She passed a housekeeping trolley and considered the cruise's empty staterooms. The chance to meet your favourite TV expert and learn a thing or two about a new collector's piece or the antiques of the future was normally irresistible to their core clientele. MVGoldstar specialty cruises were always sold out. This time there were a dozen staterooms all along the same corridor on Deck Eight that were unoccupied except for Luke, the curator of the onboard exhibition. Laura had been allocated a room there too. There was no official reason given for these vacancies – one steward told her that there was a problem with the plumbing in those staterooms. Then the captain mentioned that a tour party that was booked in them didn't show up. None of it rang true to her. And the plumbing was just fine in her room.

Her phone pinged again, with an email from Dave saying that Freya Lockwood could take over five of the antiques talks 'highlighted below.' *Did Arthur tell his former assistant what this cruise was really about?* If the answer was yes, then Freya was going to need to be very careful.

She strode down the promenade where the ship's shops, hairdressers and bars were located, weaving through the steady stream of passengers. At the end she passed the Gallery. Why was it closed? Where was Luke? But she didn't have time to investigate as she was going to miss the Lockwoods if she didn't hurry.

Even though her feet sped towards the deck, her mind lingered on the Gallery. The planned exhibition of 'Modern Artists – Future Collectables', with numbered and signed prints from artists such as Damien Hirst, Bridget Riley and the Connor Brothers had been organized through a dealer in Mayfair, London. It had been cancelled at the last minute without warning. In its place, a private collection of nautical antiques had been offered.

At 6 a.m. on the day of sailing, packing cases appeared containing Old Master paintings of maritime scenes, ancient items of celestial navigation, and cups and saucers covered with barnacles – which gave her the creeps. The official line was that they all belonged to a celebrated private collector.

Luke, the collection's curator, was in attendance. He was not like any of the other curators she had met. The antiques world had more than a few flamboyant personalities, but he wasn't one of them. He was tall, pale and softly spoken, with a small fake smile always touching his thin lips. He wore steel-framed spectacles with lenses so thick they magnified his eyes. When he thought she wasn't looking, she would catch those enlarged eyes swimming in her direction. He saw everything. She knew from experience never to ignore the instinct that told her to be on her guard. Laura promised herself to avoid him – never to be alone with him – but it wasn't always easy.

The memory made her nervously run her thumb over the engraving on the back of her wedding band. What would it be like to have someone to call when everything that might go wrong actually did go wrong? Three years ago, when Chris gave her the ring, she took it as a sign she had entered the inner sanctum of the black market and that wealth was virtually guaranteed there. But she was naive back then – she didn't understand the price she would have to pay.

Laura stepped out and held up her 'Welcome Experts' sign, trying to catch her breath. As the women came into sight, all she could think was *If Freya and Carole Lockwood now know what Arthur knew, they'll end up at the bottom of the sea.*

Chapter Eight

Freya

ITINERARY FOR THE OCTOBER ANTIQUES
CRUISE: ATHENS TO AQABA, JORDAN

Day 1: *EMBARKATION PIRAEUS, ATHENS. SET*
SAIL AT 5 p.m.

Day 2: *MINI-CRUISE AROUND THE GREEK*
ISLANDS – EXPERT TALKS

Day 3: *CYPRUS – DAY EXCURSIONS – DINNER*
WITH THE EXPERTS

Day 4: *THE SUEZ CANAL – DAY AT SEA –*
EXPERT TALKS

Day 5: *EGYPT – DAY EXCURSIONS AND*
PERIOD HALLOWEEN BALL

Day 6: *JORDAN – EXPERT HOST TOURS TO*
PETRA – EXPERT TALKS

Our taxi from Larnaca International Airport rushed towards Limassol as the afternoon heat baked the dusty Cypriot streets. I pressed my forehead to the window, wishing we were already on the ship. Questions had consumed the journey. Was the stolen painting from the Lowestoft Maritime Museum – the one photographed in the back of Arthur's journal – really the one in the Gallery? And who had brought it on board? Betty firmly believed that the man she called Mr Suited and Booted was to blame, but there was no evidence of who he was or if he was the thief.

We stood in line waiting to board the cruise, and I checked my email one more time as the late-October Mediterranean sun warmed my striped cotton shirt and chinos, making them cling to me. I tried to focus on the job ahead – I was to host a table at dinner, give talks in the ship's theatre and Library, and 'be available' to guests at 4 p.m. each day over a cream tea served in the Grand Salon. Carole, on the other hand, could do whatever she wished as my plus-one – judging by her multiple suitcases, she was planning at least four outfit changes a day.

'She looks magnificent!' Carole purred at the ship. Overhead, seagulls streaked through the cloudless sky and perched on the huge mooring chains that kept the ship tethered to the concrete dock. 'While you were packing, I used all my powers of persuasion to get a premier suite with a connecting stateroom for you. Apparently, there were quite a few cancellations for this trip.'

She tottered up the boarding ramp in her red high heels, gripping my arm for balance. 'I did try to bring sensible shoes – until I realized I don't own any.'

I was about to ask if she wanted to borrow some flip-flops when she spotted something, let go of my arm, held tight to her oversized straw hat and sped away. 'Over here!'

We came to a halt in front of a trim woman in her mid-twenties, with sun-kissed skin, red lips and blonde-streaked hair twisted on top of her head. She was wearing a crew uniform and holding a sign that read 'Welcome Experts'.

'The experts have arrived!' Carole jazz-handed at the bemused MVGoldstar representative.

'And what's your specialty – drama?' I winked at her and smiled at the crew member as we approached. 'I'm Freya Lockwood.' I pointed to the sign. 'One of the antiques experts.'

'I'm an expert too,' Carole reproved me. 'The sign did not specifically mention *antiques*.'

'Care to share your area of expertise?' The woman's Australian accent was soft but distinctive, like she had been away from home a long time.

My aunt gave her a radiant smile. 'Life, darling. I'm an expert at living my very best life, no matter what the circumstances. It's the only way, don't you think?'

I shook my head, knowing that Carole truly did believe her bumper sticker sayings, and I saw the frosty crew member thaw a little and her frown unravel.

'I'm Laura, the events organizer.' She tried to smile. 'Great hat – very glamorous.' Carole adjusted it proudly. Laura's bright hazel eyes seemed to take in every detail. 'Right, we're meeting in the Library, Deck Nine, at three thirty.' She checked her watch. 'That's in an hour. I'll give you a printout of your schedule when you get there.' She handed me a map of the ship and two key cards. 'Your suite and stateroom are on Deck Seven. Your luggage will be brought up. You can take the lift, first right through there. OK?' She took a few steps back, indicating that was all the welcome we were going to get.

Carole looked up at the ship's multiple decks, towering over us. 'This must be an amazing place to work.'

'One port is much the same as the next.' Laura seemed to catch the world-weary note in her own voice and forced a smile. 'But this ship is smaller, with around four to five hundred passengers. Some of the massive cruises have a thousand or so passengers on board. I'll see you both later.' With one wave of her hand she sped away.

We left the deck and walked into a towering, air-conditioned atrium housing the shopping parade and Grand Salon restaurant. A sweeping golden staircase led upwards, branching in two directions. Suspended overhead were at least a dozen glittering chandeliers.

'How does anything this big even float?' I asked as I craned my neck to take in the view of the decks stacked above us. 'And she's saying this is a *small* cruise ship?'

The interior of the ship evoked glamour and opulence. Perfumed air wafted down the staircase from somewhere above. Whether it was from the fresh flowers displayed all around or something added to the air-conditioning, I couldn't tell. There was a slight movement beneath my feet . . . not enough to make me want to steady myself, but my body gently began to adjust its centre of gravity.

'It is *wonderful*, isn't it?' said Carole. 'I feel so at home.'

'You'd probably need to be super rich to afford one of these cruises.' I was hit by the thought that I was going to have to stand up in front of all those passengers and give presentations, make small talk in the Grand Salon and sit at dinner.

As the lift doors opened, I pulled my shoulders back and lifted my chin – *you've got this, this is the way we get to the truth*. I stepped inside, to see it was backed by glass, giving us a full view of the ship's multi-level grandeur as we sped to Deck Seven.

I gripped my hand luggage, which held some of my costume jewellery collection and my laptop. I'd been asked to prepare two illustrated slideshow presentations and I'd spent the flight writing them. I was not experienced in public speaking, but if this hunt resulted in the stolen painting being recovered, then I would have solved my first case. Lockwood Antique Hunter's Agency might get some much-needed publicity to register on some of the larger museums' radars. That would really get the agency off the ground.

Carole caught my eye, and she must have seen some sort of trepidation in it because she said, 'It's been quite a couple of days. How about we sit down and take a breather before the meeting? Devise a plan of action.' She linked her arm through mine and squeezed.

* * *

My stateroom was connected by an internal door to Carole's large suite. There was a strange imbalance swirling inside me that had nothing to do with the movement of the water underneath. Every corner of the room seemed to scream *relax, you're on holiday*. Fluffy dressing gowns hung in the bathroom, a big bowl of fruit sat on the side table and crisp white bedsheets covered the bed, but my mind was creating bullet points on what to look out for on board. I went to collect Carole and found her bouncing on the corner of the bed.

'Just lovely, isn't it?' She beamed at me.

I smiled back, marvelling at her chameleonlike qualities. I was quite sure they were going to be very useful on this job.

'We need to find out as much as we can about the antiques experts on board. Mark Rushwell was the only one advertised with a full profile, but there was mention of "other prominent experts". We should get photos of the experts and any polished man to send to Betty.'

Carole ran her hand over the sheets. 'Absolutely, photos of everything. Give me a few minutes to change.'

I returned to my adjoining stateroom and opened the wide glass sliding door, letting the salty Mediterranean breeze sweep over me, along with the mutterings of numerous other passengers on their balconies. I leaned over the glass side as passengers farther down were excitedly taking selfies. Seagulls circled above the ship.

We were all waiting to sail.

Carole came out to join me.

'I've hung up our Halloween costumes. It's going to be so much fun!' Carole cupped my ear. 'We're undercover now, aren't we? It's so thrilling.' She indicated the endless parallel rows of pristine balconies on either side of ours as the ship's huge shadow gave shade to the seagulls bobbing on the choppy water. 'None of them will know our real reason for being here.'

'What costumes?' I was quite sure the one assigned to me would be the most flamboyant she could find.

'There's to be a period costume Halloween ball – I'm keeping your outfit a surprise for now, but don't you worry, it's fabulous.'

I laughed. 'We'd better get to the Library and meet my fellow experts.'

'Excellent idea.' Carole tapped my arm. 'I'm just going to slap on some lippy. You go on without me and I'll meet you there. You're the star, after all.'

I took one last look at the tranquil setting before me as the sun glittered over the water. The passage through the Suez Canal would begin early tomorrow, and in the meantime, the

MVGoldstar was our luxurious home away from home – two nights and a day at sea stretching ahead of us.

The ship's engines started to hum, sending vibrations through the hull.

Within minutes we were no longer tethered to dry land – and as the ship headed towards the horizon, it was clear that there was no turning back.

Chapter Nine

I knocked on the Library door and waited for someone to answer. When they didn't, I knocked again, louder this time.

Laura stuck her head out. 'Your key card will also work on the lock here.' She pointed to the key card reader with a forced smile.

'Oh, sorry.'

'Don't be, come in.'

I stepped into a long, light-flooded room with floor-to-ceiling windows down one side and marine-blue painted bookcases lining the facing wall.

Eager to see the Gallery, I asked where it might be.

Laura opened her mouth to answer, but her eyes came to rest on something behind me – what she saw drained the colour from her cheeks.

Someone nudged me aside and stepped in front of me. 'The Gallery is locked up?' The new arrival had a clipped British accent, hugely magnified eyes behind his steel-framed spectacles, and the manner of a man who believed Laura was there to serve his every whim. 'Why? Where are the keys?'

'I'm so sorry.' Laura almost rolled her eyes, both of us tacitly acknowledging he needed placating if the interaction was to be kept brief. 'This is Luke, the curator of our onboard Gallery. Now, Luke, if I could just finish helping Freya.'

Luke still didn't acknowledge me.

'I need to sort out some items from the collection for a private talk I'm giving this evening,' he said in a low, urgent tone. 'I was only gone for half an hour, and now I can't find the guard, who must have locked up and taken the keys.' His voice was strained, and the vein in his neck pulsed as if he was about to explode.

Laura's smile didn't falter; she was clearly used to this. 'I'll make a call to security and we can sort this out.' To me she said, 'I need to give you your schedule, don't I?' Her grace was evident as she glided over to a desk by the door and opened a drawer. Luke glared at me as I came to stand next to him. 'I'm Freya Lockwood, one of the antiques experts.' I held out my hand, but he didn't take it.

I should take a photo of him – he could be Mr Suited and Booted.

'Just make the call,' he said to Laura.

I decided to try and ease the tension, for her sake, and get some information on the exhibition in the Gallery at the same time. 'I believe that the Gallery on board was showing signed and numbered prints of famous artists of our times, but then it was changed?' I asked.

'That doesn't sound like a question.' I waited for him to elaborate, but he was focused on Laura.

'And where's the Gallery?' I asked.

'I need the keys, so will you please get on it – right now?' He directed his anger at Laura.

She didn't flinch but merely tilted away from him. 'Why don't you go out and say hello to your fellow experts?' she said to me, gesturing towards a sliding door at the far end of the room, which led to a private deck. A man and a woman chatted by the railing. I was eager to meet the other experts and see what I could learn.

Mark Rushwell was in his early sixties, silver-haired and darkly tanned, wearing a well-cut pink linen suit. His handsome face was familiar to me from several TV antiques and game shows. The woman I recognized as Sally Bright, a regular on *Bargain Hunt* and *Antiques Road Trip*. She was a headmistress type, with a sensible low-maintenance hairstyle and pale skin that shone red in places, telling me that she had caught a little too much sun. Her floral summer dress paired with a gold-buttoned navy jacket seemed over-the-top. Their heads were bent towards each other but their eyes scanned the area, making sure no one was listening.

Suspicious.

I nodded to Laura and was halfway to the door when someone touched my arm.

'Sorry, here are the details on the evening talk and the experts' dinner you will be taking part in tonight.' Laura handed me an envelope, and over her shoulder I spotted Luke leaving the Library. 'I'm so relieved you turned up; we have just two talking heads and they were *not* happy!' Her gaze flickered to Mark and Sally on the private deck. She didn't look relieved, she looked worried, but I put it down to the drama with Luke. 'What made you change your mind? Terrible British weather get to you in the end?'

'I think there was a misunderstanding – I was told I wasn't needed, but . . .' I paused and waited for Laura to fill in some information.

'How strange.' She rolled her shoulders and changed the subject. 'Anyway, I hear you helped bring down an international forgery ring back in the spring.' Laura's eyes were bright with curiosity. 'That must have been . . . exciting.'

The image of being locked in the Copthorn Manor vault came rushing back and I shuddered. '"Exciting" was one word for it.' I didn't want any more questions about what happened last May, so I smiled at Laura and pressed the button to open the door.

Filling my lungs with confidence I didn't 100 per cent feel, I stepped out onto the private deck, which was bathed in afternoon light and fanned by the fresh sea breeze. There was a faint hum of voices from the adjacent decks.

I headed towards Mark Rushwell and Sally Bright and was about to hold out my hand to Mark when I remembered the entry in Arthur's journal relating to a sword.

The pristine bronze 100 Guinea Sword was awarded to Captain James Rushwell of the 74-gun HMS Swiftsure for his role in helping the British to victory in 1805.

Was it just a coincidence that the sword belonged to a Rushwell? Could James and Mark be related? I made a mental note to ask Sky to do an internet search.

Mark stepped forward, beaming at me. 'Good afternoon. I'm Mark Rushwell and you must be Freya Lockwood. Your reputation precedes you, Ms Lockwood.' One hand remained in the pocket of his double-breasted jacket while he held out the other. He had the air of someone used to charming the public.

'It's a pleasure to meet you,' I said. We shook hands; his grip was strong but welcoming. 'I didn't mean to interrupt your conversation. I just thought I'd have my coffee on deck.'

Sally nodded to me. 'Not at all. I'm Sally Bright. Isn't this ship magnificent? I'm so glad you're here. We were just saying how tired we were getting, hosting everything on our own. I was only meant to be here for the onshore guided tours – my passion is Egyptology, and I'm fascinated by the Nabateans who built Petra in Jordan. Our trip there is going to be utterly splendid. However . . .' She leaned in and whispered, 'The talk I had to cover on eighteenth-century British furniture yesterday was only possible with the help of Google.' I chuckled, as I would have had to do the same. 'Promise not to tell the passengers, as they seemed none the wiser.'

'I promise.' I reached out and touched her arm to let her know that her secret was safe with me. 'It's wonderful for me to be here with you. I was flattered to be invited.' I looked between Mark and Sally. 'So, you have both been here since the beginning?'

Sally nodded. 'Did you know there were meant to be two other experts here, not including you, that didn't show up? Word on the ship is that one of them might be actually missing . . . like missing, missing.'

'What are the names of the missing experts? They didn't seem to be on the MVGoldstar website.'

'Ben Wells and Chris Prince,' said Mark, leaning back against the railing. 'I suppose as they weren't well known, not on the telly like us, the organizers didn't go into great details on their website.'

I turned my attention back to Sally. 'Do *you* know the other experts who were meant to be here?'

She shrugged. 'I'd say they're more collectors than experts.' Her lips began to curl into a smile, as if she was enjoying a private joke. 'Anyway, Mark is far better suited to schmoozing and entertaining people.' Her gaze lingered on him. Catching herself, she checked her watch. 'I think I'll go for a walk before the meet and greet.'

'But I . . .' She was gone. I'd wanted to know if she'd heard why the other two men didn't show up for the cruise, but it would have to wait.

I sent Sky a quick message and asked if she could try a deep dive on the two absent experts now that we had names.

'It was lovely to connect. I'm sure we'll see you in the Grand Salon in half an hour for our daily grilling by the passengers. Enjoy your coffee,' Mark said.

I sighed and found a seat in the far corner of the deck. I curled the fingers of my right hand until they gently touched the damaged skin on my palm – something I often did when I was thinking.

My phone pinged.

Betty: *Are you on the ship yet? Did you meet that dashing man from the telly, Mark Rushwell?*

Three more dots . . .

Betty: *Is he very handsome in real life? Could you get his autograph?*

And again . . .

Betty: *No pressure, just if you have a moment.*

*   *   *

The 'meet and greet' in the Grand Salon consisted of eight passengers and three antiques experts, me included. The passengers all crowded around silver fox Mark Rushwell while

Sally and I sat a few feet away with soft drinks at the bar. 'Are you and Mark close?' I asked.

'Known each other years. My parents had an antiques shop in Cranbrook, Kent. His parents had an auction house in Sevenoaks . . .' She shrugged. 'Kent's not a big county. All the dealers know the auctioneers. Mark took over the family business straight out of uni when his dad got sick. I resisted taking over my parents' shop, but my ex-husband was charmed by the idea. Then he shagged my shop assistant and ran off with the dog walker.'

'He sounds like a catch!' Our eyes met and we both laughed.

'You're the same as us, taking over Arthur's' – she raised an eyebrow at me – 'shop? Or are you going to . . . expand?'

She's digging for answers just like I am.

'Did you know Arthur well? He used to do these cruises.'

Sally's face paled, but she covered it with a smile. 'I've been an expert for these trips for three years now. I got to know Arthur rather well . . . but then again, he could be quite secretive. Perhaps I didn't always know everything.'

She turned away from me and caught Mark's eye as he extracted himself from his conversation. He strode over to us. 'Everything all right?'

'I was just asking Sally how she knew Arthur.'

Mark shrugged. 'Everyone knew Arthur. He was the life and soul of a party and a good auctioneer.'

I might have got it wrong, but I had never known Arthur to run an auction. We'd been estranged for over two decades though, so perhaps that was a new side to his business. Mark checked his watch. 'Time's up, folks,' he called to the room. From the corner of my eye, I saw an older lady in a mauve cashmere cardigan and skirt hurrying towards him; her hair was in one long plait down her back and she had reading glasses perched on top of her head.

'Mark, my dear,' she called. 'Come and sit with me.' I expected him to protest that the meet and greet was over, but he seemed keen to join this particular passenger. As they were about to walk away, she turned to me and held out her hand. 'I'm Patricia Henderson.' I shook and she smiled warmly. 'Mark and I have become good friends after all these cruises together . . . He's so wonderful on the *Roadshow*!' She linked her arm through his and beamed up at him as they walked away.

I took this to mean that I was now free to try and locate the Gallery and study its contents. My step quickened as I left the Grand Salon. If the stolen painting really was on display inside, then I was on the right track and might even be able to solve my very first case in record time and enjoy the rest of the cruise. But I should have known that nothing in the antiques underworld was that simple.

Chapter Ten

I exited the glass lift at Deck Eleven and spotted the Seafood and Steak restaurant, which had been taken over tonight for a 'dine with your favourite expert' event. Long tables stretched down the centre of the room, subdivided into separate areas presided over by Mark, Sally and me. Beyond them a sign indicated the Sunset Veranda deck with bar.

Over the past two hours I had found the Gallery, but it was closed, with metal shutters pulled tight over the windows. It was deeply frustrating because I couldn't even get a glimpse of what was inside. I had then spent the hours before dinner walking the ship and getting my bearings.

I was climbing the final steps to the restaurant when my body jolted and I fell forward . . . *Shit!* . . . I must have missed a step. I reached for the banister, but my hands met the carpet instead. My palms and knees burned. I couldn't tell if it was the movement of the boat or my exhaustion that had made me stumble, but blazing heat started in my neck and rushed to my cheeks.

This was not the dignified entrance I'd imagined.

'Oh dear!' came a soft voice from behind me, and Patricia Henderson, the grey-haired passenger who had commandeered

Mark after the meet and greet, reached out her hand towards me. 'Are you all right? Are you hurt? Let me help you.'

I was grateful for the hand. 'Thank you. I'm fine, I just . . .' I quickly straightened myself for fear she might try and help me up, snapping her frail frame in half with the strain.

Her eyes passed briefly over my chest, and I readjusted my emerald wrap dress, which had gaped open to reveal my bra. She stood in front of me while I checked my modesty, and I could have hugged her.

'I'll walk with you,' said Patricia, tapping my arm, her soft blue eyes flicking to my heated cheeks as I lifted my hands to cover them. 'I do love a cruise, don't you? My mother worked in a travel agency, and after school I would sit behind her desk and flick through the brochures. I always dreamt of being the type of person with enough money to sail the seven seas.'

'I haven't much experience with cruises, so I'm delighted to be here.' I followed her to the restaurant. Although she was probably nearing eighty, she was made up impeccably and her tanned skin had a pretty glow. She wore a mid-length black satin designer cocktail dress. A showstopping Art Nouveau ruby glinted on her ring finger, and a cream pearl Léa Stein Gomina, the sleepy cat, was pinned to her jacket – her style was understated, and yet there was no denying the quality and high price tag of everything about her.

'That's a lovely Léa Stein brooch,' I said.

'My nephew gave it to me. We used to have a cream cat called Snowy. He's a dear boy,' she replied. 'Snowy isn't with us anymore.'

The sadness in her eyes made me change the subject. 'You said that you've been on these antiques cruises before?' I asked.

'My husband and I used to love cruising, but now he's gone, I go alone. It was always his biggest dream to go to Petra so, like so many things, I'm doing it for the both of us. They have changed it up a bit for this latest one and I'm not always a fan of change. I do love *Bargain Hunt*, and *that* hasn't changed in eons! I fancy I could do so much better than some of the contestants, although of course . . .' She stopped herself as we reached the restaurant doorway.

'Although?' I asked.

'Oh, nothing, just that Bill wouldn't have liked me to appear on television – he was a very private person.' Patricia pushed open the door. 'Are you married?'

I scoffed. 'No, I have a terrible track record with men. I'm happily single.'

Patricia reached out and squeezed my arm. 'You never know who's around the corner. Bill was my second husband. He opened up the world for me in so many ways. I met him at an antiques fair in Oxford . . . he was a dealer in ceramics back then. He could be stern and overpowering with other people – someone at his funeral even told me that he was scared of Bill – but to me he was wonderfully kind and generous.' She spotted Mark again. 'Excuse me, I won't be a minute.' She made a beeline straight for him.

There was a small queue of passengers waiting to be seated and I stood behind them. They smiled at me but made no attempt to talk, for which I was thankful. I wiggled in my dress, pulling it closed again. *Where is Carole when I need a safety pin?* I scanned the room, trying to keep my chin up and shoulders back though my palms were sweaty. The polished cutlery and starched white tablecloths were not at all what I was used to . . .

73

'Hello, hello.' I knew my aunt had arrived before I saw her. 'Isn't this extravagant?' Carole hurried over to me and linked her arm though mine. I leaned against her, hoping that her confidence would seep into me. 'Remember, she who has the most fun wins . . . and tonight we are winners!' She slid on her oversized reading glasses and studied the seating plan on the clipboard by the maître d's desk. 'Each expert has their own section.' She sighed in relief and pointed to her own name. 'Here I am on yours. At least we get to dine together. Let's pretend we're gate-crashing a wedding . . . eat and drink as much as we can, find two handsome men and . . .'

'Ladies, a pleasure to see you both tonight.' The maître d' was around six-foot-four, with olive skin, dark hair swept back from his face and deep brown eyes. He wore an expensive Patek Philippe on his wrist. 'If you could let me know your names . . .'

Carole answered, and he made a bit of a business of ticking them off on his seating plan. He was using a gold pen, I couldn't help but notice, and wearing a designer suit. He flashed us another bright, expensive smile. 'If you would follow your waiter.' The maître d' indicated a tall man in a suit who promptly turned on his heels and led us away.

A couple of male officers in uniform entered and joined tables to our right. Carole was seated some distance from me but gave an exaggerated wink when it became clear another officer was walking towards us. I looked more carefully. I *knew* him. And by the way he was heading in my direction with shock widening his eyes, he knew me too.

Phil.

I sat up as tall as I could, shaking my head in disbelief. I mouthed to my aunt: 'This just got interesting!'

Phil was the undercover FBI agent I had met while on the Copthorn Manor case.

'Lucky I sneaked that bikini into my luggage!' Carole called out to me as Phil arrived at our table, handsome in uniform. 'Oh . . . don't *you* look dashing.'

Phil's eyes ping-ponged between Carole and me as the colour drained away beneath his tan.

If the FBI Art Crime Team had gone to all the trouble of putting an undercover agent on board the MVGoldstar, then there was a lot more going on than just a stolen painting.

Chapter Eleven

Phil stood in front of me and held out his hand. 'Good evening, I'm officer Phillip Ward. It's a pleasure to meet you.' His eyes bored into me, making sure I knew the game we were now playing. His salt-and-pepper hair was a lot more groomed than when he'd worked undercover as a gardener at Copthorn Manor. I took his hand, and he squeezed as a small smile of relief spread across his face.

Carole had made a lot of innuendos back in May about how handsome he was, how single I was, how 'friends with benefits' would be good for me. I had ignored them all. And by the twinkle in her eye as she sat watching us, it was clear I was in for round two the moment we were alone. But even Phil in a uniform wasn't going to distract me from recovering the stolen painting.

'A pleasure to meet you, Phil. Are you joining our table for dinner?'

I can play at being strangers if that's what's needed. I'll get to the bottom of why you're here.

The last time I had shaken Phil's hand he was standing in the entrance hall of Copthorn Manor watching me with amusement as I unsuccessfully tried to hurry Carole into the car. We had solved the Copthorn Manor case, and the place was swarming with police.

'Thank you.' I had walked over to him and held out my hand, trying to be professional. 'For . . . everything.'

He had taken it and stepped towards me, leaning into the shell of my ear. 'I hope this doesn't become a habit – you getting in the way of FBI business.'

'I'm looking forward to meeting again too.' I leaned back enough to look him in the eye.

I had not heard from Phil since, and I would love to say that I had never thought about him again, but that wouldn't be entirely truthful.

Phil seated himself next to Carole, but he was not paying any attention to our table – his eyes scanned the room. Carole murmured something to him, and he shook his head in despair until she made the motion of zipping her lips. His scowl made me cough back a laugh. He had clearly learned nothing from our time together at Copthorn Manor.

I had to get Carole away from him.

Four more passengers entered and took their places in between us.

Phil poured water for the table and started chatting to the elderly gentleman to his right. Within seconds they looked like they were long-lost friends. Phil was just like Carole; people warmed instantly to him when he wanted them to.

I heard a voice in my ear. 'I'm Jenny Harris and that's my husband, Archie.' The woman beside me pointed to the man making Phil laugh. Jenny was wearing a long silver sequinned dress with a Georg Jensen neck ring and matching earrings by Astrid Fog, circa 1972. I had always coveted a pair. She pulled out her chair and sat down next to me. Picking up her napkin and flipping it out, she said, 'I haven't seen you on the telly, have I? I'm an expert on all the antiques specialists on the telly – it would be my *Mastermind* topic.'

'Pleasure to meet you, Jenny. No, I ... .'

She motioned to Patricia Henderson, who had just appeared at our table. 'This is my good friend Patricia; she knows all the *Roadshow* lot but doesn't watch *Bargain Hunt*—'

'Actually . . .' Patricia began, looking like she was trying to stop Jenny in her tracks, but Jenny batted away the correction – she was on a roll and turned back to me.

'I don't believe that you've been on either of them, have you?' Her eyebrow was raised in what looked to be an attempt to make her question seem genuine. She knew perfectly well I wasn't on TV, and it was clear Jenny had decided that paying the extra to 'dine with an expert' meant dining 'with a *TV* expert'. I did not tick that box.

'I'm afraid not.' I tried to smile but was worried it came across more like a grimace. Having my inexperience high-lighted in public made me want to curl up and hide, but I tried not to let it show.

Jenny rattled on. 'On the board over there it says you're the new owner of Crockleford Antiques. You're just a dealer, then?' Without waiting for a reply, she turned to gesture to a waiter. 'Let's get some wine.'

I gave her a broad smile. 'Wine would be a great idea.' If I got her drunk enough, she might stop talking.

'Now, Jenny, let's allow the dear young lady to relax, shall we?' Patricia took one of the little artisan bread rolls from the silver basket in front of me. 'Tell Freya about your amazing collection of Lalique.' She winked at me.

Jenny leaned towards me, completely ignoring her. 'The only non-telly-expert I liked was Arthur Crockleford. I met him on one of these cruises, you know. Now, *he* was a very interesting man. Charming, even if he wasn't famous. He was like an old Indiana Jones – someone once told me the shop was a cover for his top-secret missions. Such a shame he's no longer with us. And such drama over who could possibly replace him.'

'Did you ever meet Chris Prince and Ben Wells?' I asked swiftly. 'They were meant to be experts here.'

'I have, yes, but . . .'

'Jen, are you having red or white with dinner?' her husband asked, giving her an unreadable look.

While we all waited for the wine to be poured, Patricia and Archie began a conversation in which he seemed to be enquiring about her nephew Tony. She lowered her voice when she replied, and I thought I caught the words 'stepping up'. but Jenny had already downed her wine and was focusing on me once again.

'It must be difficult for you, working in the place where poor old Arthur had his tumble?' Her expression was a curdled mix of sympathy and curiosity. It was unbearable. I gripped the napkin on my lap and twisted one corner around my finger, cutting off the blood supply. I turned for help towards the only person I trusted in the world: my aunt. She was chatting away to Patricia, and it was Phil who caught the look of panic in my eyes and nudged Carole.

I nodded to him in thanks, and he lifted his glass of wine.

'Freya, won't you introduce us?' Carole's voice boomed down the table.

She was rescuing me, and I loved her for it. 'May I introduce Carole Lockwood? Arthur Crockleford's best friend. She *was* on the telly in her glory days,' I said pointedly.

'Still in my glory days, darling.' Carole flicked back her hair and winked at Jenny. 'Shall I tell you about a brief . . . shall we say . . . *encounter* with Hollywood royalty?' She lowered her voice. 'It could be a little too much for your husband's ticker.'

Jenny glanced dismissively at Archie as excitement flushed her cheeks. 'Arch, switch seats with Patricia, will you? She needs to hear the story too.' A man used to obeying orders, he sighed and meekly stood. Jenny proceeded to move everyone around, until I was sitting at the head of the table with Phil and Archie as buffers on either side of me.

I decided this was a good opportunity to get some information out of Phil. 'The onboard Gallery seems interesting. I'd love to have a look around. Do you know why it's closed?'

He gripped the stem of his wineglass and his gaze swept over the table, checking no one was watching us. 'Why are you *really* here?'

'What's so important that . . .' I stopped when I realized Jenny had turned to face us . . . not us . . . *him*. Her gaze circled up Phil's torso to his lips, to his hairline, and back down. I reached for my wine. 'You have admirers.'

'Do I?' He looked confused, so I flicked my eyes towards Jenny.

I kept my voice as low as possible. 'Perhaps we're here looking for the same thing? Want to tell me what that is?'

Phil shifted towards me in his seat. 'This isn't a game. You shouldn't be here.'

'No. This is a *hunt*!' I said, making myself smile at him. *And I'm no child*, I wanted to add but didn't. He forced a smile and turned to focus on Carole, who was in the middle of her story. Annoyance at his last comment pinched me. It was clear he took his career seriously. Was it really that difficult to believe I did the same? My fledgling agency and the deathly quiet shop were all I had.

'Those two seem to be getting on like a house on fire,' he said, looking at Patricia and Carole laughing together. He was changing the subject.

I didn't reply – the silence between us becoming deafening – as we had reached a sort of stalemate.

I changed tack and did what Carole would do to get information out of a man: tried to use some charm. 'Arthur would've been sad to miss all this, don't you think? You might entertain the possibility that I could know something that you don't. I did last time.'

'If *he's* here and he knows you and Arthur worked together . . .' Phil stopped talking as the soup was served. 'It's not safe for you,' he growled. 'Last time I should have insisted you left, and this time . . .'

'Who's *he*?' I took a warming sip of watercress soup. The rest of the table was oblivious to Phil and me – they were hanging on Carole's every word, Archie included after turning up his hearing aid.

Phil's knee grazed mine under the table as he moved closer. 'Tell me what this is all about?' Our eyes locked. 'What's gone on since . . .'

'Nothing.' There was a look on his face I couldn't read. 'What about you?'

Neither of us wanted to give up the information we had, but I was now desperate to know why the FBI was on the cruise. Another idea came to me and I pulled out my phone. Phil could be Mr Suited and Booted if he wanted to be. 'How about a selfie?' I didn't wait for him to object and squished in next to him. His heady aftershave of vanilla and wood carvings swept over me.

His jaw clenched, and as I was about to press the button, he whispered, 'You shouldn't . . .'

'Too late.' Pleased with myself, I slipped back onto my seat and sent the photo to Betty.

He sighed and was about to say something until he focused on someone over my shoulder. 'I'll be right back.' I turned to see Luke and Laura heading our way.

Laura was nervously spinning the gold wedding ring on her finger.

Phil met them before they reached the table and put a hand into his pocket. Luke was flushed and his fists were clenched as he spoke to Phil. Laura hung back a few paces, biting down on her bottom lip, but Phil didn't seem fazed at all. He extended his arm, directing Luke out of the restaurant. Phil turned back and our eyes met as I rose to my feet. There was a faint shake of his head.

If he didn't want me to follow them, then that was exactly what I was going to do!

Chapter Twelve

Sky

Sky Stevens had been working at Crockleford Antiques for three weeks and two days and she had loved every second. But after leaving Aaron, everything had changed. Now she anxiously stood at the front door, fingers clasped around the lock.

Could she lock up early?

Would Freya mind?

Should she tell them what was really going on?

Rain beat down on the pavement outside and a truck sped past on the high street with its headlights blazing.

Someone ran towards the shop. Her heart shuddered. On instinct, she popped the latch and locked the door. The hands on the longcase clock read 4.45 p.m. It was close enough to closing time for her to turn off the lights.

Sky had one foot on the stairs up to the flat when she saw a figure in a long coat silhouetted against the pinkish sunset. The shop door handle rattled.

Bang! Bang! The man rapped his knuckles so hard on the door Sky was afraid the glass pane would shatter.

'We're closed,' she called, trying to keep her voice steady, not moving from her position by the staircase.

He banged again, and she turned towards the back door of the shop, which led out onto a cobbled back alley. Could she make a run for it?

'Come back tomorrow,' she instructed. She hoped he was just an eager customer, but she feared he wasn't. Was this to be one of those moments? The ones women knew could go either way? She pulled out her phone and let her shaking finger hover over the emergency call button.

'Sky. Open up.'

His voice brought bile up her throat, but she didn't press call.

'Now,' he barked.

She knew better than to get the police involved – it wasn't exactly legal, the type of hacking she had done in the past. A life she was trying to get away from, if Aaron would only let her. She ran to the door so that he wouldn't make any more noise.

'Leave before I call the police!' She waved her phone around to show she was serious.

Did he see her hand shaking?

'Do your new employers know what you really do? Do they know why you're here?' Their eyes locked through the glass and her stomach clenched. How did she ever think that he was everything she'd ever wanted?

'Leave and don't come back.' She kept her voice calm and firm. 'I told you . . .'

Aaron banged his fist against the frame, and she shook along with the door. But he didn't break it down. 'And I heard you. But you'll leave when I have what I need – the dossier. You know, all that computer equipment cost money. You owe me.'

'I worked for that equipment!' But in the years she'd been

with Aaron she had learned one thing: it was best to keep on the right side of him. 'How much do you want for it?'

'Do the job you were sent here to do and I'll let you walk.' He turned and strode away.

Sky had told him that she was out. That she was done spying on Freya and Carole, because they didn't have what he was looking for – and that's when he got really mad. Whoever Aaron was working for scared him. And very few people scared Aaron.

After switching on every light in the flat, she poured a large glass of icy water and downed it, trying to calm her racing heart. In the sitting room she found a wooden chair and hooked it under the door handle. Aaron probably wouldn't come back tonight, but she wasn't going to take the chance – he was unpredictable. The sofa was old and squidgy, so she put her headphones on, started her audiobook and curled up under her cardigan.

Her phone pinged. Freya's text read: *Did you find anything else about the missing experts?*

I'm on it, she messaged back, and then scrambled for her laptop and began.

Sky sighed. She liked the women she now worked for. However, all Aaron cared about was a good payday, no matter what it took to get it. So, when he'd seen a reward on the dark web asking for a full dossier on Arthur Crockleford and all his dealings, he didn't hesitate to get his best hacker involved.

But Sky had found out so little online that she had driven to Little Meddington to see the shop and its new owners for herself. She'd thought she would ask some questions and get some new leads.

The village was quiet and reminded her of where she grew

up in north Essex. There she had stood out and hated it – she was the only black kid in the small church school she attended and the daughter of the village drunk. Sky couldn't control her dad's drinking, but she could smash her grades and get the hell out of there. At sixteen she was offered a place at university to study computer science.

If it wasn't for Aaron paying her to build websites for fake businesses so he could con people into investing in them, she wouldn't have had the money to fund her first degree and her master's. The job had seemed like a good idea when she was a teenager and broke. Her work changed a few years later. She hated finding him marks – but digging around to find some banker's dirty little secrets . . . that was different, she could allow it. Some wives or girlfriends received photographs anonymously through the mail when the truth needed an outing. As time wore on, she'd realized that Aaron had no feelings for her; she was being used, was just another of his marks, but by then it was too late. She was in too deep.

What she hadn't expected was the whirlwind that was Carole Lockwood – the way her energy could make you think anything was possible. Sky had only been intending to make a brief visit, and she had to admit she was fascinated to meet Freya Lockwood – a woman who'd brought down a murderous gang and uncovered stolen antiques.

The shop was closed when she arrived, and while she was standing in her favourite pink cardigan with her hands cupped against the shop window Carole had tapped her on the shoulder. 'I know I'm opening up a little bit late.' It was past midday. 'I was at a party in Southwold last night and we ended up skinny-dipping in the sea in the dark. Freezing, darling, don't try it unless you're practiced in cold water breathing. Are you looking for something in particular?'

Carole unlocked the door and hurried her inside.

The musky smell of silver polish swept over Sky. 'I wasn't . . .' She scanned the room, and her eyes came to rest on the advertisement stuck to the front door.

'Of course, you're here for the job!' Carole promptly sat her down and gave her tea and biscuits.

'I just saw the article about the stolen antiques . . .' She didn't need another job, but a small seed of an idea had started to grow . . . the job could be a way to get more information. Getting out of her flat and out from under Aaron's watchful gaze was an added benefit.

'Come and join our team. You look bright and smart, which is just what we need.' Carole held out her arms like she was about to hug her and then thought better of it. Probably because Sky stepped backwards without meaning to – she liked her personal space.

'Don't you need to see my CV first?'

She's too trusting.

When Carole shrugged, Sky walked around the antiques shop and let herself imagine what a normal life would look like. But now, over three weeks later, as Sky sat huddled on the old sofa in a cold and musty room, she worried it had all been a big mistake. Aaron was never going to let her go.

She needed to find a way out of the mess that she had made of not only her current situation but also her life.

Her laptop glowed on her lap.

Chris Prince . . . she knew that name from somewhere. After a quick search she concluded that there were so many Chris

Princes and Ben Wellses that it was impossible to narrow down the correct ones, and there were none she could see who were directly involved in the antiques trade. The cruise company seemed only to focus on Mark Rushwell, and there was a small mention of Sally Bright and 'other experts to be confirmed'.

She set up a new email address and sent an email to MVGoldstar's Head Office, asking for some details for an article she was supposedly writing on Prince and Wells. If they didn't get back to her, she would resort to hacking their systems.

For the first time in years she was using her skills for the right reasons, and it warmed her and filled her with foreboding at the same time.

Chapter Thirteen

Freya

In a staggered procession we were all heading for the Gallery even though I had lost my sense of direction. After walking the full length of the outside promenade deck, we descended the sweeping golden staircase to the shopping parade on Deck Ten. I hung back, knowing that if I took the stairs I would be easily spotted. Laura and Luke approached a guard who was standing by the door of the now open Gallery looking sheepish. I couldn't hear what was being said, but from Luke's gestures he was livid and asking for the keys to be placed in his outstretched hand. Laura ushered Luke in without the keys being handed over.

I hurried down the steps and along the main parade of shops.

Phil stood discreetly outside looking in, but I didn't want to hang back. I was eager to see the exhibition and took a step towards the door.

'What are you doing?' he muttered, coming to stand next to me.

'I just need a quick look around.'

He looked confused and his gaze met my eyes. 'What's so urgent? What do I need to know?'

I wasn't going to tell him what I was looking for just yet. I wanted to see if I was right first – if the painting really was the same as the one in the back of Arthur's journal. Without hesitation I stepped inside the Gallery.

Hanging on the walls were oil paintings of ships and seascapes. There was an eye-catching mahogany barometer displayed at the far end. It almost looked like an upside-down longcase clock hung on the wall – a slender neck stretching down to a clock face. Although it told the weather, not the time. I recognized it at once – 'GEORGE ADAMS, LONDON, CIRCA 1765'.

'A GEORGE III WHEEL BAROMETER' – I had seen it in the first section Arthur had headed 'THE COLLECTION'.

I pulled out my phone and brought up the images of the second journal – the original was safely hidden in the shop – and found the picture with the description below it:

The case with broken-arch pediment and vase finial, hinged at the lower edge for access to the tube, the square gilt-brass dial plate with matted centre, silvered chapter ring, steel main hand, pierced brass recording hand operated by brass knob above the dial, the upper trunk inset with 'A General State of the Weather' engraved on a silvered plate, signed to the lower edge 'Geo. Adams, No. 60 Fleet Street, London, Instrut. Maker to His Majesty K. G. III'.

Mahogany and brass. Worth between £30,000 and £50,000.

It was exactly the same.

Luke had been standing in the middle of the room, facing the small painting on the wall, when he saw me.

He frowned and crossed his arms. 'Can I help you?'

I hurried to the central cabinet; I stopped in my tracks when I saw the contents. 'I'm just excited to see all these antiques.'

My phone was still in my hand, but I didn't dare check the photos again in case Luke or Laura saw them.

Inside the cabinet was a display of shipwreck ceramics and a sea sculpture – a vase and teacup fused together by coral. It was a beautiful example. An ancient sextant, a compass and some other nautical instruments were visible at the far end of the case. Along with a bronze sword.

'Is there something you are specifically interested in?' I turned to see Laura glaring at me. Her friendly demeanour in the Library had slipped into open hostility.

'Oh, hi, I just wanted to see the collection.' I tried to give her my warmest smile.

Luke stalked towards me, his eyes darkening. 'The Gallery is closed.' He pointed to the door. 'You can come back tomorrow.'

'Yoo-hoo! Darling,' called Carole from behind me. She walked into the Gallery with her arm linked through Phil's. 'I found' – she squeezed his arm playfully – 'an officer and a gentleman for you!' Phil shook his head and a deep laugh rumbled out of him.

I wasn't normally one to let my aunt's innuendos land, but I could feel my cheeks warming so I spun around and turned my attention to the items in the Gallery. Every item in Arthur's second journal was on display. None were listed on the Art Loss Register, so I couldn't be sure if they were all stolen. But there had to be a reason why Arthur had logged them all in the journal for me to find.

'We are closing up for the night.' Laura's voice was strained.

'That painting . . .' said Carole, pointing to the one Luke had been studying when I came in. 'Of the burning ship. Could we . . . ?'

Luke stepped between the painting and her. 'It's a new acquisition. I'm still refining the hang, so if you wouldn't mind . . .' He held out his arm to herd Carole and Phil to the door.

Carole huffed and shook her head, not moving. 'Where did you get it?' She arched her neck to peer past him.

Eager to see the painting, I sidestepped Laura – bringing the photograph of the painting in the back of Arthur's journal to my mind's eye. The one Betty had confirmed was the painting he had donated to the museum.

The painting before me fit Betty's description: 'big old sailing ship with cannons along one side and huge sheets which had caught the wind. A captain at the helm . . . but half of the ship was engulfed in flames and was sinking. The sea was black and stormy, and overhead there were rain clouds.'

As Luke was ushering Carole and Phil out, my aunt slipped her phone from her clutch bag and held it at waist height. But the glaring flash made Luke snap to attention.

'What are you doing?' He jabbed his finger towards the sign on the wall. 'This clearly states "No Photography".'

'I'm so sorry. I couldn't read it.' Carole smiled sweetly at him. 'These ageing eyes of mine.' And she popped the phone back in her bag, standing close to Phil as she did. Luke was standing much too close to her, yelling, 'Delete it *now*!'

Anger pitted in my stomach, and I stepped forward, but Carole threaded my fingers through hers. 'We're leaving,' she said in a calm tone.

I breathed deeply, pushing away my desire to put Luke in his place for talking to Carole so rudely, and took Carole's phone from her. In a quick motion I sent the picture to myself and then deleted it. 'See. It's deleted and we're sorry about the flash.'

Phil stepped in, telling the curator, 'We'll be on our way.'

'We will come back in the morning,' I said, trying to see if there was any attribution on display alongside the painting. There wasn't, but I got a better look at the painting itself – there was something decidedly odd about it. At the end of the ship that wasn't in flames, where the captain stood at the wheel, the paint looked brighter . . . the colours more pronounced, as if half the painting had been cleaned or altered.

Luke stared fixedly at me as if he didn't trust that I had deleted the photograph, but Phil gestured ahead of him, placing his broad back solidly in the way of any attempt to stop us.

I was buzzing with excitement. It had been the right thing to do, coming on this cruise – because the painting was on board, and I was close to solving my very first case.

'Better get back to our table,' said Carole as we began to climb the golden staircase.

But I didn't want to go back. I needed time on my own to mull everything over. 'I think I might go to the Library and have some tea.'

* * *

The Library was empty apart from a crew member who was sitting behind Laura's desk.

'I just came for a cup of tea.' I smiled at him.

'Are you sure I can't get you anything stronger?' he replied, indicating the bar by the kitchenette.

'A mint tea would be perfect.' I pressed the button to open

the glass doors to the private deck. I settled in a comfy wicker armchair next to the railing, not far from where I had met the experts earlier. The night was dark and the stars were bright; waves lapped against the hull. I was glad of the shawl Carole had suggested I keep in my bag. I looked out over the railing and realized there was no shoreline visible on that side of the ship, no reassuring glow of light. The soft, rolling advance of the ship through the dark waters calmed me until the reality of my situation made me shudder. I might have found the painting, but I still needed to get to the bottom of how it came to be displayed in the Gallery, and who stole it from Lowestoft Museum.

Did the thief bring the painting here? Was he on the ship? Was he involved in the murder behind the museum?

The hunt wasn't over yet.

I opened the photograph, hoping to find some answers, and zoomed in on the figure at the helm – and couldn't believe what I was seeing.

Chapter Fourteen

Carole

Carole and Phil walked together back to the lift. 'I have a feeling that you have something you need to get off your brooding chest.' She patted his arm. 'So, out with it.'

He stopped and his deep hazel eyes studied her – his brow furrowed. 'Why are you both here? You've no idea what you're walking into . . .' He raked his hand through his close-cropped hair. 'It's *dangerous*!'

Carole scoffed. 'I think we've proven that danger doesn't scare us! Perhaps we could offer you some help? I know that you and Arthur had an . . . arrangement . . . a trading of information. Might we also be given such a role?' she said. 'You have consultants, don't you?'

Phil's eyes widened and he shook his head. 'Arthur was an old friend. He wanted me to keep you both safe. Both of you make that very . . . *difficult*.'

'Now, listen.' Carole poked a finger at his chest. 'We don't need protection. We're strong women, quite skilled in self-defence. What we need is professional help.' Phil sighed. 'And there's no getting off this ship until we get to Egypt. We're all stuck here together . . . so . . .' Carole might have been on the wrong side of seventy, but she still had the skills to play a man when necessary. 'We're here on a case and we're not stopping until it's solved. Let's help each other.'

He nodded, but there was a look in his eyes that she couldn't read . . . as if that worried him more than anything. 'Let me walk you back to the restaurant.' He held his arm out as the lift door opened.

'Thank you, but I'll make it on my own,' said Carole, inwardly appreciating his lovely manners. 'You're both dashing and charming, aren't you? But you need to see that Freya is really coming into her own now and she's doing a fabulous job on her first case.' She locked her jaw – she had probably told Phil too much already.

There might have been a faint smile straining his lips, but he wrestled it into submission.

The Seafood and Steak restaurant was buzzing now; the wine had been flowing in her absence. Carole sat back down at the dinner table, giving everyone a cheery 'hello, did I miss any-thing?' but she was troubled. Phil was right; there was danger on board the ship, and she needed to uncover it before it found her and her niece.

There was a very small helping of cheesecake and berries already at her place setting, but she wasn't hungry. She'd pulled out her phone to tell Freya she was going to bed.

Patricia reached over and tapped her arm. 'Is Freya coming back? She left in such a hurry; I didn't get a chance to talk to her about her shop in Suffolk and about Arthur.'

'I think she went to bed. I was going to . . .' Carole paused as a wave of grief began to build. She had always believed that she had known everyone in Arthur's life, but as she started to explore the underbelly of the antiques world with Freya at Copthorn Manor, she had realized she was wrong. Her best friend had had a life far beyond their love for each other, and it pained her to be reminded of that now – for she had never even heard of Patricia before setting foot on the cruise.

Patricia was waiting patiently, so Carole cleared her throat and replied, 'Did you know Arthur well? I'm surprised we never met before.'

'I met him on these adventures at sea. I'm so sorry to hear of his passing.' She squeezed Carole's arm. 'I've lost so many dear to me, but I have a nephew that I'm very close to. Just like you and your niece . . . We are so lucky, aren't we?'

Carole's heart clenched as the memories of the people she had loved and lost over the years came crashing back. She sighed, put down her phone and turned her attention to Patricia. 'We are. Arthur and I went on so very many adventures together, but it's sometimes the small things we miss the most, isn't it? I loved popping into his shop for a cuppa and a good long chat on a cold afternoon. The way he always said "hello, dear" when he answered the phone. The twinkle in his eye when we were about to "go have some fun" . . .' Carole paused as her heart twisted.

Patricia reached over and rubbed her arm. 'And did Freya join you and Arthur on your adventures?'

'Oh, no, they didn't see eye to eye for a long time. They worked together moons ago but then . . . stopped.'

Patricia nodded. 'I could see that it could be hard working with the younger generation. So, Freya runs the shop now?'

Carole had a lightbulb moment – if Patricia had been on past cruises with Arthur, she could know a great deal without realizing it. 'I'll let you in on a secret.' She leaned towards Patricia's ear. 'I think Freya is too work, work, work and needs some fun. And this trip is perfect for that.'

'Fun in what sense?' Patricia's eyes sparkled with conspiracy.

'Well, of course she needs to focus on her job as an antiques expert, but I wondered if there wasn't a nice gentleman she could have a cocktail or two with, and you seem to know everyone on board . . .' Carole winked at Patricia.

'Oh, a bit of matchmaking will make these days at sea fly by! I might know someone.'

Carole knew this was her moment. 'I was hoping that she could meet with the other experts, Ben Wells and Chris Prince, but they don't seem to be here. Have you ever met them? Would they have been a good fit?'

Patricia bristled and she shook her head. 'Neither of them would be good for any woman. I'm afraid they are too focused on business to be serious about anyone. They leave a trail of broken hearts behind them. But I have one lovely nephew, he's quite a catch!'

Carole's phone pinged. Freya had messaged her.

Zoom in on the captain. Do you recognize anyone?

Patricia was now chatting away about how easy it was to make new best friends on a cruise ship and how much she loved seeing all the regulars. Carole murmured agreement and put on her reading glasses. Just a quick look.

Patricia leaned forward. 'What's that you have there?' Carole put the phone away. There was something weirdly intense about the way Patricia had stared at her screen.

'It was so lovely chatting to you – what a wonderful dinner. But I'm feeling rather tired. It's been quite a lot of travelling for one day,' Carole said, standing up again. 'Shall we have a coffee tomorrow?'

'Do stay!' Patricia looked around the depleted table, frowning. 'And where did the dashing captain go? If I was younger, I'd have made a play to get those strong arms around me, if you know what I mean. He could be in the running for a cocktail or two with Freya.' Her look was conspiratorial and contagious, and Carole warmed to her once again.

'I don't think Phillip is the captain . . . I think he's just one of the officers.'

'How about we demand that he comes and has dinner with us tomorrow night!' Patricia chuckled.

Carole couldn't help but smile. What would the serious FBI agent think of all this talk behind his back? 'Shall we have a nightcap on the terrace?' she asked the women.

An hour later Carole had left the terrace, her ears ringing with ship gossip. Some of the premier members like Patricia were annoyed at one of the single men, Jamie, for bringing a female passenger into the exclusive bar and not introducing her to anyone.

Her head swam with the two espresso martinis she had consumed while trying to get as much information on the passengers as possible. But when she had tried to bring up the two experts again, Patricia shrugged it off. Jenny, on the other hand, had frozen at the mention of them and then suggested they had clearly 'changed their minds'.

Alone in the lift, Carole opened her phone again and studied the photo. She pinched and expanded the screen. It wasn't the thought of being at sea while studying a painting of a ship on fire that suddenly chilled her to the bone. It was the way the captain was painted. Standing straight-backed while chaos reigned around him, his hands resting on something, she wasn't sure what – but one finger seemed to be out of line with the others. She squinted in vain at the hands but could not distinguish any more detail. Freya probably could. There was a flash of colour at his neck and another on his lapel. Carole zoomed in closer. The ship's captain wore a bright orange cravat that looked oddly familiar. She brought the phone directly to her eye and for the first time acknowledged whom she was seeing.

Hello, Arthur.

Chapter Fifteen

Phil

Phil strode away from Carole and out onto the promenade deck, pulling at his collar and taking in a deep breath. When he finally found a quiet spot in the shadows, he gripped the cool metal of the railing, willing his pulse to settle.

The spark of defiance and drive Freya had back at Copthorn Manor was even stronger now, but no matter how skilled a hunter she might be, he couldn't have her or Carole involved, could he? The Collector went to extreme lengths to keep his identity a secret and those who tried to uncover it always ended up dead. He didn't want more death on his hands.

Phil's other problem was the 'meeting' Arthur referred to last year when they had spoken on the Embankment. He had stalked the ship day and night, surviving on very little sleep, but he had seen nothing unusual so far.

The lapping sea and the hum of the engine soothed his nerves, and it gave him pause to consider his options. Should he trade information with Freya and Carole? He didn't have a team on board because he hadn't explicitly told his boss that he was there to hunt The Collector. A few months back Sloane – the young FBI agent – had been told by her informant that antiquities were being trafficked out of Egypt via a cruise ship. It was just enough to get him on board and to have requested Sloane as backup.

Once at sea he had a suspicion that the antiques and art in the Gallery were a small portion of The Collector's private collection; but why was it on show? It was either incredibly sloppy or some sort of trick. He believed the latter.

Phil sighed. First, he would find out why Freya and Carole were on board. Back in Copthorn Manor, they were following a lead that Arthur had given them. Was it the same this time?

The memory of Freya in the Gallery earlier filled his mind, her warm perfume washing over him again, and he shook his head to rid his mind of any further thoughts of her . . . like that. He was on a case, and nothing could distract him. Until he found himself wondering – why were the women so interested in that painting of a burning ship?

He pulled out his phone and messaged Sloane. *Any more information on the items in the Gallery? I know we agreed to start with the provenance of the most valuable items first, such as the barometer. But I think we should now focus on the painting of the burning ship.*

Sloane: *I looked into it already – it's on the list I already sent you of items to reclaim when we get to Jordan. It was stolen from the Lowestoft Maritime Museum nearly a week ago – the night before the ship set sail – and is linked to the murder of an unidentified man at the scene. I'm checking with the local force to find out more.*

Phil pulled out the list and read it again. It hadn't seemed important when Sloane had mentioned it yesterday, but if Freya was interested in it then there was more to that painting than he had originally thought.

The sound of holidaying passengers' drunk laughter rippled over him, and he was reminded it was late and he also needed to start his nightly search of the ship.

Over the past eighteen years, since Ed, his old partner, threw a file on his desk, he had tracked The Collector. In his notes Ed had described a museum guard who had been arrested for his part in a theft back in 2000 and had begged Ed for protection on the ride to the station. The guard had insisted that The Collector was real, and that the operation was run like a business with a CEO – The Collector – and a board of directors profiting from each transaction. The guard had died in jail a week later when a fight broke out. But from that point on Ed was convinced that the company and the position as The Collector were real and had been in operation for over two hundred years. No one ever got close enough to identify any of those involved. Or when they did, they didn't live to talk.

Over the years, every sleek and sophisticated unsolved theft had been attributed to The Collector. Every time an item was discovered in a private collection a continent away from where it was stolen, it was whispered The Collector had moved it there.

But Phil had discovered something else over his years of research. Around 60 per cent of the thefts had a very specific pattern. No fingerprints were ever found; a guard or member of staff was always blackmailed or bribed and left as the fall guy . . . there was always a van outside that could never be traced. Once or twice a line of enquiry had led to an offshore shell company that had a small one-page website to make it look legitimate. On several occasions, CCTV showed a biker in the vicinity.

The theft of a grey Ming Dynasty vase from a Greek museum two decades ago was the closest Ed and Phil ever came to the notorious figure. They had managed to track down the getaway driver to a biker cafe on the outskirts of Athens. Under questioning, he told them he was just a man for hire, but he knew the vase was on a ferry from Athens to Santorini. He tried to flee, and when caught he insisted that because he had been in contact with The Collector he would be killed for talking to the police. He produced a burner phone with messages he claimed came directly from The Collector. Phil was sceptical; they could have been sent by anyone organizing the theft, but for Ed it was one more piece of evidence that The Collector was one man.

When they tracked an odd catamaran leaving Santorini and followed it all the way to Aqaba, Jordan, in every port they heard the rumours from informants that The Collector was behind the theft of the vase. That he would be there in person to collect it. Ed was thrilled they were so close . . . but then days later even more men died to keep The Collector's identity a secret.

Moonlight danced across the waves as Phil checked his watch and decided it was time to look at the painting again, without any drama. As Phil approached, he saw that the Gallery was still open; a couple was staring into the central cabinet and the curator was, once again, studying the painting of the burning ship. Phil stopped walking and sidestepped to his previous viewpoint – to see without being seen. Luke was staring intently at the canvas, his nose so close to it that it was almost touching.

What is he seeing?

* * *

Three days earlier, the curator had arrived on board with a container full of priceless art and antiques. Phil had been informed the exhibition contents were arriving and naturally offered to help so he could take his first look at them.

He was walking around in uniform but had no real idea how the ship was run. MVGoldstar Head Office had agreed that he could introduce himself to the passengers as the events officer, but when he met Laura Scott, he realized that the cruise already had one. MVGoldstar was reluctantly supportive of the FBI's mission, but then again, he hadn't given them much choice.

Phil had greeted Luke on his arrival. He showed him to the shop off the main parade on Deck Ten that would be the Gallery for the duration of the cruise. The space had once been a jewellery boutique and MVGoldstar's fully accredited security service was in place. He hung around while Luke and another crew member started to unpack the contents, and a security guard set about hanging the paintings under Luke's close supervision. After each was put on the wall, the two men had taken a few steps back and considered its position in relation to the others. He had become absorbed in watching the lengthy process.

When Luke noticed, he waved Phil away. 'You can leave us now.'

He took his time and watched as the security guard placed a set of keys down on the central glass cabinet. With a sleight of hand, Phil dropped them into his pocket, deciding that he would find out the alarm code and come back after the Gallery was closed and the passengers were sleeping.

The first night, when he was alone in the Gallery, he had taken photos of all the items in there and consulted the Art

Loss Register and other databases on the FBI system. There was a record of the stolen bronze sword from years ago, and the barometer had also been stolen from a stately home. But other items weren't on the list, so Sloane and Phil had started with the shipwrecked ceramics.

The twist of panic settled in him from that point on – he had needed to prove to himself that he was on the right track. That Arthur had been on the right track . . .

* * *

Phil entered the Gallery to see Luke turn away from the painting and pick up a polishing cloth and begin to wipe the glass on top of the central cabinet. He strode towards the painting Freya was so interested in.

'Can I help you? It would save us both time if you tell me what you're looking for,' said Luke.

Phil kept his tone carefully neutral. 'My mother was an art curator, and being this far from home for this long . . .' Was he really just about to admit to homesickness that he didn't know he felt until he had started talking? 'I haven't seen an antique exhibition for years,' he lied. 'Have you shown this collection on a cruise before?'

The curator smiled warmly for him. 'No. The owner is personally friendly with the organizers, who begged him to exhibit here.'

'And how will all these items be shipped back to their owner?' Phil asked.

Luke shrugged. 'Safely. Please excuse me, I must make a phone call.'

He strode to the back of the Gallery and put his phone to

his ear, though he didn't appear to be talking and he kept his eyes on Phil.

Phil turned his attention to the enigmatic painting that seemed to fascinate the curator, Freya and Carole. Why was this piece of such interest to all three? It seemed strange to him. Up close, it looked kind of a mess: recent work on top of an uninspired nineteenth-century provincial copy, if he was any judge. The last time he viewed it, he hadn't paid much attention to the figure of the captain, but this time he stepped up so close his nose was almost touching the oil paint.

His eyes widened and a surprised smile tugged at the corners of his mouth.

'Hello, old man, good to see you again. How on earth did this painting get on this cruise?' he murmured.

He took it as a sign he was on the right path.

Luke coughed and Phil decided it was time to leave. He had gotten the answers he came for . . . and his respect for Freya Lockwood had swelled a little more.

Freya must have known that Arthur was depicted in the painting, and that didn't sit well with Phil. He also wanted to be annoyed with her for finding a way to get onto the cruise when he had made sure she wouldn't, but he admired her tenacity.

Maybe it was time to give Freya and Carole the information they so clearly craved.

Chapter Sixteen

Freya

The Suez Canal

It was nearly 6 a.m. when I stood on the top deck in my running gear. I couldn't summon the energy to start after watching a couple in their sixties jog past me in top-of-the-range trainers, tight shorts and matching sun visors. I closed my eyes, turning my face towards the breaking dawn and breathing in lungfuls of iodine-rich air – trying to look yogi-like and serene instead of the way I felt. I had slept only fitfully. The constant rocking movement of the ship made me restless.

The unanswered questions about the case were circling like seagulls.

I decided that I couldn't be standing here on their next circuit, so I headed to the Library in the hope that there was fresh coffee in the pot this early.

The Library was deserted but there was coffee in the pot, so I filled a cup and headed to the private deck. I relaxed into my new favourite chair in the far corner, which enabled me to see anyone who might enter the Library. I took another look at Carole's photograph of the painting. Betty had never mentioned that the ship's captain depicted in it was Arthur. Had she known all along? I decided to contact Sky next.

Me: *Have you found any photos of Chris Prince or Ben Wells yet? I'm sending you a pic of the painting that was stolen from Lowestoft – it's here! See if you can find out anything about it.*

Sky: Interesting! I'll see what info I can get.

On my phone I had pictures of each page of the second journal. The first section of Arthur's journal itemized a collection of nautical antiques. The second section documented just five rare and valuable items, none of which I recognized from the exhibition. All were documented as stolen from five big burglaries within the past fifteen years.

20 x rare Mint Error 2p coins, valued around £100,000 each – stolen from the British Museum in 2012

Patek Philippe Supercomplication Pocket Watch 1932 – $24 million – stolen from a safe in a private house in New York in 2009

Very rare pair of Duck Decoys – valued around $50,000 – stolen from a Cambridge museum in 2018

A collection of 18th-Century Qianlong jade from Qing Dynasty, $5.3 million – stolen from a private collection in Amsterdam in 2006

A grey Ming Dynasty vase – $millions – stolen from a museum in Athens, Greece in 2003

The grey Ming Dynasty vase interested me the most because it was a case that Arthur and I had worked on together in 2003.

We had never succeeded in recovering the vase, and I'd believed it was destroyed in a fire. *A fire on board a ship* . . . just like the painting that Arthur was painted into!

Betty said Mr Suited and Booted had mentioned a grey vase.

I was deep in thought when my senses prickled and I looked around to find a uniformed waiter standing in the Library doorway staring at me. He was the maître d' who had welcomed us at the Seafood and Steak restaurant, but now in a very different uniform.

He looks familiar.

Our eyes locked and he ducked his head, retreating into the corridor. I stuck my head out the door – the waiter brushed past an arriving Carole, averting his face. *Strange.*

'Is there something stronger than coffee in there?' My aunt nodded to the Library. 'I'd love to start the day with a big glass of holiday bubbly.'

I nodded. 'It's a cruise ship. There's alcohol on tap. But I think at eight a.m. there will also be French pastries, fruit, granola . . . you know, the sort of thing generally considered breakfast-appropriate by responsible adults.'

My aunt gave me one of her most winning smiles. 'Adulting is no fun. And when they say all-inclusive, it's rude not to start a holiday morning with bubbles! Were you leaving?'

'The maître d' from the fancy restaurant was just in here as a waiter. Does that seem strange to you?' Carole turned back and frowned. 'Never mind . . . I was thinking of going to see that painting again and perhaps ask Luke its provenance. It makes me think Arthur is trying to tell me something.'

Carole glanced around, checking that she wasn't going to be overheard, and led me back into the Library and out onto the private deck. 'I have something to show you. I was going to do it last night but when I came into your room, you were asleep and I didn't want to wake you.'

I settled down in my chair and she sat opposite me, ignoring the fresh sea air and the container ships chugging by.

'Right. Look at this.' She pulled up a picture on her phone and I leaned in. 'Do you see it?' She turned the photograph of the painting towards me and started to zoom in.

'I saw Arthur there, if that's what you mean.'

'Yes, but look at this on his lapel. That speck of red.' She stretched the image even more. 'It's . . . a brooch.'

Our eyes met. We both knew what that meant. 'It's the Léa Stein red fox brooch he left me in his will.'

Some favourite phrases of Arthur's came back to me: 'Ready for the next fox hunt, then?' he always used to say before we started our next job.

And I would smile and reply, 'I'm always ready, old man.'

Now that Carole had shown me that the clues were all in minute detail, I worked my way slowly over the area around Arthur. 'The ship seems to be called HMS *Lockwood*,' I said. 'I think we can safely assume there wasn't a real ship called that.'

'And see, the orange cravat has a purple edge? It was the one I bought him as a thank-you for taking me on our trip on a cruise ship from Southampton to New York back in 2005. He was invited to hold some lectures as an antiques expert and I had never crossed the Atlantic by sea. Win-win!'

'Arthur was leaving us another message,' said my aunt fondly. 'Last time he left us a letter. This time he left a painting.'

I squinted. 'The details on the newly painted Arthur are incredible. Look at each section, down to Arthur's fingers . . .

Someone would have to paint with a magnifying glass to do that, wouldn't they?'

Carole was staring at me.

'What?'

'Well . . . it's just . . . that's what you used to say about the paintings at home . . . the miniature paintings your mother did that are hung in the hallway.'

I looked at the picture again. 'It does look like that . . . but we're not saying Arthur got my mother to paint this, are we?'

She shook her head. 'Your mother's been gone a long time. Long before Arthur gave you the fox brooch or I got him the orange cravat in New York, both of which are in the painting.'

'So who painted Arthur into a Victorian painting? And why did he want it hanging in Lowestoft Maritime Museum?'

Carole shrugged. 'Your mother knew a lot of people in the miniature-painting world. Perhaps Arthur met someone through her, then went to that artist to get this painting embellished sometime earlier this year, before he died. The detail of the face, the fine crease of the trousers . . . It is such delicate specialist work,' she said, and reached out to pat my hand.

'I'll ask Sky if she can dig up miniature artists . . . Betty said Arthur had gone to pick up the painting in Norfolk, so she might try there first.'

'Special delivery!' a male voice said from behind me.

We both whipped around. Phil had appeared, carrying a tray with a bottle of champagne, a glass and some croissants arranged on it. 'An apology for how abrupt I was with you last night, Carole. Had to follow up on something.' He placed the tray on the table in front of her and set about opening the bottle. It popped and fizzed as she grabbed the glass in anticipation.

'Now, I think it's time you explain what you are really here for,' said my aunt.

Phil's eyes snapped to mine. 'If I tell you what I can, will you be open and honest in return?'

I nodded. 'As far as I can, yes.' *But I'm not mentioning the journals!*

He sat down next to me. 'First, I need to insist you keep a lower profile. No more snooping around drawing attention to yourselves.' We both nodded in agreement. Carole crossed her fingers under the table.

Phil scanned the deck and sighed. 'I'm sorry, but this is a dangerous case, and I don't want either of you in harm's way.'

'Arthur wanted us here!' Carole glared at him.

'And now you're here.' His tone was calm, but there was an edge to it. 'Even though you shouldn't be.'

'Go on,' I said. 'You first.'

'Have either of you heard of The Collector?'

A seagull called out over the swelling waves and a foghorn boomed out, but my senses were overcome by an onslaught of unwelcome memories all sliding into one.

The Collector . . . It had been a very long time since I had heard that name. Arthur and I were in Jordan in 2003, hunting the stolen Ming Dynasty vase that had been destroyed in a ship fire. Afterwards, Arthur had mentioned he had heard whispers of The Collector being involved. He relayed the legends, told me he didn't believe them. But what if Arthur had uncovered the truth while moving through the underworld? What if he had been keeping an ear open for other rumours about The Collector ever since?

I nodded as Carole shook her head. 'He's a myth, isn't he?'

I asked, wondering where all this was leading. 'What are you getting at?'

'I don't think he is a myth. And neither did Arthur. It was he who informed me that The Collector was going to be on board this ship for a succession meeting. The old Collector is to step down and a new one will take his place. Arthur told me it was a rare opportunity – both would be in the same room together and therefore I could uncover the identities of old and new.'

I stared, waiting for the smile to tell me he was joking. But the crease on his brow told me he wasn't – I shook my head in disbelief. 'You're an FBI special agent in one of the biggest art crime units in the world and you believe in conspiracy theories?' He flinched like I'd prodded him with a hot poker. 'Even Arthur didn't believe it.'

He sighed and I shifted in my seat. 'Arthur *did* believe The Collector was real. He was the one who told me to be here. The Collector acquires and trades objects all over the world, and like most wealthy private collectors of a certain vintage, when they want a priceless antiquity, they don't care how they get it. Last winter we intercepted a private plane associated with The Collector and confiscated over six million dollars' worth of art and antiques. The Collector was not on board. That's why you must be careful – The Collector prizes rare objects above all and sets no value on human life. Witnesses are intimidated into silence, informants end up dead and . . .' Phil paused and closed his eyes.

Before I had a chance to ask another question, Laura strode towards us.

'Thank God I've found you!' She gripped the back of Phil's chair while she addressed me. 'There's been a mixup and we'll need you to do your talk on costume jewellery earlier.' She checked her watch, and then her eyes came to rest on the champagne.

'I thought I had most of this afternoon to prepare?'

'I know, but today's afternoon talk was meant to be by Mark, but . . . well . . . he is exhausted. Sally, too. They have already been working overtime. So, *please*, would you do this for them?'

'I'll leave you to it,' said Phil, rising quickly and sliding his chair out of Laura's grasp, tucking it away under the table. He walked back into the Library.

Laura glared at him. 'He shouldn't have been sitting drinking with you. I hope he wasn't bothering you?'

'Oh, no, darling! He brought me champagne, and I demanded he sit down. He's just so handsome I couldn't help myself.' Carole winked at Laura.

Laura tutted. 'I'll see you at three.'

Carole reached over and grabbed my hand after Laura had left. 'This is all going wonderfully well, isn't it?'

I wasn't sure it was going that well, as I now had more questions than answers. Who was Mr Suited and Booted, and had he stolen the painting and brought it on board? Arthur had told Phil to be on the ship to uncover the identity of the legendary Collector. Was it all connected?

Excitement tingled through me as I pulled up the photo of the painting one more time – zooming in on Arthur.

'What are you telling me this time, old man?' I whispered. 'What is at the heart of this hunt you have set us all on?'

I took in a lungful of air and caught Carole's eye. She reached over and took my hand in hers. 'Whatever the danger, we will get to the bottom of this, just like Arthur would have wanted us to.'

'We will,' I assured her.

Chapter Seventeen

Luke

Luke Drummond stepped into the theatre with apprehension – his mind was racing, but when his eyes fixed on Freya Lockwood onstage he thought: *She can't really be here to take over from Arthur Crockleford, can she?*

The seats at the very back were a perfect place to ensure he had a good view of everyone. For now, the room was brightly lit, but in a matter of minutes darkness would sink over the auditorium.

Luke had grown tired of the black market years ago, but it was not the sort of life you just walked away from. He was too . . . knowledgeable. But finally . . . finally . . . he was ready to execute his long-planned exit strategy. With a new Collector on the horizon this was his chance to quietly slip away.

He breathed in deeply, wishing he was an ordinary passenger. Passengers had more fun. But he had managed to secure his place on board for one thing and one thing only. And when he had that, no one would ever see him again. Costa Rica was calling.

Freya opened her laptop and fiddled with cables to get the slideshow to work. *Amateur.* Once the logo came up on the projection screen, she began placing some small silver pieces of jewellery on a side table beside her – they looked like mid-century modern, maybe Danish, but it was hard to tell from such a distance. Next came a collection of gold costume jewellery pieces, a necklace, earrings and a bangle with ruby-red glass that caught the light and sparkled as Freya picked them up.

Perhaps she thought the showy costume variety would appeal to the masses.

He scoffed. *There are no massed crowds, no one wants to hear her talk. They want* real *antiques.*

Amateur.

Jenny and Archie walked in and sat across the aisle from him. He wasn't surprised they were here – they wanted to know why Freya was on board as much as he did. Archie gave him a small twitch of a smile. A crew member stood by the entrance scanning the room as Laura fussed with the lighting until she was satisfied and then caught his eye and came over.

'I'm surprised you're here,' she said, without looking surprised. 'Decided this is your sort of thing after all? Or are you here to cause trouble?'

'I'm here to observe.'

Laura frowned and searched his face for the truth. It was clear that she didn't believe him, but instead of questioning him further she rolled her shoulders and forced a smile, and her professional mask slipped back into place.

Luke had a sneaking suspicion that Laura wanted out just as much as he did. He wondered if she had the nerve to go through with it. Over the past few years Laura's brightness had dimmed; he might not have liked her, but even he could see that she was nothing like the young woman he had met back in London all those years ago. She was young and carefree then – always laughing and joking around. But the black market did something to a person over time, and now she had seen too much . . . they had both seen too much.

His handcrafted brogues kicked a discarded plastic champagne flute that had been missed in the cleanup after the ballroom dancing show the night before. Luke liked the sedate surroundings of a stately home or castle; he wasn't fond of being trapped at sea with hundreds of people. One of the joys his job afforded him was working for people with a clear vision for their personal collections. People with the funds to back their taste – to outbid anyone at auction – that was the sort of milieu where he belonged.

But he had to make sure the items in the Gallery reached the right hands safely before he could slip away.

Luke thought back to the events of yesterday evening. Freya Lockwood . . . the nosy expert who didn't bother to show up until the cruise was underway. She was the last person he'd wanted to see in the Gallery because she had known Arthur Crockleford – and Arthur had known far too much.

The incident of the aunt snapping a photograph of the painting was deeply troubling to Luke. He knew that locking up the Gallery again was the safest thing to do, but it meant he couldn't check everything as thoroughly as he'd intended. There was never a quiet time on board a cruise to do things unobserved. Apart from the floor where his stateroom was located.

And now he had to keep an eye out constantly for the Lockwoods. He wasn't going to let two nosy women get in the way of his payday.

Luke settled back in his seat and crossed his arms.

He was ready.

Chapter Eighteen

Freya

MVGoldstar's windowless theatre was marked by a large 'What's On' board in front of two large double doors. I had arrived early and now stood at the corner of the stage gripping the curtains to steady myself, my heartbeat pounding in my ears. Through the gap ahead of me I could see a few passengers meandering down the stairs into a sea of empty chairs.

I pulled out my phone as a distraction, hoping to see a message from Sky, but nothing appeared.

Carole opened the double entrance doors, waving to me as she hurried down the aisle. She knew where I'd be hiding until it was time for me to step reluctantly into the spotlight.

I never set out to be this sort of antiques expert. I didn't want to be instantly recognizable . . . out in the arena of public opinion and always on show. Fading into the background was what I wanted to focus on. That ability would enable me to scour the underbelly of the antiques trade and hunt down stolen items.

But if that was what it took to solve the case, then . . . *I can do this!* I breathed in all the courage I could find and readied myself to walk onstage.

The theatre seated at least three hundred, for a cruise of

around four hundred. Luckily for me, if not for the event's organizer, it was still empty apart from a thin scattering of strangers. The next time the door opened, I saw Phil. He was wearing the standard crew uniform now – navy shorts and a navy polo shirt that was too tight around his arms when he folded them over his chest. He scanned the stage and then the rest of the room, but he didn't move from the main entrance. He looked like a bouncer. The presence of one more friendly face made my chest relax a little and I smiled in gratitude even though he couldn't see it.

Carole was sitting in the front row. She lifted her chin towards me and pinned a huge smile on her face. Her pride in me never faltered and today I needed that strength to infuse me. My fingers closed around the burn scar on my palm and my index finger traced the damaged skin. I reminded myself that if I could survive a fire, I could survive this.

But this time instead of soothing me, the image of that burning ship with Arthur at the helm came rushing back to my mind. Why choose that image? He knew that any mention or picture of a raging fire made me clench my hand over my scar. If flames were contained within a fireplace or wood-burning stove, I was fine. But if some trivial ad or illustration came on the TV, like a cartoon lion jumping through a ring of fire for instance, my pulse would quicken and . . . I opened my palm and studied it.

What were you trying to tell me, Arthur?

Out of the corner of my eye, I saw Patricia Henderson from dinner last night entering the theatre and greeting Phil warmly. She walked down the central aisle, taking her seat next to Jenny and Archie and waving to Carole at the front. It was good to see Patricia there.

Phil stood straight-backed and stared at each and every member of the audience as if he were burning them into his mind. Laura hurried past the stage, tutting when she saw the way the audience had scattered around the auditorium. Like a sheepdog, she urged them to congregate forward and centre. Only Luke was resistant to her charms and stayed where he was, at the very back.

Laura stepped briskly onto the stage towards where I had been setting up the jewellery. She was holding a headset microphone. She clipped a wire to the power pack on my back and linked it to a frame set over one of my ears, supporting a small microphone that she angled towards my mouth.

It felt strange, pressing against my cheek. 'Isn't there just a normal microphone? I'm not sure I need this – we're not in the West End.'

'These are the *best* ones, top of the range for lectures.' She shielded her eyes from the glaring spotlight to try and see the audience. 'Hello, everyone, sorry for the confusion. Shall we get started?'

I picked up my notes as Phil closed the auditorium doors and the house lights were lowered.

It's time.

She clicked the presentation clicker, and the first slide of the PowerPoint flickered into life on the large screen behind me.

'Good evening, thank you all for coming' – I knew how few people were there, but 'all' was what I had written down and I was sticking to it – 'to this talk on vintage and costume jewellery.' I took a breath and began.

'In recent years, the world of vintage hunting has experienced a resurgence in popularity. People are increasingly drawn to the charm of bygone eras, finding pieces at car boot sales, charity shops and flea markets. Among the treasures waiting to be discovered, costume jewellery stands out as a particularly captivating choice. With its affordable price tag and a rich history intertwined with glamorous Hollywood sirens of the past, costume jewellery has become alluring for vintage enthusiasts.

'So, what exactly is costume jewellery? Well, the term was first coined by the haute couture fashion industry during the early twentieth century, and generally refers to pieces of jewellery made from non-precious materials and designed to embellish fashionable outfits.

'I believe that one of the most attractive aspects of collecting costume jewellery is its association with the glamorous world of Hollywood. In the early twentieth century costume jewellery became a symbol of the Hollywood dream and enabled everyday women to affordably transform into starlets in their own right.'

I clicked the button again and images of Hollywood icons appeared: Marilyn Monroe, Joan Crawford, Greta Garbo and Vivien Leigh.

'Between the thirties and the sixties, Hollywood sirens and starlets adorned themselves with these exquisite pieces, creating an aura of enchantment. The items of jewellery that graced the silver screen were often used to accentuate the actresses' elaborate costumes and gowns. Many of these pieces were custom-made or specially chosen to match a character's personality, style or storyline, further enhancing the allure of the jewellery. For example, Marilyn Monroe famously loved the sparkling pieces from Joseff of Hollywood. Joan Crawford, known for her strong and glamorous persona, frequently wore pieces from Miriam Haskell, Trifari and Eisenberg.

'Before me on the table are three pieces by Joseff of Hollywood. Founder Eugene Joseff was a leading supplier of costume jewellery to the major Hollywood studios.'

I picked up my Joseff snake motif necklace – it had a chain that attached to two slithering snakes with open mouths eager to eat the large red cabochon stone in the centre. 'This necklace, along with matching earrings and bangle . . .'

The double doors to the auditorium opened again and light from the corridor flooded into the darkened space. In a flurry of movement, a blonde woman dressed in a waitress's uniform headed for the back row. I caught a glimpse of her face in the spill of light. She looked familiar.

Carole had followed the direction of my gaze. She gave an audible gasp and waved frantically at me, pointing with one hand. But by now the new arrival had moved into the shadows. I shielded my eyes and scanned the amphitheatre-style seating, looking for her.

She was at the very back, almost hidden in the darkness, a few seats away from Luke.

A cough came from my left and I saw Laura glaring at me, mouthing: 'Talk!'

'This is a good example of Joseff's bold pieces: larger than life and easy to see on the screen. Some of his pieces were worn by famous actresses such as Marlene Dietrich in *Shanghai Express*, Greta Garbo in *Camille*, Vivien Leigh in *Gone with the Wind* and of course Marilyn Monroe. In 1939 he launched a retail line to cater to popular demand for his jewellery.'

'How on earth are we meant to see those things all the way up there?' Luke heckled me, striding down the central aisle.

My cheeks burned. 'If you give me a minute, then a picture will come up on the screen behind me.'

I pressed the clicker and waited. I pressed it again.

Nothing happened.

There was a rattling sound at one side of the auditorium, and a finger of light stretched into the theatre. Phil's wide-shouldered frame was silhouetted against it as he walked out the door.

I shielded my eyes again and scanned the audience. Luke was now standing in the aisle close to the stage. He had his arms crossed and looked distinctly unimpressed. I stared at Carole, who pointed to him. 'Take them over,' she mouthed. 'Pass them round.' I didn't know what else to do. I gripped the necklace and headed down to join the audience.

Luke stepped forward as I placed the gold metal snakes in the centre of my palm. Everyone else got up from their seats and surrounded us – apart from Phil, who, I was relieved to see, had re-entered the theatre. He mouthed 'sorry' to me as our eyes locked.

Laura crushed in next to me, and her strong floral perfume made me sneeze.

Everyone took a step back.

'Did you have to do that?' said Luke in disgust.

'I'm so sorry.' I noticed goosebumps on my arms.

Luke returned to stand next to me. His Old Spice threatened to make me sneeze again. He peered at the necklace and shrugged. 'I believed that we were on an "antiques specialist cruise" hearing from antiques experts about antiques! I was always under the impression that for something to be an antique, it had to be over one hundred years old?' He didn't wait for me to reply. 'So there is nothing antique about any of this.' There were beads of sweat on his temple even with the air-conditioning at full force. He glared at me, implying that neither my talk nor my expertise qualified me. All eyes turned from the necklace to me.

I opened my mouth to defend myself.

'Could you let my niece complete her talk and then ask questions at the end?' Anger laced Carole's husky voice.

'What can *she* possibly enlighten us on?' He glared at me then turned away, almost staggering into the nearest seat. Before I could ask if he was all right, he coughed and barked, 'Get on with it then.' He pulled out a handkerchief and dabbed his forehead.

There was an awkward silence among those surrounding me. They were all watching me. Waiting for me to say or do something.

My stomach churned.

Carole placed a hand on my shoulder. 'You continue with this marvellous talk, darling, because we all want to hear it.'

I reluctantly climbed the steps back onto the stage, a bead of sweat running down my spine, and picked up from where I had been interrupted. Fortunately, Laura had fixed the PowerPoint glitch, and this time I was able to illustrate my subject as well as talk about it.

Over the next twenty minutes my voice shook and my heart hammered in my ears, but I got through it with a sense of accomplishment. With practice I could see that these speeches wouldn't be as terrifying as I had first thought. I concluded . . .

'And finally, the overriding advice I always give to anyone starting a collection is "only buy what you love", but in this case I'd take that a stage further and say: "only buy pieces you feel really passionate about". Costume jewellery always looks wonderful, magical, hoarded away and spilling out of your jewellery box, but ultimately, it's meant to be worn. It was always intended as a bold personal statement of style and fashion. So, please, don't just collect it . . . wear your heart on your sleeve and show it off as well!

'Venturing into the world of vintage costume jewellery collecting is not just a hobby; it's a journey into the glamour and elegance of a bygone era. As a beginner, you can uncover hidden treasures and learn to appreciate the artistry and history behind these captivating pieces. With names like Joseff of Hollywood, Weiss, Miriam Haskell, Trifari, Elsa Schiaparelli and Hattie Carnegie to guide you, your journey through car boot sales and charity shops will be enriched. So put on your detective hat, seek out the sparkle and become a part of the enchanting world of vintage costume jewellery.'

When the stage lights dimmed and the house lights came on, there was a ripple of applause – or was that just Carole? – and I smiled in relief. I had completed my very first talk as an antiques expert, and apart from the brief interruption at the beginning, it had gone reasonably well.

Someone coughed in the audience.

'Help! We need help here!' yelled Patricia Henderson.

From the stage I could see people huddled around one of the seats at the front. Carole waved for me to come over. I jumped down from the stage.

Laura stepped aside and I could see for the first time what they were all staring at.

Luke was bent double and coughing, his eyes wild. He grabbed his throat . . . then slumped sideways in the chair and onto the carpet.

'Luke!' called Laura, checking for a pulse. 'Luke!'

Her face drained of colour. 'He's dead,' she said.

Chapter Nineteen

Before running over, Phil had turned the main theatre lights up. As my eyes adjusted, I saw the panic stretched over Carole's face and the whites of her knuckles as she held onto Patricia's arm. I needed to get them out of there.

'What could've happened?' Patricia stuttered. 'Heart attack?'

Carole rubbed her arm and nodded. 'We need to get you some strong sweet tea for the shock.'

'Perhaps you should both go and get some tea, and I'll come and find you with an update,' Phil suggested. The two women nodded in unison but didn't move.

Phil stepped towards me, his hand brushing around my waist as he tried to manoeuvre around me to get to Luke. 'Sorry . . . if I can just . . .'

'Yes of course . . . sorry.'

I stepped away and he quickly checked for a pulse. 'Folks, listen up, please – I have found a pulse. He is *not dead*,' he stressed to everyone. Then, to Laura, 'Maybe he fainted. Please alert the ship's doctor. I'll stay with him.'

She nodded and strolled towards the door.

'As fast as you can, Laura.' Phil glared at her and she picked up her pace to a light jog. 'Hurry, dammit!' He looked at the rest of us. 'I think it's best to give Luke some space. If you would all please leave the theatre.'

'Well . . .' said Patricia, who had slipped out of Carole's grip and bent over the curator, 'if you think that's best, but I'm worried for this poor man. Isn't there anything we can do to help him?' She tucked a stray strand of grey hair behind her ear, and I noticed her hand was shaking.

'Tea?' I asked, taking her elbow as she straightened.

'I think it's time for something stronger, don't you, Carole?'

Carole took over from me and slid one arm around Patricia's waist. 'We'll look after you. This is a shock, isn't it?'

Jenny bustled in on the other side of Patricia, clearly feeling Carole was competition, and glared at her husband. 'Arch, collect our handbags and meet us in the Grand Salon.'

The three women swept out with poor heavily laden Archie scrambling after them. 'You will let us know how he does, won't you?' Carole called back, staring straight ahead.

Phil opened his mouth as if he was about to tell me something, but snapped it shut again.

I wasn't intending to leave, and I turned my attention to Luke, knowing that the ship's doctor would be with us any minute. 'See that?' I whispered, bending down to examine the unconscious figure. 'Phil, look.' I pointed to the corners of Luke's mouth, where some white froth bubbled. 'Maybe something else is going on here?'

I bent closer, as did Phil. Our shoulders collided and he recoiled. There was a brief moment when our faces were level. His eyes were wide, his mouth tight . . . he looked afraid. But of what?

'Could he have been poisoned?' I whispered.

Luke groaned and his eyes opened a slit.

'Help is on its way,' Phil reassured him.

'Did you notice anything?' I asked. 'It was too bright for me to see the audience from the stage properly.'

Phil frowned. 'I was watching you too. Apart from when a couple of guests thought that bridge was being played in here and tried to come in. I only left for a second, to show them where to go . . . The doctor will be here soon to give her opinion.'

I agreed, and as we waited for medical help, I tried to run through events while they were still fresh in our minds. 'The only time people moved around was when everyone got up to join me once I came down to show the necklace, wasn't it?' He nodded in confirmation. 'Perhaps he was poisoned before he came into the theatre? He was sweating and coughing when I showed him the necklace.'

'Maybe . . .' Phil checked Luke's pulse again. 'Laura made most of the audience move closer to the stage.'

'You're right, she did. But Luke stayed where he was. There was a waitress sitting near him. She came in late, didn't she? Carole looked like she recognized her.'

Phil frowned. 'I didn't see her clearly.'

In a far corner at the back of the room, a woman was standing, watching us.

The waitress.

I squinted to get a better look at her. A tall, slender figure . . . olive-tinted skin under blonde hair. Unusual. Our eyes met and I knew just who I was looking at.

Bella.

Bella had been a guest at Copthorn Manor back in the spring when Carole and I had stayed there hunting for Arthur's murderer. She was a chameleon – a master of disguise, especially when she wanted something. I had never wanted to see her again.

'Bella?' I called, annoyance making my voice louder than intended.

Phil stood and ran towards her.

But Bella fled for the exit.

She was as athletic as I remembered, dodging past Phil and slamming the double doors. I was about to run after her when Phil gripped my elbow and said, 'Bella can wait. We've entered the Suez Canal and won't be stopping until we dock in Egypt tomorrow. Let's get Luke the help he needs and then find Bella and learn what she knows.'

'So, we're doing this together now?' I asked.

Luke groaned as Phil placed a hand on his shoulder. 'Help is coming, hang in there.' Phil could be gruff and stern . . . but in the moment when he reached out for Luke to reassure him I saw another, softer side.

When he looked back up at me, a smile was threatening to spread from the corner of my lips and his eyes travelled there. 'As you're not going anywhere until we dock, we might as well make use of your talents,' he said.

* * *

The ship's doctor arrived. Luke was taken away on a stretcher, and Phil went off to comb the personnel records and see what he could find out about any new waitresses who fit Bella's description. I found Carole at the cafe deep in conversation with Patricia – cocktails, not tea, in hand.

'Darling, did you know that Patricia is an adventurer? She has led the most extraordinary life and she's still in her prime.' Carole beamed at Patricia, and I saw a friendship blossoming.

Patricia shook her head and her long gold earrings swayed. 'My late husband went from working as an antiques dealer to working for the oil companies, so we lived in a lot of places. I think Carole's adventures with Arthur Crockleford were far more exciting. She was just telling me about Copthorn Manor . . .' Before I could ask her about her husband's transition from antiques dealer to oil company employee, she patted the bar stool next to her. 'Come have a drink. You look flushed.' Her forehead creased with concern, and she waved at the barman just as Jenny arrived.

I placed a hand on my warm cheek. 'The talk has taken it out of me. And the shock of Luke's collapse. Thank you, but I think I'll go back to my room.' Before Carole could spring to her feet, I said, 'I'll see you in a bit.'

I had only just opened my stateroom door and picked up a letter that was tucked underneath when Carole hurried up to me.

'I thought you'd stay and chat?' I said.

'I would have, but Jenny arrived and I'm not so fond of that one – she likes to talk about all the money her husband has.' She saw the letter in my hand. 'What's that?'

Freya, I had an arrangement with your predecessor. Do you want to continue it? If so, meet me in the promenade bar. 7pm.

'Luke asked me last night where we were staying. Do you think he wrote that, put it under your door, and was poisoned to stop him from talking to us?' asked Carole.

'You told him the room numbers?'

'He didn't look like a murderer.' Carole ran her fingers through her hair. 'And I can spot them a mile off.'

'Really?' I chuckled. 'Listen, I'm going to go to this meeting in the letter to see what I can find out. If someone was working with Arthur, they might know valuable information on what Arthur thought was going on here. It could help our case immensely.'

'I'll come too.'

'Not this time. This time I'm going alone. The letter was addressed to me, and I don't want to spook them.'

Before Carole could protest, my phone pinged with a text message.

Phil: *Luke is doing better and back in his stateroom. The doc is with him. They need to run some tests. He might be taken to hospital when we dock.*

'I won't be long,' I said. 'Trust me, I'll be fine.'

'But I've brought jeans and a T-shirt specifically for going undercover,' Carole objected.

I was touched she had envisaged just such a scenario, but I didn't want her in any danger – she was all I had left in the world. The only person I trusted.

'Stay here. I need to do this.' I reached out and squeezed her hand. She understood without me saying that I needed to prove to myself I could do it.

She flicked her hair off her shoulder and winked at me. 'You go see who wants to meet you. While you're following your leads, I might just have a few of my own.'

I wanted to ask her exactly what she meant, but there wasn't time. I kissed her on the cheek. 'I'll be back as soon as I can.'

Chapter Twenty

Phil

Even after Phil had spoken to a friendly face in HR and been given privileged access to the records of new staff members, he was no further forward. There was no entry for any member of the crew, waitress or otherwise, who resembled the striking art thief he remembered from Copthorn Manor. Was Bella a passenger who dressed as a member of the crew to gain access to areas of the ship off limits to passengers?

He changed out of uniform and put on chinos and a linen shirt rolled up at the arms, baseball cap on his head. He left his stateroom and went to sit in a quiet corner to watch passengers heading towards the Grand Salon for cocktails.

Did anyone else look out of the ordinary?

He had concluded some time ago that the idea of The Collector 'retiring' was misleading. It gave the impression that The Collector was of retiring age, late sixties perhaps, or maybe older. But there was no reason to think that The Collector wasn't in their fifties or younger. It made the hunt that much harder, because Phil believed that much of the gossip around The Collector was spread on purpose – it was a clever way to stop the law getting a grasp on what was true or false.

His former front-running suspect – Luke Drummond – was now gravely ill in his stateroom. Phil had suspected Luke after Sloane informed him that Luke had been an associate of the private collector whose Shakespearean First Folio was stolen.

But now it seemed he had been dosed with a dangerous amount of a recreational drug, probably MDMA, that had caused him to suffer temporary seizures and disorientation. The ship's doctor thought she should be able to stabilize him on board, but she would review Luke's condition again once they docked in Egypt. Had someone tried to take Luke out believing that he was The Collector, as Phil suspected? Or was Luke someone who knew too much, flew too close to the flame?

If Luke wasn't The Collector, could he identify who was? Phil pulled up the passenger list on his phone and went over it again. Phil also wondered if there was any passenger on the list with a connection to Greece or the Athens Museum, where the Ming Dynasty vase was stolen. Chris had told Arthur that he suspected the vase held some sentimental value to The Collector, so that was another clue to look out for. And then there was the painting . . . What was Arthur trying to say by painting himself onto that canvas?

The operation wasn't going to plan – the unanswered questions just kept piling up.

He raked his hand through his hair and rubbed his face – he needed to talk this through with Sloane. With his phone in his hand and his finger poised to press call, he saw Freya walk across the lobby and pause for a second to look out over the canal. He slipped his phone back in his pocket and followed her. He was reminded of the first time he had seen her in the woods of Copthorn Manor. From his vantage point between the trees, slightly up a hill, he had noticed Freya and her aunt as they hurried down a path they shouldn't have been on. Freya had that same look of pure determination now, and it meant she was on the hunt for something or someone.

In the months since Copthorn Manor, Freya appeared to have grown taller somehow, her shoulders straighter, her head held a little higher, and she met everyone's eye when they talked.

Freya dodged the passengers around her and he picked up his pace. He didn't want to lose her.

* * *

On the promenade deck was a small bar at one end with large faux leather armchairs and mahogany drinks tables. Phil watched Freya order something and head for the rear corner, her back to the window.

Who's she waiting for?

He was just about to step towards her and ask what was going on, when someone grabbed his arm.

'How's Luke?' asked Laura, looking up at him from under her eyelashes. He inwardly recoiled. Not for the first time he wondered if Laura knew who he really was – she'd been wary of him ever since the captain introduced them, saying that Head Office had created a new role of 'events officer' and that Phil was there to 'learn the ropes for some other cruises in the pipeline.' But by the end of the first day at sea, Laura had shown Phil everything and clearly believed her part was done. She had mainly avoided him ever since.

'Will Luke be taken off the ship and to hospital when we reach Egypt?' She gave him a look that he couldn't read – because it didn't look like concern. It looked like fear.

'I believe so,' said Phil, playing a hunch and overstating the seriousness of Luke's condition to see how she would react.

'Did you see that waitress that snuck into the talk? She looked off to me,' she said, swiftly changing the subject. 'Maybe she slipped him something and that's why he's sick.' Laura was garbling her words, her face looking much paler than usual.

'Are you OK?' Phil asked, worry beginning to build in his gut.

'Oh, I'm good, thanks. Just tired. My shift is over. I'm going to head to the crew cafeteria and then early to bed.' As she walked away, her shoulders slumped, and it didn't look like it was tiredness; it looked like worry mixed with defeat. Laura was involved somehow, and he wanted to get to the bottom of it. But Phil couldn't help if she didn't talk to him, and it was clear she wasn't ready to do that. He turned his attention back to Freya.

How did she get a place as an expert on the cruise in the first place? Does she have Arthur's journals? Is the information about The Collector in there? Or did she really just follow the painting?

Either way, there were only a few nights left on board to find the Collector . . . and time was running out.

He would never forgive himself if he let this opportunity slip by.

Chapter Twenty-One

Freya

Watching Phil and Laura talk, I assumed that one of them had sent the note and would soon appear at my side. Instead, an older lady in a tweed jacket and skirt limped towards me carrying a tumbler and then pulled out a chair at the next table.

'I see you took up the invitation to be an expert on the cruise after all, did you?' she mumbled out of the side of her mouth.

I knew that voice. I looked up and recognized those dark brown eyes.

Bella.

'Hello, Bella. So, you sent me a note asking me to meet you?' She lifted an eyebrow, almost as if she was impressed that her disguise hadn't fooled me.

'I don't know what you're talking about. I didn't send any note.' Her voice was low and her lips barely moved as she spoke. 'Before Arthur died, he asked me to do some . . . things for him. One of them was to recommend you as an expert on this cruise. He must have really wanted you here.' Bella took a sip of her whisky. 'You've no clue *why* Arthur wanted you here or what to do, do you?' She downed the last of her drink.

'Of course I do.' I hoped the lie was convincing, but from the way Bella shook her head, I could see it wasn't.

'Then why haven't you been to the stateroom on Deck Eight?' Her tone was matter-of-fact, and I hated the feeling that I had missed something important. What was in there?

'I'm following other leads,' I replied, hoping she wouldn't ask me to elaborate. 'Was that you dressed as a waitress in the theatre earlier? Did you talk to Luke?'

Bella sighed. 'If you don't interfere with me, I'll keep out of your way.'

'Why are you here?' I leaned forward. 'Back to your old tricks of stealing from the black market?'

'I'm not here to steal.' Her voice was tinged with a sadness I hadn't heard there before. She rose and hunched herself back into character. 'Arthur asked me to help you back in the spring . . . I owed him a lot.' She sighed, her conscience getting the better of her. 'There's a meeting arranged in an Egyptian museum when we land – probably a pickup, I'm not sure. You might want to be there. And watch Deck Eight. Believe me, I had nothing to do with Luke.' And with that, she hobbled off.

I had barely had time to take another sip of my mint tea when Phil strode over.

'Evening. Are you here to see me?' I asked, wondering why he would send a note when I had given him my number after the Copthorn Manor case.

He frowned at me as he sat down. 'Why do you ask?'

'Someone sent a note asking me to meet them here.' I raised a questioning eyebrow at him.

'And you thought it was a good idea to meet this mystery

person on your own?' He shook his head and sighed. 'What part of "it's dangerous" didn't sink in?'

'Calm down. I'm in a public place.' I glanced quickly around the bar. 'You need to leave; otherwise you might scare them away.'

Phil relaxed back in his chair as if he were settling in for the night, and a smile twitched at the corners of his lips.

'Really?' I glared at him, annoyed that he was somehow now taking control of the situation.

'Yes, really. I have a question for you.'

I huffed. 'Not *now*. Now I want you to . . .'

He leaned forward, putting his elbows on the table between us. 'Do you have Arthur's journals? You looked surprised when I told you about The Collector, but were you really?'

I wasn't going to discuss the journals, so instead I explained about the note under my door and what Bella had just told me about a meeting in Egypt. In a quid pro quo, Phil mentioned his brief exchange with Laura and how she was acting off.

'Do you think Laura sent me the note asking for a meeting here, and then saw you and was scared away?' I asked him.

'I've no idea. Did Bella tell you why she was here?'

I shook my head. 'But I'll be going on the museum tour when we get to Egypt.'

Phil straightened. 'How does Bella know that?' His voice was low and urgent.

'She didn't say.'

'Let's check it out and see if we learn something.' Phil's use of the word 'we' wasn't lost on me.

'I don't trust Bella, but . . .' We both knew that we were going to the museum anyway.

'Each night I've searched the ship and uncovered nothing of the meeting Arthur mentioned.' He sounded worn down by the weight of the hunt. 'I've checked out all the passengers, but proving someone is The Collector is a needle in a haystack.'

I thought about the idea of a clandestine meeting and said, 'If I wanted to meet without anyone knowing about it, then the night of the Halloween party would be good, wouldn't it? When everyone is distracted.'

Phil nodded. 'And in costume. That thought had crossed my mind too.'

It was time to test this new alliance. 'Sally said she's leading the tour to the Egyptian museum. I don't know either of them well enough to trust her or Mark. But next time I see Sally, I'm going to try and talk to her about the museum visit. See if she lets anything slip.'

'And I'll try and find our friend Bella – we need to know what she knows.'

'Divide and conquer?' I asked, and our eyes locked. An unspoken agreement was made between us in that moment.

Phil sighed and looked away. 'You're walking into the lion's den.' I beamed at him, as I knew that was exactly where I needed to be to get the answers I sought. Phil was on the hunt for The Collector and I firmly believed that was the reason Arthur wanted me on the ship in the first place. That meant that I was now on the hunt too. Wherever that took me.

* * *

The two antiques experts were back in their usual spot on the private deck off the Library, faces in silhouette against the full moon. In the distance, the navigation lights of container ships danced on the flat, almost lifeless, darkening water. The land to either side of the canal was arid, still, but beyond that there was a glimmer of life: lights of cars rushing home and a glow of villages. I straightened my shoulders and made myself look in control.

What do you both know?

Sally saw me coming and indicated to Mark. It was almost a replay of yesterday, and yet there was a change in their attitude – before, they had been welcoming. Now Sally wore a frown, and Mark breathed in and straightened his back as if getting ready for a performance.

They're worried.

'Hello.' Did Sally's voice shake or was I imagining it?

'Hi, I was just wondering if I could ask about the tour you're leading tomorrow?'

'Is there news on Luke?' asked Mark, abruptly changing the subject.

'Did he have a heart attack?' asked Sally, with a sidelong glance at her companion. The dynamic between them was so confusing. 'We haven't heard anything.'

They are being evasive. How do I ask Sally about the Egyptian tour and if there is to be some sort of meeting there?

In the distance a horn sounded from one of the other ships on the canal. Thick, humid air seemed to pin us in place; it was now or never.

'No idea, but I'm sure he'll be fine. Listen, I'd love to see the Hurghada National Museum when we dock,' I lied, and tried to look casual. 'I was wondering if you wouldn't mind me tagging along.'

'The tour is fully booked.' Mark's voice was low and flat.

I'd been told that at the tour desk on my way to the Library. Bella was right; something was going on tomorrow at the museum. Was it the meeting Arthur had told Phil about?

'I'm sure I could squeeze in?'

'I'm afraid that won't be possible,' said Sally.

There was an uneasy silence between us, and it was clear that I was going to have to make my own way to the museum tomorrow.

I tried a different tack. 'Are you also leading the tour to Petra when we arrive in Jordan?'

'Um, well . . . yes . . . I lead that tour too. But Mark and local guides are taking groups too. It's quite popular.' Her fists clenched, but I didn't miss the small shake in them.

I turned to Mark. 'You deal in antique swords, guns, and other weapons, I believe? But you also lead a tour of Petra?'

He shrugged. 'It's an all-hands-on-deck situation.'

As I had Mark in front of me without his fans hanging off his every word, I decided to ask the question that had been niggling away at me. 'I was just wondering if you'd seen the bronze sword in the Gallery? It occurred to me that Captain James Rushwell, who was awarded the sword for his bravery at the Battle of Trafalgar, shares your name. Very few of them were ever made.' I didn't want anyone knowing that I had Arthur's journal and the information inside it, all photographed and stored in my phone.

Mark tried to shrug this off, his expression openly hostile.

I continued. 'How did it come to be in the Gallery?' I knew it was stolen, but I wanted to see his reaction.

'I'm not sure this is any of your business.' He smiled warmly. 'If you will excuse me, I'm turning in for the night.'

Sally watched him leave while pulling the gold disk on her necklace from side to side. 'Was there any point in dragging that up?' she whispered to me. 'That theft was a long time ago. There are quite a few of those swords in existence . . . you don't know the one in the Gallery is the Rushwell sword.'

My mind scanned the picture of the sword in Arthur's journal alongside all the other items in the Gallery. The only reason Arthur would have compiled that list was if they were stolen or black-market antiques.

'The Rushwell sword was the only one that was reported as stolen.'

Sally paled. 'Let sleeping dogs lie.'

'Freya.' I recognized the voice that came from behind me. *Phil.* 'I thought we might discuss the onshore excursions?' He smiled at me, and Sally took the opportunity to leave.

'That was' – he raised one eyebrow – 'an interesting line of questioning.'

I wondered how much he had overheard and bit my lip while he watched me – I might have pushed too far. 'The bronze sword was stolen from Mark's family . . .'

'The sword in the Gallery isn't attributed to Captain James Rushwell, so how did you come by that information?' He stepped closer to me, his lips close to the shell of my ear. 'Wouldn't have anything to do with Arthur's journals, would it? The journals which have never been found? The ones that might have lists of stolen antiques inside them?'

My blood ran cold. Why did he keep asking? 'No. I . . .' I hesitated and turned to meet his eye, trying to look convincing. 'I've told you, there are no journals.'

He sighed. 'Very well, if that's how you intend to play it . . .

According to the research we have conducted on the items in the Gallery, you are correct about the sword. It was stolen. Not all the items inside are recorded as stolen, but that doesn't mean that they haven't been at one time. It doesn't mean that they are not part of the black market.'

Phil pointed to a nearby chair, and we both sat in silence for a moment watching the water dance in the darkness. 'Let me start somewhere near the beginning. Not long after the Jordan case you and Arthur worked on, he came to me and asked if I would look into a prominent black-market *collector*. He wanted to know if the FBI Art Crime Team knew their real identity and the identity of the people who worked for them.' He paused and ran a hand through his hair. 'Of course we had a file on him, and I had an added interest in finding The Collector or his associate Chris Prince, because back then I believed one or both of them murdered my partner. It's why I was trying to keep you away from here.' His hand flicked around the deck. 'I can't . . . I won't have the deaths of you and your aunt haunting me, like Ed's death has.'

Phil's eyes glazed over as he became lost in the past.

'You won't.' I reached out and squeezed his arm, really hoping that what I was saying was the truth. 'Tell me what happened.'

Chapter Twenty-Two

Phil

The Library had emptied out as people headed to bed, but Phil wouldn't be getting much sleep that night. He would once again be stalking the corridors keeping an eye out for the meeting.

He checked his watch. It was 9.45 p.m. 'I'm going to make this as fast as possible because I have things I need to be . . . doing.'

It was hard to know exactly where to start, but he told Freya about his meeting with Arthur on the Embankment over a year ago and his discovery last year that neither Chris Prince nor the vase went down on that catamaran. After talking to Arthur, he now suspected that Chris was responsible for the fire all along – probably because he was working for The Collector – or he was trying to steal the vase from him.

'But I don't understand,' Freya said. 'I mean . . . I understand that Arthur believed both old and new Collector would be here. What I'm confused about is, what's Chris Prince's role here and in all this? We thought he was meant to be an expert on the ship. Why isn't he here now?'

'Chris Prince.' Phil breathed deeply, trying to quell his

anger – learning from Arthur that he had not died decades ago was still raw. 'He was charming and well-mannered, with the type of bad-boy good looks that women seem to find irresistible. But he was manipulative – rotten to the core.'

Freya sat quietly watching him, the whites of her eyes like a beacon in the darkness, giving him space to order his thoughts and conquer his rage.

'He had a privileged upbringing: boarding school, large country mansion, South of France in the summer, skiing every winter. By all accounts, when he finished his education he worked in finance in the City of London for a time – that's where he got his taste for fast money and started a side gig selling antiques and antiquities to City boys who believed Chris was legitimate. Or else didn't really care how he came by the items he sold – most of them were either stolen or fake. Then he vanished from England and turned up in sailing circles in the Med and the Middle East. The seagoing lifestyle suited him. He helped to shift illegal cargoes, some of them human, by boat. He had no loyalty to anyone but himself.

'It was only after reading Ed's notes that I learned all of this – it wasn't official, but Chris gave bits and pieces of information to Ed – mainly selling secrets on his competitors. He seemed especially focused on supplying information on, and therefore taking down, other antique trafficking rings.'

'How did Ed die?' Freya's voice was low and hesitant and her eyes moist. She had connected the dots and remembered what happened to that boat, and the men on board, as well as he did.

Phil shook his head. He hadn't talked about it for decades. The lapping waves and cool salty air reminded him of that morning. 'I haven't . . .' He paused and fixed on the lights of a cargo ship in the distance. Talking about it again would crack open the wound, but keeping it locked away from everyone had meant that the information (and the justice) he sought had also been elusive. 'Ed said he had been told, "by an informant", that there was to be an exchange of black-market antiques at sea and that The Collector would be on one of the boats. So we jumped on a plane to Jordan. Ed would always take calls . . . he had never been secretive about an informant before.

'He told me when and where the trade was to take place and that he had secured a place on the boat as a deckhand. I told him he was too old to be a deckhand – that they might think it odd, and that I should be the one to go. But Ed was on the way to retirement and wanted this case to be the one that made his name. The uncovering of The Collector. I should have insisted . . .'

'You believe that Chris Prince got Ed a place on the boat . . .' She paused, deep in thought. 'And Arthur was in contact with Chris in Jordan too, if he later asked Arthur to help him hide the vase. We were all working the same case, but from different angles.'

Phil caught Freya's eye and hummed. 'I didn't know Arthur well back then. He wasn't working with us, and I didn't realize until a lot later that we were there at the same time. We were not informed that the museum's insurance company had employed Arthur to get the vase back. There has always been a disconnect between law enforcement and the insurance companies. The FBI is interested in the retrieval of stolen items *and* the apprehension of the thieves – whereas the insurance companies focus solely on getting the item back so they don't have to pay out.'

'Ed was on that boat in Aqaba.' Freya placed her hands over her face. 'God, I'm so sorry. We were there watching from a distance – waiting for the trade to take place. And then when the fire started . . . we tried to help but . . .'

'I remember seeing another couple of boats trying to get close enough, but I didn't know until years later one held you and Arthur.'

Freya looked up at him and her eyes widened. 'But that's it, isn't it? Arthur had himself painted into a picture of a boat in flames. It can't be a coincidence that a burning ship means something to you . . . that fire is the thing I most fear. That we were both there the day the catamaran was set alight. An image that would've caught my attention and yours.'

'The painting, of course, I hadn't . . .' Why hadn't he put two and two together before now?

'Arthur wanted us on this cruise . . . both of us. The place where he knew the retiring Collector and Chris Prince would be. A lot of people believed Chris died in Aqaba in 2001. Who has he been hiding from? The Collector, everyone who works in the black market, or just the law?'

Phil shook his head. 'I think he's been working with The Collector all this time. Back in 2001, Ed was like a dog with a bone when it came to uncovering the identity of The Collector, so I think Chris and The Collector devised a way to get rid of Ed and make Chris disappear. Perhaps Chris believed Arthur was the best person to get the vase out of Jordan with the FBI breathing down their necks. Arthur would get it back to the UK and Chris could collect it from there when the time was safe. But then, a couple of years later, when Arthur started working with the black-market vaults owned by the powerful Metcalf family, he became protected from Chris's threats by his association with them. At that point, Chris had no way of pressuring Arthur into giving back the vase.'

'There is another thing we need to consider. Arthur couldn't have known the painting he had donated to the Lowestoft Maritime Museum would be stolen and end up here, which means that the painting isn't a clue as to The Collector's identity . . . but it could reveal the location of the vase, which he had hidden from Chris. And someone knows the painting is a clue and stole it!'

'Arthur said, "the clue to where it's hidden will only mean something to the right person". That person is you . . . you were in a fire as a child, you were in Aqaba when the catamaran went up in flames,' said Phil.

'And also you. I think he knew we needed to work together on this.' She rested her head on the back of the chair. 'He was always planning ahead.'

Phil studied Freya. 'But how would Arthur know that you would go looking for the painting?'

Freya rolled her head away to watch the shore. 'I'm not sure.'
She's lying.

'If Chris Prince was your informant, do you have a photo of him?'

She's changing the subject.

'He wasn't my informant . . . he was Ed's, but I do have an old photo of him from back then. Since that meeting with Arthur, I've been searching for him, but he's a ghost.' Phil pulled out his phone and showed her the photo.

Freya sat bolt upright. 'Can you send this to me so I can show Betty at the Lowestoft Museum?'

He nodded and sent her the photo, and she sent it straight on. Her phone pinged within seconds and Freya gasped. 'Betty says it looks very like Mr Suited and Booted. I think it's a good bet that Chris Prince stole the painting. And maybe he killed that other man . . .'

Phil let the new information sink in. 'If you believe that Chris stole the painting and it's now here, then Chris must be too.' Hatred swelled in the pit of his stomach along with a deep desire to come face-to-face with Chris and finally apprehend one of the men responsible for Ed's death.

'So, it was after talking to Arthur that you realized that Chris planned for the boat to go down? You're not just out to catch The Collector, are you?'

'Do you know that they never found Ed's body?' Phil murmured, that familiar ache in his throat returning. 'Arthur promised me that I would get justice. This cruise was his way of helping me.'

Freya reached out again. 'We'll get to the bottom of this. You'll have your justice . . . Let's hope the museum trip tomorrow gives us some answers.'

Chapter Twenty-Three

Freya

Shadows of the past darkened Phil's eyes and stripped them of their normal glow. He gripped the arm of the chair as if he were trying to steady himself from crashing waves of grief. It was clear he mourned his friend and Arthur too. Talking about both of them made Phil feel their loss keenly.

But as we sat in silence, my memories also flooded back.

Arthur and I had witnessed the trade taking place from shore, and I had frozen in terror as the catamaran erupted in a sheet of flames. My nails had dug into the scar on my palm like I was reliving my childhood, the terror of a fire all over again. We had convinced a fisherman to take us towards it to search for survivors, and my lasting memory was tormented images of the flaming vessel and the smell of diesel and soot pungent on my skin.

Arthur had insisted that I leave immediately after our little fishing boat reached the shore, having been unable to save anyone on board the catamaran. With smoke clinging to my clothes, I had hurtled down the Desert Highway through Wadi Rum in a beaten-up 4x4 to get to the Amman airport and catch my flight home.

I pulled myself into the present and looked over at Phil . . . Fire had taken a lot from both of us. My parents had died in a tragic accident from a faulty electric heater, and yet I still wondered what would've happened if my mother hadn't caught my cold and insisted the house was freezing. I was more determined than ever to get to the truth after hearing what had really happened back in Jordan all those years ago.

'When Arthur returned home from that trip, he was secretive about what he'd uncovered after I'd left. He told me that all four crewmen on the boat had died – atomized in the explosion – and that he believed the deal had gone wrong. I think he blamed himself for it, but I never really understood why. Much like at Copthorn Manor, Arthur seems to be trying to atone for his mistakes in the past by making sure we are both here.'

Phil looked up at me and nodded grimly. 'If the painting is on the ship and Betty has identified Chris as Mr Suited and Booted, it means that Chris handed the painting over to be shown in the exhibition. Why would he do that?

'And just because I haven't seen him on board doesn't mean he's not here.' His deep hazel eyes met mine as a steward came on deck to clean the tables. He pulled back and gazed out to sea. While he was watching the sea, I watched him . . . the way the vein in his neck pulsed as he clenched his jaw. 'Let's go and examine that painting again. It's the one clue we have to what Arthur was up to.'

'Won't the Gallery be closed for the night?'

He smiled and placed a set of keys on the table between us. 'Why didn't you say so earlier?'

'I was waiting for most of the passengers to be having dinner, in the casino, or too drunk to notice!'

Just then my phone lit up.

Sky: *Spoke to a Head Office employee – Dave – who said that a Susan Jones phoned him and recommended you. BUT she wasn't the first person to do so. Arthur put you forward for this cruise back in May.*

I showed the text to Phil. 'You have another person on your team?' There was a strange expression in his eyes. 'Who is it?'

'Sky's a great help.'

Sky: *I looked into who might have learned the same techniques of miniature-painting as your mum. I found quite a few options. Did you know she taught artists back in the 80s? Shall I send you a list?*

Me: *Betty told us that Arthur had come from Norfolk the day he brought the painting to the museum. Anyone on your list from there?*

Sky: *Yes! Miranda Clive was one.*

I turned the phone towards Phil and we both watched the three moving dots.

Sky: *She lives in Norfolk and on her profile page there's a pic of this village . . .*

Sky sent through a picture of Burnham Market – it was a beautiful north Norfolk village with pubs and boutique clothes shops, bookstores, butchers, fishmongers. Then another photo of a small art gallery in a cobblestone courtyard. I looked over at Phil and he nodded – we were thinking the same thing.

Me: *Any chance you can get up there tomorrow? I think face to face you might get more information.*

Sky: *Sure.*

'What clues did you see added to the painting?' asked Phil.

'I haven't had a chance to study the original in great detail.

But Arthur had a highly skilled artist – who paints tiny paintings that are so detailed they look like photographs – paint him onto the burning ship, so I assume there are other things painted there too. We saw the brooch Arthur left me, and Carole identified a handkerchief she gave to Arthur painted there as well.'

We both stood. 'Let's go,' said Phil, placing his hand on the small of my back, and I fought the urge to look up at him. There was no time for the complicated feelings swelling inside me. I needed to get to the bottom of why the painting was so important.

*   *   *

It was approaching ten thirty when we unlocked the Gallery. I stood watch as Phil pulled the metal shutters enough of the way up that we could duck inside – I also hoped that Phil's uniform would make it look like we were in some official capacity if we were seen.

I stepped inside to look for the light switch.

Phil stopped me. 'I need to turn the alarm off first.' He tapped some numbers into a keypad dimly visible on the wall. 'It's silent,' he said when I raised a questioning eyebrow. '*Now* let's look at everything in here, including the painting.'

I switched on the lights as Phil pulled the shutters down behind us.

'We can't be long. Don't want anyone looking too closely at the Gallery and seeing the lights through the shutters.'

I nodded and hurried to Arthur's painting, lifting it by the ebonized frame and carefully placing it image side down on top of the glass central cabinet. It wasn't lost on me that without Luke stalking the Gallery we now had the opportunity to have a proper look at the painting. My fingers traced the back of the canvas and then the wood. I was sure a more tangible clue would be hidden somewhere on it, but if there was one, I couldn't see it.

'There's nothing here,' I murmured. Disappointed, I turned the frame back over so I could see the painting up close.

I squinted at the tiny depiction of Arthur and then at the way his hands were resting around something. A book of some sort, I thought, propped on the ship's wheel. The spotlight above me helped me to make out, in the smallest imaginable writing, 'No. 2.'

The second journal.

'Perhaps Arthur thought that we would get answers on this cruise that would lead to the Lowestoft Maritime Museum . . . to find this painting. The order in which Arthur planned things might not have worked out the way he intended.'

Phil hummed. 'Perhaps.'

I noticed the index finger on Arthur's left hand was raised and pointing away from the scene depicted. Why?

'What are we looking at?' asked Phil, coming to stand close to me. I showed him Arthur's hand.

'You saw the place where Arthur hung it, right? Can you remember what was displayed nearby?'

I thought back. 'There's nothing much. Some lobster pots. An old diver's suit and helmet. Posters on the other walls advertising fishing nets. An anteroom leading to a kitchen extension.' Then I remembered what Betty had said. 'He hung the painting himself, seemed determined it should go in one particular place. Perhaps if it were in its original location then it would make more sense. I'll send Betty a message in the morning and check with her,' I said.

Phil's eyes shone. 'When we reach Jordan, we'll impound it there with the rest of these items and make sure it gets a speedy return – the painting is now the one item we can prove has been stolen.'

'Great. If we believe that all the other items in the Gallery are owned by The Collector, which seems a fair bet, then what is the relationship between The Collector and Chris Prince? Are they one and the same?'

'I don't think so. After meeting with Arthur, I've begun to believe that Chris Prince was working for The Collector all those years ago. That might still be the case.' He sighed and dug into his jacket pocket and pulled out some black discs. 'I'm going to put some more of these around so I can hear anything that can help us.'

'Listening devices?' I asked.

I took some more photos of the painting, this time lying flat, before I rehung it. The shipwreck ceramics inside the case caught my eye next. Without Luke breathing down my neck, I had the opportunity to study them closely. Beautiful examples, all of them. 'Do you have the key for this case?' I asked.

Phil nodded and opened it.

'Good thing the CCTV is having "technical issues", isn't it?' He winked at me, and I realized with a twinge of admiration that he really did think of everything.

'I'm quite sure these items here,' I said, indicating a small grouping, 'are from the collection known as the Hatcher Junk – specifically, Jingdezhen blue-and-white ceramics.' I turned over a wine cup embellished with the coral that had grown over it at the bottom of the sea. 'See here the original orange-red Christie's Amsterdam label reading "Hatcher Collection June '84"? Christie's Amsterdam was the first auction house to sell shipwreck ceramics. The provenance in this case is exceptionally clear and it's what makes the pieces additionally valuable.' I put the wine cup down gently and picked up another item. 'And here are some excellent examples of sea sculptures – the curator's label next to this one states that it is from the Hôi An wreck. I expect you know a bit about its history?'

He nodded.

Moving with great care, I picked up the sculpture. It was more blue-and-white porcelain, Vietnamese this time, a medium-sized vase and teacup, fused together at right angles by barnacles. The original shiny glaze had worn off and the once bright blue surfaces were now soft and mellow.

My eyes came to rest on a tiny teacup . . . which reminded me of the one Arthur was holding in the Lowestoft Martine Museum guidebook. It was a clue . . .

Think! When had Arthur ever talked about shipwrecked ceramics or a case involving such items?

'How do you know that these items are stolen? They could have easily been purchased on the open market.' Phil gently ran one finger over the fossilized remnant of the creature that had once made its home on the submerged treasure, then raised an eyebrow at me. He admired them as much as I did.

He's testing what I know.

'It was the dealership case,' I blurted out.

Phil frowned. 'I don't follow.'

I met his gaze. I wasn't going to tell him that these exact pieces were in Arthur's journal and that I had now realized that he had found items that were stolen forty years ago. 'It was around the time I had lost my parents and wasn't talking much – I would go to the shop with Carole, and Arthur would tell me stories over a cup of tea. He described a case where a large number of dealers – and one very prominent London dealer specializing in shipwrecked ceramics – were robbed back in the late eighties. He used to bring it up every so often, as it was one of the cases he never solved . . . although perhaps he did.' My fingers stroked the small teacup. 'This spate of thefts happened before the Art Loss Register was set up in 1990, so perhaps they didn't make it onto the register?'

He nodded. 'Almost everything here was stolen before 1990. I will have Sloane dig deeper into those cases.'

'That would be great.' My index finger snagged on a rough crustacean. 'Some people who have no knowledge of ship-wrecked ceramics and who don't like the look of the barnacles have been known to try and take them off. I once heard of a cleaner scrubbing away the Christie's sale stickers. In doing so, she massively reduced the piece's value.' I set down the sculpture and walked around to view it from several angles. 'I find these so evocative,' I continued, almost to myself. 'Just the idea that this cargo was lost to the world for so long, and we fortunate few can touch it and feel connected to the past.'

As I carefully restored the sculpture to the lined display case, I felt a bump under the fabric. I was about to take a closer look at it, when I heard the shutters screeching upwards behind me.

'What are you doing in here?' demanded Laura, slipping inside the Gallery.

'We're checking that everything's in order.' Phil slipped a coin-sized disc between my fingers, and I knew exactly what he wanted me to do. I peeled off the backing and stuck it under the cabinet as I bent to lock it. Phil stood between Laura and me, blocking her view.

Adrenalin tingled down my spine. This was what I loved, this was what I was meant to do! And it wasn't lost on me that it was Phil who had helped me get here.

'You don't need to do that.' Laura arched her neck to peer around Phil and at the same time held out her hand for the keys. I shot a questioning look at Phil. If we handed them over, we'd lose access to the painting. 'You're not the only person with a link to Head Office – you're just here to learn the ropes,' she told him, suspicion etched into her brow. 'It's been decided at the highest level that the Gallery is now my responsibility – and so are those keys.' She snapped her fingers at me. I expected Phil to protest but he simply nodded at me. She snatched them away, eyes sharp with satisfaction.

'Good night.' She stepped to one side so we could leave.

Phil nudged me forward. 'Let's go.'

I glared at him as he hurried me out and around the corner then brought us to a halt on the main concourse, yanking me into the doorway of a darkened shop. 'Let's see what she does now.' He pulled out some headphones and gave me one earbud.

I placed it in my ear and couldn't contain the smile that broke over my lips.

'You didn't bug the place before now?' I asked.

'I did, but I believe Luke found them . . .'

'Hello?' The speaker had a familiar Aussie accent. I cupped my hand around my ear to hear Laura more clearly. My elbow bumped into Phil's chest but I didn't pull away.

'It's all fine, I've sorted it . . . No, you don't need to do that!

I have it all under control. Everything will go ahead . . .' There was a crackling sound and then, 'Yes, the first meeting is in place. Tomorrow. The museum.' More crackling. 'And then it'll all go off in Jordan, of course. Had to be the Treasury, didn't it? Exactly.' She laughed. 'No, I won't be there. Too much bloody walking for me . . .'

Phil was so close to me in the dark that I could feel his muscles tighten when the meeting place was confirmed.

The Treasury in Petra.

How would they surveil a site like that?

Dazzling memories of one of the great sites of antiquity, one of the new seven wonders of the world, in an isolated part of the Jordanian desert. The wonder of my very first visit decades ago came rushing back to me. Laura was right, the walk through the desert was a hot and dusty one. Why schedule a meeting at a place like that?

'The Deck Eight room will be ready for tomorrow. You don't need to worry . . .'

I met Phil's eye. 'Is that *three* meetings we now know of?'

Phil nodded in agreement. 'Arthur knew about one on board the ship, Bella knew about the one in the Egyptian museum, but it seems something else is happening when we reach Petra.'

'Then we have a plan.' I smiled, and started to step away.

'There is something else I need to tell you,' he said, and I stopped.

'What?'

Laughter came from behind me. A couple walked past us, heading towards the casino, energy drinks in hand.

He moved us deeper into the darkness. 'When I saw you and your aunt here, I wondered who was watching the shop and asked a colleague to look into it. Earlier this evening, Sloane messaged me informing me that Sky is a hacker. She can't be trusted.'

'But she's out of it now. Sky got caught up with the wrong man. It's easily done . . . Why exactly are you checking up on a member of *my* staff?'

'Because I'm worried.'

I don't need his worry, I need his faith. But that didn't stop the pinch of concern in my chest. I wanted to trust my instincts and Sky.

I shook my head. 'I'm perfectly capable of doing this on my own. I can even . . .'

'That's not what I meant. People are searching for Arthur's journals, so I . . .' He raked his hand down his face this time.

'I don't have any journals . . .' I looked him in the eye and hoped my lie would hold. That's why he was wondering who was looking after the shop. Would he have arranged a search for the journals if no one was there? It wouldn't surprise me if he did.

He gave a half smile. 'And I've no doubt that *if* you have them, they are so well hidden that no one would ever find them. Even if they have the run of Arthur's old home and shop while you are conveniently out of the country.'

Was he just trying to spook me? I was beginning to doubt my own judgement in hiring Sky and letting her stay in the shop, but there was little I could do about it from a cruise ship in the Red Sea. And then I remembered. The third journal was sticking out from behind a beam in the corridor. The one that can catch you on the head if you forget to duck.

Is that hidden enough if she really does go on the hunt?

'I have an early morning tomorrow . . .' I pulled away. 'I'm going on the tour of the Hurghada National Museum.' I didn't wait for a reply and instead headed towards the lift, hurrying to tell Carole what Phil had said about Sky. Were the shop and the journals hidden there in danger?

I didn't want to believe that my instinct about Sky was wrong, but I knew that one way or another I was about to find out.

Chapter Twenty-Four

Carole

Carole had left her stateroom in search of Freya, but had only gotten as far as the Grand Salon when she ran into Patricia and was persuaded to join her for a drink in the Library. Martini in hand, Patricia looked over at her. 'Cheers.'

'Aren't we lucky to be here?' said Carole, looking out over the water and taking a fortifying lungful of sea air.

'Oh, we are. This is the life, and we have to live it, don't we? It's why I've been telling my two nephews that there'll be no inheritance. They'll have to make their own way as I'm going to blow the lot!'

'Good for you, darling. What are you going to blow it on? Lots of lovely cruises and vacations? See the world in luxury?'

'Strippers! Big beefy ones . . .' She winked.

Carole nearly choked laughing. 'Brilliant! And how did your nephews feel about . . . the strippers?'

'Oh, Tony is bemused. He's a bright spark, quick to laugh and good with numbers. He thinks I'm too old for adventures, but I'm not dead yet.' Patricia chuckled. 'Sometimes he's just too serious for his own good. We took my nephews in when they were teenagers, as my late husband's side of the family

167

were no good at all – got their money the wrong way and then blew it all on fast cars until the law caught up with them. So they came to live with us, and we straightened them out by sending them to a very good boarding school and on to university. Tony is very clever, but I think he needs a lady friend. He's been kept busy so much recently that he hasn't had time to really find the right type.'

'Oh, we do have so much in common, don't we? I took in my niece when her parents died, and she is the best thing that ever happened to me. Had a disastrous marriage but now is truly back on her feet. So, you think we should set Tony and Freya up?'

Their eyes locked and the seed of an idea was planted.

'We could put our love of matchmaking to good use,' said Carole. 'I tried to get Freya to consider dinner with the dashing officer, but she doesn't always listen to my fabulous ideas. I'm also trying to make her a little more flamboyant in her clothing – she thinks her job needs her to blend in, but . . .'

'Oh, she sounds like Jenny. She needs to be more daring with her outfits.'

'Was Jenny the one at the "meet the expert dinner"? Wasn't she also there at Freya's talk?' asked Carole.

'She was.' Patricia sighed. 'She's sweet, but her husband, Archie . . . it's always the quiet ones you have to look out for.' She gripped Carole's arm and her gaze became serious. 'Don't spend too much time with him. I like you.'

Carole was bemused by the sincere tone in Patricia's voice and had opened her mouth to say more when Patricia changed the subject.

'Freya is running Arthur's antiques shop now, isn't she?

How is following in Arthur's footsteps going for her? It looks like she's taken to it like a duck to water. I like to see women thrive.' Patricia drained her martini and waved at the bartender to get another round in. 'The art and antiques world were very much a man's world when I met my husband forty-five years ago. He loved his antiques, but when he got into the oil business, he didn't always have time for our passion for collecting and dealing antiques. Sometimes these far-flung places can be a bit lonely . . .' She tapped her head. 'Turned out that I was the one with the eye for a good deal and had a head for numbers. His name was above the door, as it were, but the rest was all me.'

'Bloody fantastic,' said Carole, as another glass was placed in front of her. 'I can't keep up with all this drinking!' She took a sip. 'It's been a joy to see Freya finding her way back to what she loved to do. The antiques shop is just the tip of the iceberg when it comes to what Freya and Arthur used to . . .' Carole stopped herself and took a large gulp. She knew that she shouldn't really talk about these things with people she didn't know well enough to trust, so it was time to change the subject. 'And she's slipped back into Little Meddington like she never left.'

'I'm sure Arthur would be proud of her. Does she enjoy it back home?'

'Oh, I hope so. It's been wonderful having her close since Arthur passed away.' Before grief dug its claws in, she said, 'We have a wonderful new assistant who's super with computers and getting our stock on the internet.'

'Things have changed so much since our day, haven't they? When it was all in-person interaction. When things were done with a handshake, and people kept their word. Tony says I'm out of touch, but I think I'm just nostalgic for a time when I knew the rules.'

'Sounds like you're a lot more involved in the antiques world then you let on,' said Carole, but Patricia frowned, and it made Carole wonder what she had said to offend. So she reached out and squeezed Patricia's hand. 'I truly marvel at what the younger ones can do nowadays.'

Patricia smiled warmly. 'You see the brightness in everything, don't you?'

'I'm always trying to tell Freya, life's too short to sit in the shadows. And slowly but surely, she's truly coming into her own. When she's on a hunt, she never fails.'

Carole lifted her cocktail glass to Patricia.

'May we never go to hell but always be on our way,' said Patricia.

'May all your ups and downs be under the covers!' said Carole.

Patricia laughed. 'Here's to being single, drinking doubles and seeing triple.'

Clink!

'Absolutely to being single, darling, but friends with benefits are the way forward. I do keep trying to tell Freya that.'

'I've no idea what a friend with benefits is?'

Carole placed her drink down and clapped her hands together. 'You're in for a treat . . .'

Their eyes met and Carole smiled to herself – the mischievous spark in Patricia's eyes was a rare gift, and Carole was grateful to have found a kindred spirit.

Chapter Twenty-Five

Freya

Egypt

I woke up to a hammering on my door. 'Just a minute.' I pulled on a dressing gown and checked the time. It was 6 a.m.

The banging continued until I opened the door to find Laura standing before me with her hands on her hips.

'Was it you?' she began, eyes boring into mine.

'I don't know what you're talking about.'

'I saw you there last night. This morning when I opened up . . . the sword was missing. Please, put it back before anyone else notices.' The anger in her tone had been replaced by fear. 'Do you even know who you're dealing with?' Her crew polo shirt was crumpled as if she had slept in it.

In the calming tone that I had only ever used on my ex during our disastrous marriage, I said, 'I haven't stolen any sword.'

She ran her hands down her uniform shorts. Her brow was etched in lines of panic.

'Perhaps I can help. Tell me who else has keys and the alarm code. Or could it have happened when the Gallery was open and someone's back was turned?' I knew there would be no CCTV as Phil had turned it off.

She pushed into my stateroom and closed the door behind her, leaning back against it. 'Luke was meant to oversee the Gallery . . . then the charge was given to me.' She ran her nails up and down her arm – it was her nervous, unconscious tic – leaving nasty red scratches behind.

'Who owns the collection?'

She violently shook her head, her eyes wild. 'I don't know – I'm not stupid enough to ask. I need to find the sword . . .'

Bella is the only thief I know on board. 'Why don't you come and sit down? When did you notice it was missing?'

'This morning . . .' She went pale, as if she had remembered something. 'I can't stay.' Laura opened the door and then turned back. 'I would keep a low profile today – stay on the ship when it docks. Your presence seems to be making some passengers uncomfortable.'

'Laura, you look . . . scared?'

Her knuckles were white as she grabbed the edge of the door. 'Do you still have my note? You need to destroy it . . .'

'You sent it?'

I had an arrangement with your predecessor. Do you want to continue it? If so, meet me in the promenade bar. 7pm.

'You used to give Arthur information? Let me help you.'

She opened the door and scanned the empty corridor.

'Wait, Laura, please. Tell me how you knew Arthur.'

'It doesn't matter anymore. He was trying to help me out of all this. Get away from Chris. But now it's all going to shit.' Without looking back, she ran down the corridor.

Laura's note was hidden in the back of the crime novel I was reading, so I pulled it out.

'Carole?' I called as I entered her stateroom. 'We need a

better hiding place for this.' I held up the note. After placing the note behind the fabric in one of her suitcases, I told her everything Laura had said. 'If Laura's telling me not to get off the ship in Egypt, then we are on the right track.'

'Absolutely, darling.' Her long, bright green kimono billowed out behind her. 'This will not do at all.' She pointed to my outfit. 'You need to find the right things to wear for our big day out in the Land of the Pharaohs. We cannot visit an incredible museum with you dressed in the first thing you lounge in. I can show you what I have in mind for myself, if it would help? Oh, and I know the tour is full, but we needn't let a little thing like that get in our way. I'm sure we can be resourceful. As a suite guest and you being an expert, we get priority disembarkation. So, let's hurry.'

'Laura is right in the middle of whatever is going on here,' I called to her while I was busy flinging on a sundress and long-sleeved shirt and hurrying to brush my teeth. 'Do you think Bella is right? That there is an important meeting at the Hurghada National Museum?'

'If the meeting happens, we will be there to see it. We are' – Carole let her voice slip into her overly dramatic actor's whisper – 'going *undercover*.'

When I saw what she had chosen to wear, I very much doubted it.

* * *

The Safaga port was built for purpose – industrial and modern – with concrete buildings and trucks in every direction. Crystal-clear waters still lapped the ship. We stood on the quayside with two other cruise ships towering over our smaller one.

Soft, humid gusts swept a lock of curls over my eyes. I brushed it aside and studied the people around me. The clamour of the Egyptian passenger terminal, overflowing with tightly packed cruise guests, was overwhelming after the cool and calm of my stateroom.

We lined up for passport control, Carole with a fan in her hand, and tried to see any sign of the Egypt that we had come to see. With our passports checked, we were through the other side and standing in a massive car park.

Carole nudged my arm and tilted her head towards Mark and Sally to our left.

Sally produced her phone, talking rapidly into it and nodding her head. She walked away and Mark followed on her heels. Next to him was a male tourist who was clearly friendly with Mark. He looked familiar but I couldn't place him. They all seemed to be heading for one of the far coaches, but out of the corner of my eye I spotted someone else.

I grabbed Carole's arm. 'Stay close to them and I'll meet you at the museum.'

'But . . .'

'There's no time.' Sally and Mark had boarded the coach, with Jenny and Archie right behind them. 'I think I've seen Bella. I have to talk to her.'

'Last time you followed Bella it ended badly.' Carole placed a hand on top of mine, but her eyes flicked back to the coach. She knew I was right . . . we needed to split up.

'We both have tracking apps on our phones . . . I'll see you there. Go!'

I scanned for the woman in the large hat who had kept walking after she met the end of the line of buses, and desperately hoped that I was right . . . that it was Bella in yet another disguise. She seemed to have a better understanding of what was going on, and I was determined to find out all she knew.

Upon reaching the last coaches, I found myself before a row of seven taxis . . . Bella had to be in one. As I cupped my hands over the first window, I noticed a large straw hat disappear into the taxi behind me. There was no way I was going to let Bella get away, but the taxi started its engine.

No, no, no.

Without thinking, I sprang forward, intending to reach for the door but ending up with my hand on the hood and my toes alarmingly close to the front wheel.

'Let me in!' I demanded with as much authority as I could muster while trying not to draw too much attention to myself.

My heart thumped, but I wasn't going to budge.

The driver threw his hands in the air and shouted at me to move. 'You're crazy, aren't you?' Bella reached over and opened the passenger door. I threw myself inside. Her olive skin, perfect bow lips and slender frame were all poised with amusement.

'OK, we can go,' she purred.

The car took off, and I collapsed back on the plastic-covered seat, allowing the air-conditioning to cool me.

I glared at her. 'Was that necessary?'

She shrugged. 'It's best when I do things on my own.'

'Are you going to tell me why you're here? What you're searching for?'

Is Bella on the hunt for The Collector as well?

Bella pulled off her hat and set it down between us. 'Um . . . no, I don't think I will.'

'I could give you some valuable information in return?'

Her large hazel eyes took in every inch of my face. 'OK. I know that Arthur left you some journals cataloguing stolen art and antiques. And there is one on a Scottish collection.'

I refused to let the shock pulsing through me show, and I bit my bottom lip trying to keep my face neutral. *How does she know about the third journal?*

'You want to know what is happening today, correct?' She pulled out some lip gloss and a mirror. 'That's the deal. You let me see the Scottish catalogue.'

I didn't 100 per cent trust Bella – she was always out for her own gain – but this case was more important, not just for me but for Phil.

Our taxi sped into the desert.

Chapter Twenty-Six

Set between two roads and a large number of big hotels, the Hurghada National Museum was a sprawling low-rise stone building with darkened windows stretching around the front. I could see scaffolding erected at one end, telling me this was a new build, probably designed to encourage the package holiday tourist to experience some of the history all around.

Bella had spent the journey telling me about her chance meeting with Chris Prince along with Arthur in Edinburgh. It was Chris who had helped Bella transport items in and out of the UK, and they had 'got close over the summer'. She sighed and turned to look out the window.

'We were the same . . . I thought . . .' She picked at her nail. 'I was tired of doing all this on my own. I thought I'd found someone to . . .' She looked over at me and scrubbed a tear that was threatening in the corner of one eye. 'He was using me for information.' She gave me a knowing look and my heart twisted. I didn't want her to think that I was using her too, but I was, wasn't I? She changed the subject.

'He's the best there is in black-market logistics. Chris can move anything to anywhere. But that wasn't enough for him. He had money and respect, but he wanted more. He wanted power. I think that was when he began to believe that he could be the new Collector . . . He started to mention ways he could do things differently or better. Maybe someone got wind of his plans and decided to stop him. Followed him to a museum in Lowestoft . . .'

'Oh Bella, you think he's dead?'

'No one has seen or heard from him since.' She straightened herself in the seat and peeled her legs off the plastic – she kept her gaze straight ahead.

'I don't know if he's alive or not.' I reached out, got hold of her arm. 'Look at me.' She met my eyes for a brief second and then dropped her gaze. 'Bella, Chris Prince is not the murder victim who was found behind the museum. We showed a museum volunteer his photo. He was there, and he had looked around the museum, but . . .'

'He's alive!' Bella reached for the car door. 'Go back to the ship.'

'Why? What's wrong? Do you think . . . ?'

She was out of the taxi, looking back at me. 'You know how I know this meeting is taking place? Because Chris planned it.' She slammed the taxi door, and I sprang out after her.

'Bella. Stop!'

'This meeting is to cement who'll be "on his team" when he takes over . . .' She scoffed. 'Really, it's about who he might bribe. But the end result is the same.'

Then I realized what she was saying. 'Who is he bribing?'

Her stride was that of a lioness on the hunt, and I had to jog to keep up. 'It's set up like a company – you know, like they have directors and shit.' She paused and grabbed my arm, her fingers digging into my skin. 'Don't get in my way; this is between me and my ex. If he's alive, I want to know why he left me out of his business dealings when he promised me I'd be included. I want to know why he ghosted me.' Then I understood what Bella wanted. Revenge.

To the right of us the coach door hissed open and a murmur of English voices reached me. I scanned the passengers for Carole.

Our taxi driver came running towards us, shouting. We had forgotten to pay! I was torn watching Bella stalk away. I flung too many dollars in the direction of our driver.

Catching up with Bella, I reached out for her wrist to slow her advance. 'You think Chris will be here? Then you can't just storm in there.' When she tried to pull away, I tightened my grip. 'Stop. Bella. Think. This isn't the way to get the answers you want.'

She spun on me and twisted out of my grip, her eyes blazing. She was probably about to let rip at me when the coach passengers started to walk past us. '*If* he's here, he will wish he wasn't,' she hissed. 'He used me . . .'

'Control your rage!' I caught her eye and tried to infuse logic into her just like I would with my daughter, Jade. 'Don't you dare let some man get the better of you. I saw you with Giles back in Copthorn Manor, how you played him to get what you want. Channel that energy. If you storm in there, we won't learn anything. We had a deal, and I'm here to try and get any information that might help stop The Collector and the trail of death in their wake.'

More passengers from the ship flowed around us as Bella cocked her head to study me . . . working out if what I'd said had any merit. And then she straightened her dress and squared her shoulders. 'OK.' Her gaze was still fierce, but she started walking slowly, in step with the tour group from the cruise. 'Have it your way. I suppose your fancy man will be here too? The one you need to tell to stay away from the auction tonight or he'll get himself killed.'

'Fancy man!' I coughed out a laugh. 'I've no idea who you mean.'

Auction? Was that on the schedule?

'Isn't that what you old people call lovers or something? You know, that officer who's not actually one.' I shook my head. Her eyes crinkled with a smile. 'Oh, I've seen the way he watches you.'

'He doesn't . . . it's not.' *God, am I blushing?*

Instead of continuing the conversation, I focused on following the group of about twenty cruise passengers heading to the front of the museum. The morning was already humid and my skin became clammy, but I hung back just enough to not draw attention.

Sally was pulling a blue headscarf over her hair. Mark Rushwell was next to her. Carole was front and centre, as always, and the rest of the crowd behind them.

'Two hours. Be back in two,' the bus driver called after the passengers as he lit a cigarette and walked away.

Carole turned back and lowered her sunglasses. I knew what she was thinking – *we're on a hunt* – because I was thinking it too.

Bella and I were the last to head through the large glass door, but as I looked around the reception hall there was no sign of Sally. Mark walked past us, heading for the ticket booth.

Carole came to stand beside me. 'Did you see where Sally

went?' I asked her. 'I thought she was meant to be our tour guide here.'

'She slowed as we approached,' said Carole. 'I don't think she came inside. There is a local guide leading most of the passengers from the coach.'

We turned and walked back out into the sun and scanned the area, but it seemed deserted until I caught sight of a flash of blue heading around a corner. 'She's going around the side.'

Carole grabbed hold of her hat as we both hurtled after Sally, stopping when we reached the corner of the building shadowed by some scaffolding. I was about to peer around it when someone grabbed my arm and pulled me back against the wall.

Bella.

Her eyes were wide, almost fearful. 'If they see they're being watched . . .' She pointed at Carole's brightly coloured outfit.

'No!' a woman's voice shouted from somewhere nearby. Bella stepped around me and we all angled our necks around the corner together. 'I didn't! I wouldn't,' was all I could make out after that, but the voice was familiar. Sally was standing alongside, wringing her hands.

'Laura?' whispered Carole. 'She wasn't on the bus.'

I strained to hear what was going on.

Laura was muttering to a tall, broad man in chinos and a white Henley T-shirt, a Panama hat and aviators hiding his face. Bella stared at him intently. Laura was trying to explain something to him when he seemed to lose patience and grabbed her by the shoulders. He shook her – his voice too low for us to make out what he was saying. Laura tried to push him off and Sally protested loudly.

'We need to help,' I whispered to Bella and took a step forward.

But Laura twisted herself free. *She knows self-defence.* And ran.

She struck out across the sand without a glance behind her. Her face was twisted with fear, almost unrecognizable. *What did he say to her?* But there was someone running after her – my aunt.

I didn't have time to call out and stop her. Carole reached Laura as she was flinging herself into one of the taxis waiting outside.

'Your aunt doesn't miss a beat,' said Bella with admiration. 'But we need to be quick. They might've seen Carole get in the taxi with Laura and will wonder if they're being watched.'

I stuck my head back around the corner. 'Right, well, as Carole has taken it upon herself to follow Laura, it's down to us to see what they're up to.' I motioned to the man and Sally, who were now walking away from us to the back of the building.

Bella's eyes never left the man.

She slipped around the building, following after them – her footsteps grating on the gravel path.

A fire escape door was opened from the inside, and Sally and the man slipped into the museum. Before the door closed, Bella caught it with her foot and opened it again.

Our eyes met and I thought that she was going to wait for me. Instead, she mouthed, 'Sorry.' And the door closed.

Fury swept over me as I stared at the locked door.

'Bella! Let. Me. In,' I hissed and tried to pull at the door, but it was locked. I ran back to the front of the museum and in through the main entrance. Once I was in the cool interior, I stopped to gather my breath and my thoughts – I needed to find that man, find out where Sally and Mark went and where Bella was. I paid for entry and tried to decipher the direction the fire exit door might lie in.

To the back left?

I sped past tourists milling around the sarcophaguses, towering stone statues and hieroglyphs that filled the cavernous space. The galleries were linked by wide arches so that it was possible to see through several of them at once. No sign of anyone. The moment I stopped, about to lose hope, I saw Sally's blue scarf flickering at the end of the final gallery. She was almost running.

I rushed towards her. With each new room I entered the atmosphere became quieter as the crowds of tourists emptied; the sound of my trainers squeaking on the stone floor made me wince. But as I caught up, I realized that Sally was also following someone – the man in the Panama hat.

My noisy trainers echoed in the deserted gallery as I turned to follow them into the next room but ended up having to fling myself back behind the door frame as the man turned around. I waited, pressed against the wall. Listened for footsteps.

I peeked around the door frame.

Sally and Panama Hat had stopped at a cabinet in a far corner, where they joined three people – Mark Rushwell and a couple I recognized from our first dinner on board: Jenny and Archie. They all tilted their heads back as though viewing an exhibit, talking all the while.

Panama Hat took off his hat and sunglasses with one hand and reached over to shake Mark's hand with the other. He then dug into his pocket and gave Sally a cloth bag.

I stretched my arm out to get a photo, but I was distracted

watching Sally pulling at the strings of the bag. A shiny gold serpent-shaped bracelet slipped onto her palm. It was too far away for me to be sure, but it was shiny, and it didn't look old. She smiled in delight and put on the bracelet.

Click! I took a photo.

Is Panama Hat Chris Prince? I couldn't get a proper look at him, but the man bore a good resemblance to the photo Phil had shown me.

As I raised my arm out to take another picture, they all turned in my direction.

Run!

Panic sped through my veins, and I skidded back through the room I had just come from. Footsteps beat on the tiles behind me. I could sense them closing in.

My heart hammering in my ears, I looked over my shoulder to see Panama Hat following me. I reached the next room, hoping to find some tourists or Bella to ask for help. But it was empty.

I was alone.

'Freya Lockwood. Stop!' I froze. There was something about his voice, deep and cold like the depths of the ocean. 'No one wants a scene.' He had a navy jacket slung over his arm to disguise the fact that he gripped something in his hand – a gun.

How does he know my name?

Once his eyes had swept the room and confirmed we were alone, his shoulders relaxed.

He's enjoying this.

Now that I could see all of him without the hat and sunglasses I knew it was indeed Chris Prince standing in front of me. He fit Betty's description of Mr Suited and Booted as well as the old photo Phil had shown me.

The man who had convinced Arthur to hide the stolen Ming Dynasty vase we were tracking decades ago.

The man who had avoided the flaming catamaran where all souls on board died.

The man whom Bella loved and thought she had lost.

The man Phil wanted answers from.

Chris Prince.

Standing close enough that I could smell the sunscreen on his pale skin.

'What do you want?' I asked, trying to sound confident though my voice cracked. I took some steps nearer to the next room and heard a reassuring chatter of voices coming towards me.

'Arthur took something from me. Do you know where it is?' He had a clipped public-school accent and the air of someone used to being listened to.

'I don't know what you're talking about.' I met his eyes, trying to convince him. 'Arthur and I didn't speak for over twenty years.' I held up my palms and took a few more steps away. *Nearly there.*

'There is no running from this.' A smile touched his lips.

My phone rang, cutting into the tense standoff. Then someone shouted 'Hey!' and Chris looked back over his shoulder. The gun went off with a muffled *pop!*

And I dived to the floor as a lightning bolt of searing pain drove through me.

Chapter Twenty-Seven

Phil

Since the moment he had seen Freya and Carole on the cruise, he had known it was down to him to protect them – even if it was from their own recklessness. He could begrudgingly accept that Freya was a damn good hunter, but that didn't make her arrival any less frustrating.

Now Freya and Carole were off the ship and getting into God only knows what trouble while he was stuck trying to get some private ambulance EMTs, going against the flow of passengers, to Luke. All thanks to Laura – who had cornered him as he stepped onto the dock and insisted this was part of his nonexistent job description. The sick curator needed to be taken ashore to a hospital, it seemed. By the time Phil reached medical with the paramedics behind him, Luke was already on a stretcher, covered in sheets up to his chin, with an oxygen mask over his mouth and nose, sunglasses over his eyes.

'He won't be back on board for the rest of the voyage.' The doctor nodded to the paramedics that their patient was ready. 'He's not in a good way.'

After seeing Luke loaded into the ambulance and driven away, Phil rushed into the car park beyond the port buildings.

Most of the coaches had left, and the last two were headed for the beach.

Bella had told Freya about a meeting in the museum, and he knew that she would be there to see it – but the last person Phil trusted was Bella. The last person Freya should have trusted was Bella.

Phil hailed a taxi as dread twisted like a boa constrictor around his heart. A fifteen-year-old, dust-covered Ford pulled up. He rubbed his sweating palms down his chinos and gave the driver directions.

The taxi left the port building and sprawling concrete behind and joined the highway, heading past the huge five-star hotels that resembled small towns and flat blocks all fighting for a sea view.

The Hurghada National Museum was shoehorned into a large, barren triangular section between two main roads, as if someone in town planning had had a bright idea about culturing the drunken tourists.

There wasn't a tourist in sight – only coach and taxi drivers seated in the shade smoking or sleeping. Two stray and mangey cats hissed at each other before scampering away. To Phil's left, four abandoned shops led to sweeping steps and a modern sandstone-coloured building with a turret-like entrance. As he passed some half-dead palm trees, he nodded to himself. It was the perfect place for a covert meeting – a public place but with very few people to see or hear anything.

The heat of the morning sun burned the back of his neck as he sprang up the steps and into the cool entrance. It was empty apart from the man behind the ticket booth. Phil picked up a map and then scanned the rooms around him to get his bearings.

Where are they?

Bella came strolling towards him. '*We've* got this.' She looked him up and down. 'You don't need to be here. It's not like you're ever going to arrest any of them . . . this isn't even your jurisdiction.'

Phil's jaw clenched but he managed a bored smile; Bella didn't need to know the arrangement the FBI had come to with the necessary authorities. 'I'm not the one who shouldn't be here. What's going on, Bella?'

He could make an educated guess, but he wanted to hear what lie she would tell. There was a lot one could learn about a person from the misdirection they chose.

Bella stepped uncomfortably close. He crossed his arms over his chest but held his stance. Her eyes widened at the challenge, and she took another step until she was pressed against his chest and her floral perfume caught in his throat. She cupped her hand to his ear. 'Arthur told me to come too . . . You're not the only one he trusted.' Her hand swept down his neck and came to rest on his bicep. She squeezed.

'Stop with your flirtatious games,' he murmured. 'They don't work on me. Where are Freya and Carole?' It was always the same with Bella – using her beauty to get what she wanted.

'I could be in mortal danger and all you care about is where Freya is.' She used an overly sweet tone that grated down his spine like fingernails on a chalkboard. He stepped back, seeing the flash of a smile on her lips when she won the point. 'Freya and I have an agreement,' she continued. 'She trusts me too. I'm going to be seeing one of Arthur's journals quite soon.'

The words were a sucker punch to the stomach, but he made sure his posture didn't change. 'After I'm done here, I might put all my energy into making a case against you. Tracking you down . . .'

'I'd love to see you try.' Bella rolled her eyes – but there was also a flicker of fear. 'OK . . .' she said, crossing her arms to mimic him. 'God, don't be so uptight. I'm looking out for her too, you know?'

'Bella.' His tone was low and rough – a warning. He didn't have time for this. 'You and I both know she's out of her depth. You should've kept her away.'

'I *tried*.' She pointed a finger at Phil. 'You're the cops, that's your job. But I also think you're underestimating her.'

Phil huffed a laugh. He wasn't underestimating Freya. He knew exactly what type of trouble she could get herself into if left to her own devices. 'You're going to help me find them.' He brushed his hand over the back of her elbow, making it clear without pushing her forward that he wanted her to move with him. Bella studied him with disgust, but sighed and met his step.

'I want you to show me where they are.'

'For God's sake.' She groaned. 'Carole has gone back to the ship already and Freya has probably gone too. This place is a rabbit warren.'

The cruise tour group was being led by local guides and was being shown a map of the museum and informed about the local history.

They walked around them and through the large, cavernous hall and into a low-lit gallery. The gallery was long and thin and lit by the floor-to-ceiling glass cabinets on each side, which were filled with Egyptian jugs, bowls – Phil didn't like darkness.

'Freya and I came here together, saw an argument outside. Then Carole raced after Laura and I followed Sally in here, leaving Freya out there.' Bella gave him a satisfied look, but there was something else behind her eyes – deceit.

'You left her alone outside? Why am I not surprised.' He scanned the empty gallery but kept moving towards the opening to the next.

'Whatever you think of me—'

'I think you're a thief and one day you're going to get caught.' She batted away the insult. 'You have no idea who I am.'

Phil shrugged. 'And you seem to know quite a lot about this cruise.' He let the statement hang in the air as they entered a larger gallery but with no more light than the last. This gallery had glass display cases around the sides and down the centre – coffins and burial items in an exhibition about how they decorated their tombs in ancient Egypt. But there was no time to admire the display.

Too many dark corners to hide in.

He left Bella's side to check around the corner of a towering display case with a brightly lit golden statue of an Egyptian pharaoh inside.

'I knew . . .' Bella stopped as her eyes fixed on the large opening to the next gallery, her fists clenched – *she saw something*. Phil reached to grab her before she fled but she was already running.

By the time he reached the room at the end there was no sign of Bella. He had swept around the large cabinets filled with ancient hieroglyphs when a man he recognized crossed the adjoining room.

Chris Prince.

Ghosts of his past awakened, ones that he had forced to slumber for decades, and fury filled his veins – until he saw Chris was holding a Glock 19.

Chapter Twenty-Eight

Carole

Carole sat in the back of the taxi smiling down at Laura, who had insisted on sitting in the footwell. 'Are you sure you're all right? Who are you hiding from?'

Laura tried to return the smile, but it didn't reach her eyes. 'I'm fine. It's cooler down here.'

Carole rolled her eyes. 'Said nobody ever, darling.'

Laura glared at her and then squirmed around until she loosened her phone from her back pocket and started tapping a message.

'In all the rush after you, I didn't double-check that you were going back to the ship.'

'I am,' said Laura, resting her head on her knees. 'And you shouldn't have followed me.'

'I was worried.' Carole reached out and tucked a stray strand of hair behind Laura's ear as a tear tracked down her cheek.

'I'm so tired.' She sniffed.

Conversation over.

But Carole wasn't one to give up. 'We are on the main road now, come and sit up here.' She tapped the space next to her. 'Perhaps a trouble shared is a trouble halved?'

When Laura didn't answer, Carole tried the age-old British tactic. 'The weather is awfully hot here, isn't it?'

Laura slid onto the seat next to Carole and arched her neck to check where they were, fixing her eyes on the window. 'Where I'm from it can feel like all the seasons in one day.'

'You're very far from home.' Carole reached out to Laura as another tear fell.

'I want to go home but . . .' She seemed to catch herself and scrubbed the tear away, trying to smile.

'I'd have loved to live on a ship at your age, but I can see it can take its toll. Do you know that I've never felt homesick? I don't have the homing pigeon gene. I could live anywhere for however long . . . but I stayed put for Freya – so that she could grow up with a sense of place after her parents died. You know what I realized? It wasn't a sacrifice, deciding on a different direction in life than the one I had planned, because Freya made my world bigger and brighter without having to set foot on a plane. My life has been richer because of those I have loved.'

'Even when you've lost them?'

Arthur's crooked smile and low rumble of laughter rattled her memories, and her chest clenched, readying itself for a crushing wave of grief. 'Everything ends, but trying to hide away because you fear the pain of loss means you might never experience what it is to truly live . . . to love . . . That's where the best bits of life are.'

'My mum is ill . . . She's been ill a long time, but now . . .'

'It's time to go home?' Carole understood the bravery it takes to watch those you love fade away.

Laura dipped her head and pulled off her ring, placing it on the end of her thumb. 'I have homing pigeon genes. I never intended to be gone this long. I got caught up in things I shouldn't, fell for a man I shouldn't. But the money was good . . .' She trailed off and slipped the ring back on her wedding finger. 'I needed the money.'

'You're married?' Carole pointed to the ring. 'I was always the bridesmaid by choice. Never wanted to be locked into any sort of agreement.'

'Not married.'

'Widowed?' asked Carole, but the scowl she got as a reply told her no.

'I've been wearing this for years . . . It's a reminder that everything I've done has been to build a new life.' Laura's phone pinged.

Carole saw the message: *meet on the Sunset deck in 20 mins.*

'You and your niece shouldn't be here. I like you. I don't want anything to happen to you . . .' She twiddled the wedding ring as she placed it back on her finger. 'This cruise is full of vipers.'

'Are we talking about passengers or crew?' Carole asked. The distressing image of the man grabbing Laura outside the museum popped into her mind.

Laura turned to study Carole. 'Someone stole the sword in the Gallery from a very powerful person and they're mad it's missing. It's been held in that collection as collateral for many years. I need to get it back or . . .' She bit her lip.

Carole's heart went out to her. Laura seemed lost and fragile in that moment, and Carole wanted more than anything for her to get out of whatever trouble she was in. 'You know, Freya is quite brilliant at finding stolen antiques.'

Carole was always one to help a fellow woman in need and so was Freya. Her firecracker niece called it 'girl code'.

There was a glimmer of hope in Laura's eyes. 'Do you think she could find it?'

'Probably.' Carole raised an eyebrow at her. 'If you let her in and trust her.'

* * *

It wasn't like Carole to rush into getting swimsuit-ready, but needs must. She was determined to see who Laura was meeting, and therefore she needed to settle on that deck before Laura arrived.

The Sunset Veranda deck and bar was smaller than the front decks. Sun loungers hugged the outer railings or circled the two hot tubs as they bubbled away. Carole found a spot in the shade, even though she was already protected under her large hat. Soon she spotted Laura beeline for the bar.

Carole waited eagerly to find out who Laura was meeting – maybe a male passenger? She pushed her oversized Dior sunglasses up her nose and attempted to lather on sunscreen while keeping an eye on Laura. If anyone caused the poor girl more distress, Carole was ready to pounce.

So, at first, it was a surprise to see Patricia Henderson place a hand on Laura's shoulder and turn her around. But then Carole was relieved Laura was with Patricia – Laura seemed upset and Patricia was a grandmotherly type filled with humour and wisdom, just what Laura needed.

Laura's shoulders had slumped forward as she was talking, and Carole fought the itch to join the conversation. There was something in the way they were huddled together that made her believe they would stop talking if she joined them. Still, her curiosity was tugging at her. What were they talking about?

Just a little closer.

She pulled her oversized hat down over her face and wrapped her poolside silk robe tightly around her body, unable to talk herself out of sneaking over to get closer to the conversation. She had only taken a few steps when she noticed a couple had put down their books to watch her pass. Going incognito was not what she was used to.

She turned abruptly and sank down on the nearest deck chair facing out to sea.

'If he knows . . .' Laura was muttering.

'Stay calm, my dear, it's going to be all right in the end. You'll see. He might suspect, but he doesn't *know*.' Patricia rubbed her arm. 'Tony is looking into it. Keep an eye on that so-called ship's officer. He's always hanging around.'

Laura nodded sadly.

Carole sighed. Phil really wasn't the very best at this under-cover thing – he was too handsome to go unnoticed!

Their voices dipped to a level she couldn't hear, until Laura mumbled a goodbye and hurried away.

'Here you go.' Carole nearly jumped out of her skin as Patricia arranged herself on the chair next to her and pushed a mojito across the table. 'Thought we could use some refreshments. This cruise is nonstop drama.'

Carole smiled and took a sip. 'To your good health.' But she was worried Patricia knew she had been snooping.

'I thought you'd gone ashore.' Patricia's gaze flickered to where she had been sitting at the bar with Laura.

She knows I did!

'Oh, yes, I came back with Laura. It was *so* hot.' Honesty was the best policy with a friend, which was what Carole had come to see Patricia as. It wasn't easy making good friends at her stage in life, so she valued each one she made. 'Laura did seem upset. I didn't want to interrupt you two as she wouldn't confide in me.' Carole let silence build and hoped that Patricia might give her a little information on what was really wrong with Laura.

'It was nothing.' She tutted. 'Man problems. Always the way with the young, don't you think? We are better off out of the dating game.' She tapped her mojito against Carole's. 'Cheers.'

Patricia must have sensed that Carole wasn't buying the explanation, and their eyes met over their low-ball glasses as they each took a sip. 'She'll be fine,' Patricia smiled.

But who were the 'vipers' on board Laura mentioned?

Chapter Twenty-Nine

Freya

The tiled floor of the Hurghada National Museum was as cold and hard as death – my eyes opened and fixed on a tomb in a glass case above me. *Get up!* I screamed at myself.

Burning . . . stabbing . . . blazing pain shot up and down my arm. My arm struggled to take my weight – deep, dark liquid seeped through my shirt, creating a small pool on the tiles.

Where is Chris?

I pushed myself up onto my feet as a rumble of footsteps and a murmur of voices echoed down the hall and I looked around. Chris was standing in the same spot by the entrance, gun still in his hand, but had turned towards a tour group headed our way. He pulled his jacket back over his gun as they spread around him.

Our eyes locked.

There was a beat in time – one where I could decide to cry out to the tour group, or flee as far from Chris Prince as possible.

I ran.

Adrenalin thumping in my ears.

I heard the muffled Chris demand: 'Get out of my way.'

But I didn't look back.

When I reached the next room, I bumped into a glass case, leaving a bloody smear. I gripped my left arm and kept going. Where was the exit? The large anteroom I had entered was empty, and a brief wave of relief washed over me, but standing in the doorway to the entrance hall were two tall, broad men with their backs to me. They were dressed as tourists, but their demeanour made them seem like bodyguards.

'Freya,' Chris barked from the gallery behind me.

I was trapped between the two men in front – their heads making small sweeping motions – and Chris, who was about to enter the gallery.

With the exit blocked, I spun around and stepped away. I had seconds to find another route. There was an opening in the back corner leading to a corridor, but it would have meant going back to where Chris was about to enter.

In the far corner in front of me was a tall ancient statue of Anubis – the Egyptian god of mummification – a black dog's head, its ears pointed and alert, on a man's body.

I could have taken it for a bad omen, but I also believed he was the patron of orphans and lost souls . . . As an orphan, I hurtled towards him.

Hide! he seemed to call to me.

My arm pounded and my trainers thudded on the stone slabs as I ran behind Anubis and slipped down the cool tiled wall, trying to catch my breath. *Not my day to die!* I told myself over and over.

I was pulling out my phone to call Carole when Bella's voice rose above my thundering heart and rasping breath. 'Chris!'

Sliding across the floor, I peered around the statue. Bella strode out of the corridor in the far corner from where I hid – with eyes full of rage, her fists clenched and her cheeks burning.

Chris shook his head vigorously and hurried over to her with the gun still in his hand. Bella squared her shoulders and stuck a finger into his chest.

'Freya left that way,' she said loudly enough for me to hear, pointing down the corridor. 'This is between you and me.'

She's going to get herself killed. But there was no doubting how impressive her bravery was . . . or how blinding her rage.

Her eyes snapped to my hiding place and my stomach flipped – she knew where I was hiding. She said something else, and he reached out and grabbed her arm.

'Bitch!' he hissed. 'You wouldn't.'

I need to help her. But as I tried to stand, Bella locked her eyes on mine and gave one, almost unnoticeable, flick of her finger, telling me to stay put. It was clear that I didn't need to help her – she was helping *me*.

'It wasn't like that.' Chris was pleading with Bella. 'But there is only *one* night. My *only* chance.'

'Why couldn't we . . .' Bella's voice was quiet, but it was filled with pain. 'You said we would do it *together* . . .'

I couldn't hear the rest of what was said as Chris was dragging Bella to the other side of the gallery and back down the corridor she had entered from.

The moment they left, I ran across the gallery towards the exit, but my legs were weak and I stumbled and slipped. I crashed back down onto the cold, hard floor and a cry escaped my lips. A trickle of blood ran down my middle finger and dripped onto the tiles.

Shouts echoed through the museum and my pulse shuddered.

'Freya?' I looked up to see Phil bending over me. His fingers gently lifted my chin to him. 'You're shaking . . .' His eyes swept over my arm. 'Bleeding . . . We have to get you out of here. Can you walk?'

'I'm fine.' He came around behind me and helped me to my feet. 'It's just shock. Just a graze, I think.' We took a step towards the door. 'Phil, Chris Prince is in there with Bella.'

He glared over my shoulder, his teeth clenched. 'What?'

'We need to help Bella.'

'I need to get you out of here.' He spread his arm back around my waist and his pace picked up. But there was a look in his eye that made me think he was fighting the urge to turn and find Chris.

My phone started its jingly tone again, telling me it was Carole. I sent her a message: *I'm on my way back*.

'Bella thought he was dead. Seems to me that Chris likes having people think he's dead, considering it's the second time he's tried that ruse,' I said.

Phil grunted and pushed open the front door of the museum, as steaming, soup-like Egyptian air hit my lungs.

'Get in.' The taxi had been basking in the heat for too long and was suffocating inside. I lowered the window as Phil grabbed a load of tissues from a box behind us.

I pulled my shirtsleeve up to see the damage. 'It's a flesh wound. The bullet grazed the skin.'

He gently leaned down and inspected the weeping wound. 'Reckless,' he muttered.

'Sorry?' Was he calling me reckless?

His eyes bored into me. 'He'd have killed you . . .' The pain of loss creased his brow. 'What could have happened if I wasn't there?'

'I would've been all right.' But in all honesty, I didn't know if I would have been able to get out of there without Bella or Phil. The idea that I had needed both of them burrowed into me. The discomfort at the reality that I had relied on other people made me anxious.

'Chris caught me taking photos of the meeting, where he gave a bracelet to Sally. I think he was bribing her for something.'

Phil pressed the tissues against the inch-long wound. 'Hold that there. You will need to get it stitched.' I hissed at the pressure, and he raised an eyebrow at me. 'Recklessness has consequences.'

'I wasn't . . .' But I sort of was, so I turned away from him and rested my head against the cool glass. 'What about Bella? We can't just leave her there.'

'She knows how to handle herself. Or have you forgotten how well she manipulated her last boyfriend back when we were at Copthorn Manor?' His words were cutting, but there was a hint of admiration in them.

The taxi driver slammed on his brakes when a pedestrian crossed in front of the car. I gulped down a groan as my arm stung again. The driver leaned out of the window and started shouting at a delivery van. I gripped my arm and closed my eyes as the adrenalin that had kept me moving ebbed away and was replaced with exhaustion.

'Still OK?' Phil murmured.

'I have to be. We need to get to the bottom of what Chris Prince is doing here. We have to stop The Collector, old and new, once and for all.'

* * *

Our taxi stopped at the quayside. I managed to hide my arm with Phil's jacket as we got through passport control and security check. As we walked back to my stateroom, Phil insisted that he could deal with the wound. 'We don't need awkward questions,' he said as I went to the bathroom to change out of the bloodstained shirt.

Phil was propped up against the dressing table when I came out pushing up the sleeve of my old T-shirt to rest on my shoulder.

He leaned in to study the cut, his breath a cool breeze on my wound. 'I have field dressings in my cabin and some antibiotics. But no swimming until it heals, and keep your eyes open for signs of infection.'

I chuckled. 'I'm not here for the sunshine and swimming. Although my aunt will be very disappointed that I won't be wearing the polka-dotted string bikini she gave me.'

His eyes widened. 'You let Carole buy you a bikini?'

'I think "let" is pushing it. Now I have a very good reason to never wear it.'

'Glad my medical advice could be of service. If only you could always follow my directions . . .' There it was again, the glint of worry in his dark eyes.

He left to fetch his medical kit after handing me some paracetamol, and I collapsed back on my bed. My mind was racing.

The image of Chris pointing the gun at me. The shuddering fear that gripped my heart as I crashed onto the floor.

I needed to find out if Bella was all right.

I needed to make a plan.

When Phil returned, he sprayed some stuff on my arm that hurt like hell. 'Sorry,' he mumbled but didn't look up to meet my eyes. Next came a cotton ball and skin closures. Each time I flinched he paused, watching me regain control of the stinging pain and waiting for me to say he could go on. His hand was steady and gentle and he bit his lip as he concentrated.

He looked up and our eyes met. 'Where's Carole?' he asked.

I pulled out my phone and messaged her – a reply was instant. 'Up on deck but on her way. I don't want her worried.' I glared at Phil until he nodded in agreement. 'We'll just tell her that I caught my arm on a . . . nail?'

'You should tell her. Chris knows who you are and that you are on the cruise. You're both going to have to be very careful from now on. Chris was meant to be an expert on this ship, and men like that don't change their plans unless they have been forced to. Stay here until we dock in Jordan.'

'Not going to happen. I came here to hunt a stolen painting and find a thief. Then I realized that it's all connected to the legendary Collector, who Arthur clearly wanted me to find. And you want me to just sit here when I'm getting closer?' I scoffed. His eyes darted to my arm. 'Even with this . . . I'm not stopping now.'

My arm was stiff and throbbing, but painkillers would keep the pain at bay.

'In the taxi to the museum Bella mentioned an auction tonight that *you* shouldn't be at – that you would get yourself killed.' I raised an eyebrow at him. 'I'm not the only one in danger, it seems. Do you think that "meeting" Arthur told you about was the same thing?'

'The Halloween Ball is tonight . . . I suppose it would make a good cover. Fancy dress and everyone preoccupied.'

The door flew open, and Carole hurried in. 'Why didn't you answer my messages?' She filled us in on what she had overheard Laura and Patricia talking about. And then she gasped as her eyes fixed on the bandage Phil had just finished wrapping. 'What happened?' Her eyes widened with fear, and she ran to me, cupping my face in her hands and pulling me into a hug.

'I'm fine. We have come up with a new plan.'

'No, we haven't,' said Phil.

I ignored him. 'Bella mentioned an auction tonight, but there is nothing about one on the schedule. I think that it could be the meeting The Collector attends.' Carole and I looked at each other with understanding. The hunt was on.

Chapter Thirty

Sky

Sky's message to Freya went unread, so she checked her watch and calculated the time difference between the UK and Egypt. Two hours. It was noon for Freya, so she opened her laptop and hacked into the ship's computer system, hoping to see if Freya was still on board.

She's probably having lunch, she told herself. *Don't bother her. You're fine.*

But she wasn't.

Her heart was still hammering in her ears hours after she'd ripped open the letter delivered by the postman earlier. Inside was a picture of documents. To a casual observer it wouldn't mean anything, but to Sky it was blackmail. It showed some of the dirtier jobs she had done for Aaron . . . It said *get all the information to me on Arthur Crockleford; your time is running out*. Without him having to write down any words.

She paced the length of the shop, up and down, until it echoed like a cage she had no key for. Her tear-filled eyes locked onto her bag hanging on the back of the desk chair and she grabbed for her car keys and flipped the shop sign to Closed.

Time to leave.

To London? Like she had originally planned, or maybe abroad . . . get on a ferry to France?

She had nothing to give Aaron. She had searched the antiques shop, been through the handwritten records and the computerized ones, and there was nothing to find! Whatever the client thought Arthur was hiding wasn't in the shop. The dossier she had compiled on Arthur, which included Freya and Carole, was a very thin one.

She had no leads – or perhaps one vague one.

Sky had called Miranda Clive in Norfolk and told her where she worked. Miranda chatted about Little Meddington, the antiques shop and Arthur, but when Sky asked about a 'special commission', Miranda hesitated.

When Sky asked about the last time she had seen Arthur and how they knew each other, Miranda became downright vague.

Sky's very old and battered Ford Fiesta was parked behind the shop. She climbed inside before she had a chance to think it all through. She needed information on Arthur for the dossier, and Freya wanted to know about the painting. Freya had asked Sky to go and see Miranda in person and ask why Arthur wanted to be depicted in an old painting and why he then donated it to the Lowestoft Museum.

The drive from Little Meddington to Burnham Market took over two hours, but with the cool autumn sunshine lighting her journey Sky didn't mind one bit. It was good to be on a mission again.

Her GPS told her she was getting close to the village, and the seagulls overhead told her she was near the sea. It turned out that Burnham Market looked like many other well-maintained

East Anglian villages Sky had visited – one wide road flanked by a mix of Victorian and Edwardian houses and shops, and two lovely traditional pubs. She would have liked to linger for a while in one of them, but she had an artist to find.

Miranda Clive's gallery wasn't on the high street but down a small lane leading to a cobbled courtyard with her premises behind. It was a tiny shop filled with warm light. A grey-haired woman in a smocked dress sat behind a desk facing the crimson-painted door.

Sky straightened her pencil skirt, checked her hair in the window and hoped she didn't look too much like an estate agent.

The bell tinkled as she opened the door. She instantly noticed that three walls of the tiny shop were lined with black-framed paintings.

The woman behind the desk looked up and smiled broadly at her. 'Let me know if there is anything I can help you with.' She wore a string of large red beads over her smock and her blue eyes were steady and kind.

Sky smiled at the warm welcome and proceeded to be mesmerized by the paintings. She stepped even closer to get a better look at a seascape and a fisherman on a boat – so small and yet so perfectly realized. Next was a small boy with freckles, eyes wide with wonder, looking directly at the onlooker – Miranda's painting style had an awe-inspiring photographic quality to it. 'Are you the artist?' asked Sky.

'Yes, I'm Miranda.' She rose from behind the desk and within three steps was on the other side of the shop standing next to her visitor.

'I'm here to ask for your help,' said Sky, convinced that only

209

a miniaturist of such quality could have captured Arthur so well. She pulled out her phone and brought up Carole's snatched photograph of the painting. 'We spoke on the phone earlier. Did you paint Arthur Crockleford onto this nineteenth-century marine work in oil?'

But Miranda shook her head vigorously and said, 'I didn't,' then hurried back to shelter behind her desk.

Sky thought back over all she had researched. 'You were a student of Grace Lockwood?'

Miranda's eyes strayed towards the door. 'I think you should leave.'

Which made Sky believe that there was something more going on. 'Grace's daughter, Freya Lockwood, asked me to come on her behalf. She's inherited Arthur's shop and wants to know why he had you paint him into that painting.'

Miranda fiddled with her beads and fixed her eyes on the door.

She's afraid, thought Sky. *I'm going to need a different approach.*

'How about we phone Freya and get her to confirm that what I've just said is true?' Sky suggested, praying that Freya answered this time.

Miranda bit her lower lip but didn't say no.

Freya answered her FaceTime call almost instantly, and Sky let out the breath she was holding. 'Hi, did you get my message?' Sky saw the bandage on Freya's arm and tried to keep her tone as light as possible, but the sliver of panic was now threatening to consume her. She cleared her throat. *Concentrate.* 'I'm with the painter Miranda Clive. I thought it might be good for her to meet you. So she knows we are who we say we are.'

210

Sky flipped the phone around to introduce Miranda Clive and Freya.

'You look just like your picture,' Miranda said, narrowing her eyes to peer at Freya on-screen. 'Arthur was so very proud of you. He left something for you with me, and a message.'

'I'm so sorry but you've frozen,' said Freya. 'Sky is working for me at . . .' It cut out.

Sky and Miranda stared at the phone. 'I'll try her again.'

Freya answered again, but the call cut out seconds later.

Miranda looked over at Sky and nodded. 'Let me dig out what Arthur left for Freya and then we can try her again.' And she rose to her feet.

She searched through the bottom drawer of her desk. Finally, she handed over a small photograph of a battered blue Louis Vuitton trunk.

'I don't understand.' Sky peered at the photo and then zoomed over the shot of the painting Carole had taken. 'You didn't paint the trunk into the painting, did you?'

Sky called Freya again and handed the phone to Miranda. 'Just under a year ago Arthur came here with an old painting under his arm, begging me to help him. He was very specific about what was to be painted. He told me that if you ever came asking about the painting, I should give you that.' She held up a photograph of an old trunk. 'He said it was the last piece of the puzzle, but whoever came would also need to remember this clue: "It's like the first trunk". He was most particular that I should memorize those words. Please do the same. But . . . take a closer look at that painting.' She told Freya, 'I'm not sure what Arthur was up to, but he was a clever old goat and everything that I painted had a meaning to him.'

For an older lady she had some presence about her. Sky knew this conversation was over. She placed the photo in her bag.

'Thank you,' she said, as she left the shop. 'Your paintings are wonderful.'

She sent a photo of the trunk to Carole and Freya and hurried to her car.

Freya: *Not sure why the painter has a photo of a trunk but please be careful and lock the shop up well when you get back.*

Afternoon sun softly lit the high street as Sky opened the back door of the Crockleford Antiques shop. She glanced briefly at a black SUV parked across the cobbled alleyway with its engine idling. A man sat inside, his face covered in shadows. Her pulse raced as she hurried inside and secured the door behind her.

Chapter Thirty-One

Freya

I must have slept for a few hours through the afternoon because the sun was already setting and Carole was standing at the foot of my bed. 'You just wait until you see your costume for the Halloween Ball tonight. I've ordered room service to give us some more time. It will help you go unseen,' she whispered. 'Phil will be knocked off his feet as well.'

I rolled my eyes, but Carole was too excited to notice.

Phil had demanded that I stay in my stateroom until we docked in Jordan, 'for your own safety'. But I silenced him with a look. 'I'm not dressing up for Phil. We're here on a case, and he can help us with that. Help us get the painting back once we dock.'

Phil had explained that the contents of the Gallery would be impounded when the ship docked in Jordan. The authorities there were on standby.

'Betty can identify that Chris was at the museum the day before the man died. As we know Chris Prince is alive, the question remains, who is the dead man? Phil and I have discussed this and he's having someone look into it.' I gave Carole as stern a look as I could muster. 'You see, we are working together. Nothing else.'

'We still haven't found out what happened to the missing expert Ben Wells. Could he be the dead man at the museum?'

'We would need a picture of Ben or some identification to be sure.' I ran through what I had learned so far. 'I don't believe that the Lowestoft Museum case was what Arthur was pointing us towards when he got me a place on this cruise and left me the second journals. In a way, the case of the stolen painting has been a distraction. There is more going on here, bigger implications to this cruise, and I must see it all through. For Arthur.'

Carole reached out and grabbed my hand. 'Then that's what we're going to do.'

'I'm going to have a walk around. Maybe down to Deck Eight before we get ready for the ball. I want to see if I can find Bella.'

After watching Bella argue with Chris Prince in the museum, I was worried for her. From what I had seen at Copthorn Manor, she preferred volatile men.

First, I scoured the main areas and decks, but with four hundred passengers and a lot of crew, it wasn't an easy search. And Bella could blend in if she wanted to. The sun had begun to set, and I knew time was running out before I needed to get ready for the ball and I'd lose the one chance to find out if there was to be a 'meeting' at the same time.

I ran up and down the corridors of Deck Eight, which I hadn't explored, but they looked exactly the same as Deck Seven, where my stateroom was.

Carole would probably be doing her elaborate pre-party

routine by now, and I understood that time was slipping away. I admitted defeat and began to walk back down the corridor to the lift.

Footsteps pounded behind me and I spun around.

A steward hustled past me. The outfit was different, but the eyes were the same. I smiled with relief.

Bella.

'You're OK?' I whispered. 'I've been looking for you.'

Her blonde wig looked real, and that soft pink lipstick really suited her – it was a great disguise. I needed to learn how she managed to change her appearance so completely. Inhabiting a different persona was a daunting prospect, but it must also be intoxicating when you pulled it off. I needed new skills if I was to get the agency off the ground.

'What are you doing?' She checked over her shoulder. 'You can't keep walking up and down these corridors.'

'I was worried. What happened?'

She glared at me, but there was also a flash of thanks in her eyes and the crease of a smile on her lips before she hardened herself again. 'I'm always fine. As you can see. Now go.' Without an explanation she turned, but I grabbed her arm. I needed to know what had gone on at the museum.

'Bella, I need answers.'

She shrugged me off and huffed. 'Not here.' Walking behind her, I saw that her entire body language was different now, mannerisms as well as looks, and I wanted to ask her how she did that. How she made every part of herself fit the role she was playing. We stopped outside a stateroom and Bella scanned the corridor. 'In here.'

The stateroom was similar to mine, and I went to stand

next to the balcony window. 'Thank you for what you did in the museum.' My hand found my arm, which was still throbbing.

'Hard for you to keep our deal if you're dead.' She tried to keep the hard edge to her voice, but it cracked. 'I was trying to keep you out of it, but you won't stay out, will you?'

'It's unlikely, seeing as it's my job. What went on between you and Chris Prince at the museum?'

She stood in front of the mirror and readjusted her wig, avoiding eye contact. 'I thought Chris was dead . . . or maybe . . . I just didn't want to see he used me and left me. I don't do *real* relationships, but he sort of . . .' There was no anger in her words – only sadness. 'He's such a cockroach.'

'What did you talk about, Bella?' I placed my hand on her shoulder.

'I wanted to know about Ben Wells,' she muttered, picking up a lipstick.

'Ben Wells the missing antiques expert?' I asked.

'I've never met him, but I heard Chris talk to him on the phone. I thought Ben Wells would be at the Egyptian museum. He was in line to be the next Collector and wanted rid of Chris. Kind of wish he'd done that now, but seems it went the other way. Chris said he's "gone", which can only mean one thing. There were three of them in the running to be the new Collector, but I don't know who the third is.'

'Chris Prince killed Ben Wells?'

'It's likely.'

'And do you know anything about what happened to Luke?'

Bella shrugged. 'Someone wanted him out of the way, and now he is. Chris didn't mention anything about it, but I don't think they get on.' She straightened her tunic.

'Would Chris want to hurt Luke?'

'Anything's possible, but there'd be a good reason if he did. He wasn't on the ship at the time, so someone else would've had to do it.'

'Now you know Chris is alive, what are you going to do?' I asked, dreading the answer.

Her eyes flashed pure fire at me. 'I'm going to take them *all* down.'

'Then let's do it together. Get proof of illegal activity and have them arrested.'

Our eyes locked and she sighed. 'My way would've had more flair.' She rolled her shoulders as if she were about to step back out on stage.

'If you want to see the information that Arthur had on the Scottish art and antiques, then I need to close this case first . . . within the law.' I hoped.

'Fine.' She strode towards the door. 'But you'd better keep your word, or I'll go back to doing it my way.'

Bella pressed her cheek to the door and her eye to the spy hole. She reached for the handle. In the corridor voices could be heard and she froze.

She spun back around and dragged me towards the wardrobe, pulling out a number of wigs and placing them on a dressing table. 'Better you're not recognized after the museum. Chris could have people searching for you.'

I reached for a wig and tried to pull it over my head, but Bella rolled her eyes and strode over. 'We need to be faster than that. I'll do it.' Within minutes she had pinned my curls to my head and pulled on a hairnet. It was how I imagined being backstage at a theatre would be. It wasn't just a hairnet

217

that was needed, but also glue along my hairline to attach the lace front. When Bella had finished her work twenty minutes later, the long blonde hair looked almost natural on me. I went to the mirror to check out my new persona. Would I like her? I ran my fingers through the shining strands and flicked them over my shoulder like Carole always did. Changing identities could be fun.

It had gone quiet outside. Bella had thrown me one of the crew uniform shirts and frowned at my leggings. 'We might get away with it.' Dressed in a crew uniform and my new hair, I slipped out of the room after Bella. We stayed flat against the wall and cautiously turned a corner. Towards the end of the deck where I knew Luke had been staying, Archie and Jenny were entering a stateroom. 'That's one of the largest suites they're going into,' said Bella with a nod of her head. 'It's not their room.'

Jenny whispered to a man in a dark suit who had opened the door to them. Even from this distance he looked like a night-club bouncer.

Once the door was closed behind the guests, Bella strode out as if she owned the place.

'Look, the crew swans around this ship and no one really notices them. But they do notice the ones who behave sus-piciously, OK?' She raised an eyebrow at me, and I stuck my chin in the air and put a swagger in my shoulders. 'Better. Now listen.'

We placed our ears to the door, but my eyes focused on a stack of room service trays sitting outside a stateroom five or six doors down. Faint voices pulled me back to the stateroom beyond the door and I pressed my ear harder against the cool metal.

'This can't go on. What did Arthur tell these women?' Archie said.

'Where are the items you agreed to trade? Do you have them?'

'I do. I will need to look over the items to trade before the deal is made,' said Archie. 'This operation was a lot slicker when Arthur was here.'

'So, tonight . . .' said Jenny. 'Quite thrilling to have new blood in the chair, isn't it?'

There was a low murmuring that did not sound friendly in tone.

'OK, OK.' It was Jenny's voice. Her usual irritating drawl sounded shrill with panic. A threat had clearly been made. 'To business.'

A trade was being undertaken, but we didn't know for what.

There was the click of something opening.

'There's not much talking at these deals,' I whispered.

'My guess is they're worried they are being watched or over-heard. I got lucky earlier today. I saw a couple of suits leaving this room when I returned from the museum and managed to get in there before they came back.'

'We're done then?' asked Jenny, her voice still shaking.

'Done.'

Approaching footsteps made me jerk backwards, and I was about to flee when Bella placed a hand on my arm. 'Slowly,' she mouthed. We were only a few steps away when the suite door opened and closed behind us, but Bella kept a slow pace.

Jenny, Archie and the bouncer walked around us without even looking.

'We should move this again,' Jenny was saying to the bouncer.

'I'll notify Tony and he'll get someone to come back with housekeeping trolleys.'

When they were out of sight, we both turned around and headed back to the stateroom. Bella pulled out a key card and grinned. I wide-eyed her, but I shouldn't have been surprised that she was a master pickpocket. 'Impressive. How about you teach me that trick?'

Bella placed the key card to the reader and the light turned green. 'I might actually do that one day.' The door swung open. 'If you teach me how you know things are a fake?'

I smiled. *Maybe*. 'Let's see what's in here,' I said.

What we saw when we opened the door and stepped inside was like the moment Howard Carter peered into Tutankhamen's tomb.

Chapter Thirty-Two

Sky

Sky sat behind the desk in the Crockleford Antiques shop studying the photo that had arrived in the post that morning. Sometimes she had to wonder how Aaron made so much money and instilled so much fear into people when he could also be stupid enough to photograph information such as that.

It had taken her hours to research each document and compile a dossier of her own – one that would turn the tables on Aaron and his associate. She was feeling quietly pleased with herself when she heard a scratch and a click from down the corridor.

Her pulse picked up, and she threw her research between the pages of a catalogue and into the desk drawer.

Someone's here.

Before she could reach for her phone or dive into the kitchen for a knife, Aaron stepped into the shop. His eyes were dark and menacing . . . cruelty twisted his lips.

'We need to talk.' Within a couple of strides she was pressed up against his chest as he reached for the strap of her shoulder bag. Sky flinched, but she refused to step backwards. Aaron had caught the action and the edges of his eyebrows rose – her fear was fuel to him, but this time his calm intimidation wouldn't force her into submission. 'Where have you been all day?'

In the weeks working at Crockleford Antiques, Sky had witnessed two women thriving without any man . . . It was an example she wanted to follow.

He reached for her shoulder, and she tightened her grip on the bag's strap.

'Calm down. I'm just relieving you of your bag.' Aaron's icy-blue eyes glinted at her – *he's enjoying this* – and his smoke-stale breath reached her nose and brushed against her cheek. 'Don't give me any trouble. I'm not in the mood.'

'What do you want?' She glared at him. 'You sent the photograph of all those documents this morning. You trying to blackmail me, Aaron? If I were to go down, you would come with me.'

He hummed in agreement. 'But I wasn't telling you I would shop you to the police, little nerd, I was trying to remind you of the type of people you work for.'

She forced her mind's eye on the photograph again. The invoice for the hosting site of a company website she had created years ago was one of the most interesting – a van hire company? No, that wasn't it, it was a moving company – King and Sons Ltd.

'Look, Aaron, I get that you want me to keep digging, but I'm no miracle worker.' She knew that he wouldn't stop until he believed he had all the information he could get on the Lock-woods and Arthur Crockleford. Running away would've been the smart choice, but she was going to do the exact opposite – she was going to convince Aaron that there was nothing to find and get him to leave for good. 'Those women are clean.'

'But they're not!' He almost shouted the words. 'Otherwise how did they know about the cruise? Our employer is raging that we didn't tell him they'd joined it. We . . . *you* . . . are meant to be watching them. Apparently, they showed up at some meeting and he had to *shoot* one of them to get them to leave.' He ran his thumb along her cheekbone and down her neck, stopping on her pulse point. 'We need to keep the client happy. So you're going to be useful and find what he's looking for . . .'

Freya had a bandage around her arm – was she shot?

'You were clever finding out about each and every museum Arthur had an affiliation with, and when we passed that information on, he was very pleased. But he followed all the leads and still hasn't found it. Chris is livid and he isn't someone you want focused on you.' His fingers stretched around her neck and rested there – he didn't need to start squeezing for her to understand the threat. 'Now he's focused on me . . . because *you* didn't do *your* job.'

All the nuggets of information slotted into place as if Sky were writing a beautiful line of computer game code that made a locked door open. Could it all be connected?

The son of a King is a Prince . . .

She took a gamble in the phrasing of her next sentence. 'What has Chris Prince got against Freya and Carole?'

There was a menacing twinkle in his eye. 'How does my little nerd know that name?'

'You just told me . . .'

'No, I didn't. What do you know?' His fingers dug into her neck as his other hand grabbed her wrist. He dragged her up the stairs to the sitting room and threw her onto the sofa. 'What. Do. You. Know?'

'Nothing, just that there was a Chris Prince who was meant to be on the antiques cruise and didn't show up.'

He tutted and slowly shook his head. 'You're in over your head.'

Aaron's phone rang and he put it to his ear. 'Yes, I'm here. I'll get whatever information you need. I've had someone on the inside for a few weeks, and I'm quite sure that she'll tell us what we need to know. Oh, she's very friendly with the Lockwood woman . . . Good idea.'

There was a pause.

'Arthur's journals and a vase, got it?' He held Sky's gaze until she nodded.

'I haven't found either of those things. You know I haven't,' she said.

'Do I?' He sat down next to her and pulled out a switchblade. 'Since working here you've been different. Those women have got under your skin in such a short amount of time.'

I was on my way out the door long before I started working here.

Aaron picked up the laptop from the coffee table. 'Now, where did you go this afternoon? What led you all the way to Norfolk?'

Shit! Shit.

Lie.

Fast.

'Chris believes Freya and Carole are on the ship because they know something they shouldn't. He doesn't trust them . . . and now he doesn't trust me. Thinks I'm holding out on him. I told him I never would because I didn't . . . you did!' He pulled out a gold Zippo lighter and a flame sparked. 'Did you know that Chris likes flames? Has a real reputation for burning shit down?' He scanned the small sitting room above the shop. 'And now that he's cruising the Red Sea, I think he's probably into giving people watery graves. Now, why are they on that ship? Or this place won't last the night. And your friends will be taking a swim.'

'Chris Prince is on the cruise ship with Freya and Carole?'

Shit!

Aaron didn't answer, but she knew him, and the smile on his face told her that she was right. The thought filled her with terror. She had to find a way to warn them. She had to get them help.

Sky reached for her laptop. 'I'll keep digging into the Lockwoods, if that's what you want, but everything I have is already in the dossier.'

Aaron settled back on the sofa and Sky quickly scanned her emails. She found a draft email on Luke she had started and remembered something interesting.

'What are you doing?' Aaron grabbed the laptop, but Sky had already pressed send.

Chapter Thirty-Three

Freya

Bella and I stood in the large stateroom. She nodded at me as I took in the scene before us. 'Not quite what you thought, right?'

'I didn't expect a museum! How did all of this get here?' I walked around the suite, which was almost triple the size of the one I had been allocated. Propped on easels were small paintings on a sea theme: sailing ships, tropical islands, storms at sea. They were hanging off clips, not stretched on canvas. 'How did they make it on board without being detected in Greece, Cyprus or Egypt?' I wondered aloud.

'I imagine a lot of bribery has gone on,' answered Bella.

On a dressing table were velvet-covered jewellery boxes. The bed had been covered in a huge collection of shipwreck ceramics. I picked up a blue-and-white sleeve vase decorated with delicate flowering branches and flying insects. It had no damage. It was a beautiful piece and far superior to the ones in the Gallery. In between some of the other pieces was a folded piece of paper.

'It's an inventory.' I showed Bella and realized something.

About 60 per cent of the items in the room were listed in Arthur's second journal.

'What's the Hatcher Collection?' asked Bella. 'These all look a bit faded and beaten up to me.'

'A well-documented shipwreck cargo.'

I reached out and picked up a miniature vase no bigger than the palm of my hand. It perfectly covered the scar that always reminded me of my parents. I took out my phone and started taking photos to check against those I had of the second journal.

Bella threw down the piece of paper and headed for the jewellery. It was clear that she preferred sparkly things that weren't part of the nautical collection. They weren't listed in Arthur's journal, but they were probably still part of the black market being traded instead of bought . . . Money is far easier to trace. 'These are nice.' She opened a small box and pulled out a pair of Art Deco pendant diamond earrings.

I flicked through a book of coins and then opened a few boxes to see compact Old Master studies – *small enough to fit into a suitcase.*

Bella grabbed my arm. 'They're coming back.'

There was a low muttering of male voices outside the stateroom and our eyes locked in panic. 'Balcony,' said Bella, tugging the curtain over a little more as she opened the door.

I hurried after her and closed the door behind me. My heart hammered in my ears, and I pushed my back against the cool frosted glass that divided this balcony from the next. My wounded arm brushed the wall, and I bit my lip, hard, to stop from crying out in pain. Bella reached down and grabbed my hand. 'You OK?' she whispered, her eyes never leaving the glass door. Metallic blood reached my tongue, and I nodded.

The clattering of ceramics made my eyes jolt open, and Bella's arm whipped across me to stop my movements. I didn't like standing aside while precious items could be damaged.

'That old stuff isn't worth getting yourself caught. We have bigger fish to catch right now – we have a deal.' She was right: if we could take down a black-market dealer like The Collector, halt a new Collector taking up position, then we would stop many antiques and paintings being stolen to order.

'How the hell did you lose the card?' one of the men inside demanded. There was a mumbled reply. 'Then from now on I'm dealing with it personally.'

'Chris?' I mouthed to Bella.

'No.'

'Then who? I recognize that voice.'

She shrugged in reply.

I placed my hand over my arm to try and numb the throbbing, but it made all the energy drain from my legs. I reached out for the wall to steady myself. I closed my eyes and felt an arm around my waist.

The stateroom door slammed shut and Bella crept forward.

'They've gone. We don't have long.' She took my elbow and made me move.

Back in the room some paintings had been removed and I saw a broken teacup on the side table. 'Arthur would've played this all so differently.'

Bella pulled me with her to the door and opened it a crack. 'You're not him. You'll do things your way, but that doesn't mean that you won't seek the same justice he did.'

I had no idea why I was opening up to Bella at that moment; perhaps because my wounded arm was making me feel vulnerable – as fragile as the broken teacup I was unable to rescue. And she was wrong, of course. Doing everything exactly like Arthur would have done was exactly what I was trying to do. I was trying to live up to the faith that he had in me by leaving me all the journals.

'We need to go.' She pulled open the stateroom door and motioned for me to follow her. 'They might check the whole room once they have removed all the items.'

I tried to smile, but I think it came out more of a grimace.

* * *

Back in my stateroom I drank some water, took some painkillers and opened the connecting door to Carole's room.

'Just in the shower, won't be a minute,' she called. 'Have you heard from Sky? I tried her phone, but my signal was bad.'

'I'll check on her,' I said through the bathroom door and retreated to stare out at the dark sea and collect my thoughts. I had two hours until the ball. The balcony of the stateroom on Deck Eight had the same view as mine, but after seeing all the stolen items in person and being shot at, everything felt different to me now. Or perhaps it was just the blonde wig I was still wearing.

I thought about Sky, and Phil's warning about her ex. I tried the shop number even though it was after hours.

The phone rang twice.

'Hello?' said Sky, but she sounded distant, like the receiver wasn't close to her mouth.

'It's Freya. I'm just checking in, is everything OK?'

'It's . . . um . . . How's the cruise? Are you safe?' she said, with an edge to her voice.

What's wrong?

'Are *you* safe?' There was the low mumble of a male voice in the background, which made my stomach tighten. 'Sky? Who's there?' I gripped the railing.

'It's just the TV. I'm fine. Perhaps we could chat tomorrow?'

'You would tell me if it wasn't? If there is someone there, tell me something like "I'm just going to make dinner". And I could get Agatha to—'

'I hear you lost your . . . key card. Perhaps you should go and check if you left it in 825? Good night.'

What did she mean about 825? It wasn't my suite or Carole's. I stared at my phone for a few seconds. The conversation with Sky felt very wrong. Sky had been measured and careful with her words, in a professional and almost stilted way. Normally she was our impulsive, brightly coloured, coat-cardigan-wearing, computer genius Gen Zer. Normally she was chatty and relaxed on the phone.

However, within five minutes I had her research about the curator (which I didn't remember asking for) in my inbox. Perhaps I was reading too much into it.

Luke Drummond was born in Brighton in 1965, making him fifty-nine. He studied history at Oxford before working for Sotheby's and as a television researcher. There was some scandal six years ago with a break-in at one of the houses where he was cataloguing antiques – the only lead they had was a removal van leaving the area. A witness said one of the drivers had a snake tattoo on his arm.

231

The van was registered to a company called King and Sons.

From that point on I could find no documented mention of any employment for Luke Drummond, though he is believed to work for private clients. He has vanished from the web and turned up.

Be careful, I think that

The email ended mid-sentence.

Chapter Thirty-Four

The Halloween Ball

After an hour of being dressed and preened by a ridiculously excited Carole, I was ready for the ball. My costume was a Victorian version of Dracula's bride with my breasts overly exposed and two dots of blood on my neck. Carole had done my eyeliner, and the way she swept the black line over my lids and got them to flick at the ends was impressive. I'd left the bodice as loosely laced as possible so that I could still breathe, hopefully without it falling down. I had kept the blonde wig Bella had expertly put on me, but covered it in a long red veil and a decorative black mask.

Carole was Morticia Addams in a long, slinky black dress that pooled on the floor, coal-black wig and very smoky eyes. She looked utterly enchanting.

The ballroom was on the top deck, decorated like Dracula's castle in a 1980s film set. Windows swept around one end of the room and black night stretched out beyond. The lights had been dimmed and ultraviolet tassels hung from every chandelier.

I scanned the room, but it was impossible to tell who was who – there were werewolves, witches, ghosts, several headless Marie Antoinettes and more Dracula brides than I cared to count. Carole and I headed for the bar, and as we waited in line I wiggled my dress upwards in an attempt to regain some modesty. 'Wait until Phil sees you in this. His eyes will *pop*.' She ran a hand down her wig. 'I'm also a great matchmaker.'

'I'm not here for him.' I needed him to treat me like a fellow professional, and I was not sure the dress was giving off that particular vibe. 'We need to locate Mark, Sally, Jenny . . . Archie. Keep a lookout for Chris.' She wasn't looking at me anymore, so I grabbed her arm and caught her eye through my mask and veil. 'Yes?'

'Absolutely.' But she still looked like she was on the hunt for Phil.

The bar was overflowing with blue dry ice; a skeleton overcome with fumes was in the midst of a coughing fit. Huge cobwebs shrouded the chandeliers and doorways.

'Oh dear,' Carole said while staring across the room. I followed her sight line and saw that someone else was wearing the very same dress and veil as I was. 'Sorry, I didn't think there would be quite so many people in the same outfit as you. I've counted five so far. Should I go over and suggest that we put different armbands on?'

'It's fine. Might be good that there are more than one of us.' I was inwardly debating whether I should go back to Deck Eight and see if anything was going on there yet.

'It must be a very popular design, as it looks like the exact same costume.' Carole shook her head. 'Perhaps if you take the veil off and put on some bright red lippy, that would make you stand out.'

I turned away and tried to make it look like we weren't actually talking. 'After the museum it's better if I don't draw attention.' Something that my aunt would probably never understand.

'It's not a sin to shine, you know,' whispered Carole. 'But . . . yes . . . we don't want you hurt again.'

'When you bought this monstrous costume, did you not think it was a bit revealing?' I tried to pull up my dress for the hundredth time.

'Of course I did, darling. But back then I was thinking of getting you some action, not helping you go undercover. Unless it was bedcovers!'

'Oh, please stop!' I cringed. 'We're here to discover . . .' *The identity of The Collector*. I didn't finish the sentence; I didn't trust that we weren't being overheard.

She leaned towards me. 'But it would have been a great bonus, wouldn't it?'

I shook my head, as she would only go on and on about me having a 'fully rounded life with lots of different types of action'. We'd had this conversation only a week ago. Instead, I scanned the room as two other women entered the ball wearing identical outfits to mine.

I saw Phil before he saw me; he was dressed in his officer's uniform with a joke-shop rubber dagger through his neck – I couldn't deny how very good he looked. How calm and confident. A woman dressed in a striped black-and-white Beetlejuice costume – which had a low bodice and a very short skirt – was next to him. She looked amazing, and I understood why Phil stopped to talk to her. She had reached out and was now gripping his arm. I wondered if he fancied her, if he was flirting, but his eyes roamed the room until they stopped at Carole and me. My pulse tingled. He said a few words to the Beetlejuice woman; she giggled, and he excused himself. Within a few strides he was standing in front of us.

'Good evening, Morticia,' he said, smiling at Carole. 'Freya?' His eyes flickered up and down my dress and he leaned in. 'How's your arm?'

Before I could answer, Carole threw her hands skyward. 'A dance! That's what you both need.' She placed a hand on my back. 'Make an old lady very happy and show me how it's done.'

We both knew she was the best dancer in the room and had the stamina of a kid, but when I didn't move, she pushed me. I reached out to stop myself falling forward and my palm crashed onto Phil's chest. When I looked up, he was looking down at me with a small glint in his eye. His lips turned up at the corners in amusement and his arm wrapped around my waist.

'At least on the dance floor I can keep an eye on you,' he murmured.

'I'm perfectly—'

'Fine on your own. I know. But we can probably see quite a lot from there, observe everyone who's here. And we wouldn't want to disappoint your aunt, would we?' I turned back to Carole, who mouthed, 'Go have fun.' Like I was still the shy child who didn't talk much.

'I haven't danced since childhood,' I whispered. I needed to keep this relationship professional, and the image of having Phil pressed close to me brought up feelings that were really quite . . . unprofessional. The orchestra was halfway through a waltz and the dance floor was full. 'We don't have to . . .'

'Just follow my lead. My mother taught me,' Phil replied, pulling me close. 'She's Mexican, so I'm better at salsa, but . . .' He was so close I couldn't concentrate on what he was saying.

I focused on the passengers and tried to ignore the warmth between us. I didn't mention the lessons I'd had with Carole when she decided I was going to be an actor in a costume drama because I 'loved the past so much'.

Phil spun me outwards and then swept me towards him again.

'Is this really so bad?' he asked.

I didn't reply, worrying that my voice would betray me.

We were moving effortlessly together in time to the music. 'How is your arm?' he asked again.

'It's better. Thank you for getting me out of there.' It was like there was an electric charge between us as his hands entwined with mine and he pulled away to turn me again. When the music stopped, I let go of his hands, feeling self-conscious and flustered. A strange longing trickled in, one I had not felt in a very long time, and I wanted to keep on dancing, but not because I wanted to dance. 'I should get back to my aunt.'

I walked away, instructing myself to keep all thoughts and feelings towards Phil platonic. I noticed a woman in the same dress as me forcing her way through the crowds. She approached a man dressed like someone out of a Jane Austen novel who was also a zombie and squared her shoulders and started poking her finger at his chest. She looked livid.

It was only when I was closer that I realized it was Laura and Mark, standing by the bar. Mark was shaking his head, his eyes creased with worry. Laura was tugging at her dress, the tension in her shoulders palpable. I manoeuvred around some dancers to observe them as the music started up again.

Mark said something, and Laura's eyes widened with shock and then understanding.

I had to get closer to hear what they were saying.

Mark reached out for Laura's arm; there was an almost pleading expression on his face, but she curled forward under his touch.

I was nearly on them when Laura twisted free. 'You can't do this. Not now.'

Mark laughed and downed his tumbler of whisky before turning towards the bar to ask for another.

I sped after Laura as she ran out of the ballroom.

Chapter Thirty-Five

Laura

Laura rushed down to the Gallery to try and mitigate the damage, but she had no idea how to do that. A few passengers in full costume were milling around, and she fought the urge to shoo them all away. She didn't need anyone looking too closely at the central cabinet.

Her fingertips swept over the glass top and she sighed. This morning, Laura had thought it was Freya who had taken the sword, but now she knew differently. Could she trust Freya enough to ask for her help in getting it back? Things weren't the same without Arthur Crockleford's affable presence. She missed his calm authority, his humour, his knowledge. He was never ruffled, always had a solution, and paid well for information. He would have known what to do once everything started to go wrong. Freya was nothing like her predecessor; she didn't acknowledge the passengers on board who traded in the black markets, nor did she head to the 'storerooms' to verify the antiques as Arthur would have done. It was as if she didn't know what was expected of her.

So why is she here?

Laura gripped the top of the cabinet and tried to calm her

racing pulse. Every other antiques cruise she had organized had run smoothly, but the tide was turning and everything was changing.

One more night . . . Tomorrow it'll all be over and I'll be gone.

Luke's continued illness was also deeply troubling. Laura hadn't liked or trusted the man, and she knew that he worked for The Collector. But she also got the feeling he wanted out – that he wanted to retire. Live a life where he wasn't always looking over his shoulder. They had that in common.

Laura had needed him out of her hair temporarily and had slipped him something in the water bottle she had handed him in the theatre. It was meant to disorient him for a few hours. She needed to handle the Gallery 'problem' on her own. But it seemed he was now ill enough to be taken to the hospital and that was far worse than she had intended.

The painting of the burning ship had been handed to her as she left a cafe in Athens the day they set sail, and she knew what that meant – get it to Jordan. It was the way it always happened – 'be at this place at this time' and she would be given something to smuggle. But never anything as large as the painting, and it took some doing to get it on board. In the end, she told the authorities that it belonged with the Gallery items.

She hadn't banked on a curator overseeing the Gallery quite so closely, no curator ever had before, and she hadn't intended for it to go up on the wall or anything like that. Now that Chris was on the ship, she needed to take it down immediately. Before he realized that it was on display for all to see. Especially since Luke, Freya and Carole had taken an interest in it. What was it about that painting they all so admired? Chris was already fuming that she hadn't told him the women were on the cruise.

Laura sighed and looked at her watch. Time for her to do a final check and move the painting into the storage room in the back. Then get back to the party. She soothed herself by picturing her new Melbourne flat, and living a normal life full of coffee shops and good wine. Not long now and she would be home and dry.

As soon as we dock, I'm gone.

She opened the cabinet, pressed the felt on the display surface and heard a quiet click. She peered inside – and screamed.

Chapter Thirty-Six

Phil

Freya was swallowed up by the Halloween Ball crowd and panic itched at the corner of Phil's nervous system. At the far end of the room, he glimpsed her following someone in a similar dress – they both left by a side door.

Freya was the taller of the two women, and he kept his eyes locked on her as he rushed through the throng, trying to keep up with them.

Even with the ship's air-conditioning, Phil was sweating. A gust of salty night air swirled around him as two vampires swept inside, their long cloaks filling the corridor. When he'd disentangled himself, both the women were gone. *Did they take the lift?*

He went to the twin lift bank. Both busy. One had just stopped on Deck Eight and the other on the parade deck, where the shops were. He didn't have time to waste. He flung himself into the service stairwell, but once he reached Eight, the corridor was empty. After checking that no one was observing him, he hurriedly went up to the parade level, annoyed with himself for not starting there.

Was she heading to the Gallery?

When he reached the parade, he was out of breath, but there was no one there other than two men drinking at the bar in the Grand Salon, looking very much the worse for wear.

Phil forced himself to slow his pace. No matter how much he wanted to find out what was going on – and where Freya had gone – he couldn't show it to the watching CCTV or onlookers. He had always been able to control his emotions, shutting them down at will, but there was something about Freya that got under his skin. He was used to people doing what he asked; he was used to being listened to. None of that was true with Freya.

When he had slowed his breathing, he placed his hands behind his back and took long strides towards the Gallery. The door was open but the lights were off.

Phil stopped.

The only sound was the pounding of his heart until he heard the rapid drumming of footsteps – he turned to scan the parade, but there was no one visible. He switched on the flashlight on his phone and stepped inside the Gallery. Above him, the security camera no longer blinked red. Three feet in front of him was a red veil pooled next to the central cabinet. And beside that . . .

Is that a foot?

He turned his phone towards it as bile rose in his throat.

Freya?

He ran around to the other end of the cabinet.

'Oh God, Freya,' he rasped.

Chapter Thirty-Seven

Freya

Phil was calling my name, his voice rough and strained, but as I looked around I couldn't see him. I ran in the direction of the sound and stood peering into the Gallery. It was dark apart from the stream of one flashlight. He was bending over someone . . . their dress identical to mine.

I gripped the open door, trying to catch my breath. 'Phil? What's happened?'

He startled, and then in one swift movement he stood, turned around and strode towards me, to grip my shoulders with his hands. 'You need to leave.' I winced under his touch near my bandage.

'Sorry.' He dropped his hands to his sides, but his eyes were wild with fear.

I stiffened my stance because I wasn't going anywhere. 'What happened?' I asked again.

'You don't need to see . . .' But we both knew that wasn't going to stop me. He sighed. 'Don't touch anything.'

I glared at him. 'I wouldn't. Is that . . . ?' I bent down to look at the red veil on the floor.

Laura? No, no, not Laura.

Phil placed one hand on my shoulder. 'You're wearing the same costume . . . I need to get you somewhere safe.'

I shook my head. 'Laura pushed me out of the lift,' I said. 'When I arrived on the promenade, I saw a man in coveralls running away from the Gallery. I tried to follow him up the main staircase, but he vanished somewhere on Deck Eleven. I thought he was stealing something . . .'

She's dead . . .

'I'm afraid she's . . . At first I thought . . .' He ran his palm down his face.

He thought it was me.

I walked over and instinctively reached out to Laura's lifeless body before clenching my fist, remembering not to touch anything. 'Oh, Laura, why?' I murmured. Laura looked like she was asleep, but her neck was twisted at a strange angle. My heart clenched and bile burned my throat.

Phil was standing over me watching the door, his arms crossed. 'I need to report this to the captain.'

'I'm so sorry, Laura,' I whispered and had stood to leave when I saw that the top of the glass cabinet was slightly open. The interior was almost empty.

'Was this a robbery?'

I should have been faster. My chest tightened at that thought.

Phil reached out and placed his hand on my back. It wasn't lost on me how many times he had reached out and touched me, but it was only when his steady hand rested on me that I realized I was shaking. 'I'll deal with it. You need to get out of that costume and go back to your stateroom. Lock the door.'

'She was planning on going back to Australia.' Phil pulled off his jacket, swept it around my shoulders. I rubbed at the edge of my wig and then wiped my eyes.

'Once I've got this under control, I'll come and find you.'

I couldn't move. I didn't want to leave Laura on the floor like that. 'I want to stay with her until someone comes. She's all alone.'

Phil stood and folded me into a deep hug, but I pulled away. 'The answer has to be here,' I told him. The Gallery seemed to be at the heart of it all. I stepped around Laura carefully. 'Can I have your flashlight for a second?'

Phil handed me his phone and I peered into the depleted central cabinet. 'Where would all these be taken?' From what I had overheard with Bella in the stateroom filled with antiques, the men were using housekeeping trolleys to move items around. It was clear that art and antiques were being hidden and transported inside ordinary-looking furniture. I reached over and fully opened the glass top of the shallow display cabinet. The cabinet was large and yet the display case was small. Could something be hidden under it?

'What are you doing?' said Phil.

'I'm not leaving until I find out what Laura was doing here. She was scared. Scared at the museum when talking to Chris Prince and scared this evening when talking to Mark Rushwell. What was she mixed up in?' I looked inside the top of the cabinet and ran my fingers around the edges. In four places down one long side there seemed to be cylinder shapes. I knew what these were: hidden hinges.

I took out the few remaining antiques scattered around it and began to heave.

'We don't have time for this.' Phil ran to the Gallery door and looked out, checking that we were not being observed.

The lid to the concealed compartment was heavier than I'd expected. 'Help me,' I called to Phil. 'This is concealing a storage space of some kind.'

Phil helped me lift it. The hinges were strong and, along with foldout metal arms, easily supported the weight of the top glass cabinet.

We both peered into the large space underneath the display level. 'Do you think something has been taken out?'

Phil took a couple of steps back. 'So *that* changes things.'

'How?' I asked as Phil crossed his arms, his reluctance obvious. I stepped towards him. 'I can't help if I don't know everything.'

'The Collector is famed for their nautical collection.' Phil indicated the contents of the room. 'But these are not million-dollar items, and therefore I doubt that dealing in these items is the way they make their money on the black market. It was why I wasn't focused on it until you and your aunt arrived.'

'Being a collector and being a dealer are two very different things,' I said, catching on. 'This sort of collection would've given him a certain reputation and credibility.'

'While also serving as a useful smoke screen. For that.' He pointed to the central cabinet. 'Hiding something that possibly was exceptionally valuable.'

'It's been moved already.' I looked inside the padded compartment. 'This is almost body- . . . or coffin-sized. And Laura knew about it, perhaps even helped with it, and . . .' Suddenly a small cartouche on one of the sides of the void caught my eye. I paused. In the top corner I saw a stamp bearing a serpent design – an Ouroboros. 'I saw Chris hand Sally a gold snake bracelet at the museum. Is this related?'

Phil stared at the symbol. 'I've no idea. Perhaps. There was a case last year when a Shakespearean First Folio was stolen in New York. A van seen leaving the scene was discovered, burned out, with an Ouroboros key chain a few feet away. I don't know the connection between that case and Chris Prince handing Sally a bracelet. There might not be one.'

'Arthur never believed in coincidences and nor do you.' I gave him a knowing look and he nodded.

'True.'

My eyes fixed on Laura again. 'What went wrong tonight for her to end up like this?' I shone the flashlight back on her, and the wedding ring glinted in the darkness. Laura's left palm was facing upwards, and I saw that there was something engraved there.

Phil, watching the door, said, 'In the world of The Collector, probably not much. He values wealth above people and the associates around him – his "board members" get rich from all the black-market trading he facilitates – for a cut of the proceeds. He arranges events like this cruise; probably has a network of mules to ferry items between buyer and seller. Maybe Laura was one of them. They're well paid, but they take all the risk while The Collector keeps his distance and the profits keep rolling in.'

'Laura was talking to Chris Prince. So are we to believe that Chris intends to be the new Collector?'

'There will be a meeting on Deck Eight tonight. Our only hope is if The Collector reveals himself as Arthur said he would. Everything that has happened in the past week seems to lead back to The Collector. And until we stop him, I don't believe this will be the last death we see.'

Before he could stop me, I pulled off Laura's ring. *A snake's head.* And then her crew lanyard. I stood and put the ring onto my finger – it fit perfectly – and the lanyard in my pocket.

I now have a way to get into the meeting.

'If there is to be a meeting on Deck Eight, then we need to get down there. Laura deserves justice . . . We can't let someone get away with doing this to her.'

Phil gave one quick nod and pulled out a key card and handed it to me. 'It's the card for a stateroom on Deck Eight – 822. You can't be seen walking up and down the corridors all evening. If there is to be some meeting on that level, you will see passengers flowing in one direction. Wait for me in the room.'

It was a room number close to the one Sky had told me, so I made a mental note to have a look around when I was there. I looked down at the key card in my hand. It was a good place to start, but there was no way I was going to sit around in some stateroom while a meeting with The Collector, a murderer and a lot of black-market traders might be taking place.

But Phil didn't need to know that. 'I'll see you there.'

Chapter Thirty-Eight

Deck Eight was quiet apart from the hull, creaking with the movement of the ship as it sailed towards our final destination.

This was the last opportunity to find out The Collector's true identity and catch Laura's murderer before the ship docked and everyone could walk away.

I stopped frequently to check I wasn't being followed, although I had no idea who I was looking for. When no one else was around, I pressed the key card onto the pad of room 822. Down the hall and across the corridor, exactly where I had seen it before, a different room service tray had been left outside a stateroom. This time there were two cloches over two plates and two wineglasses, and an empty bottle of Louis Latour Châteauneuf-du-Pape.

Someone has expensive taste!

It was the same room number that Sky had given me, but why?

As soon as I closed the stateroom door behind me, I pulled out my phone and called the shop again. I still had the niggling feeling something was wrong. And after seeing Laura's lifeless body, I was now even more worried about Sky.

No answer.

I called her phone.

No answer.

I pulled off my ridiculous veil and mask and let them fall to the floor. My thumb found Laura's ring on my wedding finger and traced across the engraved snake. Was there a connection to the bracelet I had seen Chris give Sally? Was Laura given the ring by Chris? If so, then perhaps she had dealings with him too.

The most reckless plan was now fully formed in my mind. I picked up the veil as someone knocked on the door.

'Open up,' Phil whispered.

I unlocked the door and he hurried in. 'I saw Bella dressed as Marie Antoinette as I was locking up the Gallery.'

He considered my dress. 'Are you still going through with this?'

'Pretending to be Laura is the only way in.' I held out my hand to show the ring.

Phil sighed. 'We have no idea that it wasn't you they were targeting.'

'I don't think it was. I think Laura was there to meet someone or retrieve something for tonight's meeting and the killer cornered her. If only that person knows she is dead . . .'

'And you go in there impersonating Laura, you'll be making yourself a target,' said Phil.

'It's the only way. Because they're not going to let *you* stride in there. I'll just go down and see if I can get in and take one of your listening devices with me so we can hear what's going on.' I pulled the veil back on. 'I'm not asking permission. Laura is dead and this all needs to stop.'

He stood in front of me, arms crossed.

'Do you make a habit of trapping women in rooms?' I raised my eyebrow at him, and he glared back at me. 'Should I start calling for help or shall we test out my self-defence training?'

'I don't make a habit of fighting unarmed women,' he said.

'Then I suppose you're going to have to move.'

There was a pause as Phil weighed his options, but before I could press my point we both heard a muttering of voices beyond the door.

'This is our only chance,' I whispered. It was now or never. 'I'll get in and out of there as quickly as possible.' I sidestepped around him as he pulled a small listening device from his pocket and placed it in my hand.

'Be quick or I won't hesitate to come after you.'

I patted his arm and tried to still my hammering chest. 'I'll be fine. I wonder how good my Australian accent is.'

He groaned and shook his head but didn't try and stop me again. 'If you're not back in twenty minutes . . .'

I didn't reply; instead I slipped out the door and fell into step behind nine or ten men and women, all in Halloween dress, headed down the corridor.

* * *

The passengers were filing through an open door at the end of the corridor. A man in a black suit was checking credentials. A woman showed him her phone and he stood aside for her and her companion to enter. A zombie held up a signet ring and was allowed in.

I tried to keep my distance, my head down, and held up my lanyard with the ring in full view.

My chest threatened to contract as my confidence faltered. *This isn't going to work!*

The bouncer looked at the lanyard, shaking his head. I waited to be sent away, or worse.

'You're late, Laura.'

'Yeah, I . . .'

'Get in there.'

I nodded in reply. *I'm in.*

The door was closed behind us. If I didn't come back, would Phil and Carole hunt for me?

This stateroom was huge – the largest I had ever been inside, more like a few suites joined together. I kept myself against the wall and moved along until I reached a console table that I could place the listening device underneath.

Around me sixty or so men and women in fancy dress and masks were standing in a semicircle. I rose on my tiptoes to see what they were all doing.

On a side table a large television screen had been set up. A display cabinet held some small antiquities. I moved closer and recognized some of them from Arthur's second journal and the Gallery.

It's a private auction!

An auctioneer walked through the passengers and stepped onto a podium, his back to the curtains covering the balcony doors. His costume reminded me of the Phantom of the Opera, with a long black cape and a white mask stopping at his nose. He clearly didn't want to be recognized, but there was something familiar about him. Before I could move closer to get a better view, I sensed eyes on me. I scanned the room. In the far right-hand corner was a tall, dark-haired woman dressed as Marie Antoinette, with a huge pink dress and half mask.

Bella.

To be honest, I would've been surprised if she wasn't there! She caught my eye and shook her head slowly – as if I was a naughty schoolgirl who had been caught smoking in the playground.

'Good evening, ladies and gentlemen. I'm reliably informed that this will be the last year of the antiques cruise, so we are going out with a bang!' I knew the confident voice of the man on the podium. It was Mark Rushwell. 'I'm sure we were all saddened to hear of our friend Arthur Crockleford's passing. He was a firm favourite within our community, and I know I'm stepping into giant shoes, but the show, as ever, must go on. This evening our theme is "nautical and the exotic" and we have the immense privilege of having some prized possessions from The Collector up for sale.'

Arthur had been the auctioneer on this cruise? Of course, it would have given him unfettered access and allowed him to gather information. Clever Arthur. You really did intend on taking them down, didn't you?

'And we will get to an unlisted last-minute item very soon. I promise you won't want to miss that! But first let's have lots one through thirty. All these larger items' – Mark motioned to the computer screen – 'are currently held in international vaults or private collections. They will be transported by specialist removers to your own strongroom or wherever else you desire. At additional cost, of course.

'First, the two items from The Collector's own collection – the watch and the painting. The funds from this sale will be used to secure their new ventures outside of the organization. I can confirm that the new successor will be appointed shortly and the board members will learn of the direction they're taking the company at lunch in Petra tomorrow.'

The crowd murmured with excitement.

As the double doors at one end of the room opened, I stood on my tiptoes to get a better look.

The bidding was fierce. The Patek Philippe Nautilus 5711/ 1A-018 Steel Blue 40mm 2023 fetched £2.1 million, and a Turner sketch for *The Fighting Temeraire* another £3.4 million.

'And this . . . is our last-minute addition, ladies and gentlemen. We didn't think this item would make it, but well . . . why don't you take a close look?'

Two men rolled in a stretcher. On it, a coffin-shaped item was covered in a velvet drape. I shivered as I recalled Laura's body on the Gallery floor. The men slid back the cloth. At the unearthly splendour of the sight before us, a collective gasp rose up.

I was looking at an Egyptian mummy in a modern Plexiglas coffin! If it was real, then it would be worth millions and millions . . .

'Last year we all read about the discovery of the mummified remains of a man named Hekashepes, who lived circa 2300 BC, in a limestone sarcophagus in a burial shaft in the ancient necropolis of Saqqara, near Cairo.' Mark's cloak swept outwards as he gestured towards the mummy. 'Ladies and gentlemen, what the press did not report was that a smaller but no less impressive tomb a little farther away was uncovered. I give you . . . the gold leaf-covered mummified remains of Hekashepes's son!'

The dull shimmer of the gold leaf, even after millennia, still caught the light.

The head had painted-on eyes and mouth and dark hair. The body had been wrapped in such a way that it looked lifelike even after all this time. Hekashepes and his son were clearly very wealthy men in their time. The Egyptians believed that gold was the colour of the gods. To wrap a body in such grandeur expressed the desire that the man acquire divine status in the afterlife.

I stared in astonishment at finding myself so close to a priceless antiquity like this. A human being, I corrected myself. He didn't belong in a black-market auction; he would have graced one of the finest Egyptian collections in the museum world. He belonged, at the very least, with his father.

I had hoped that the black-market trade in antiquities of this size and quality had stopped since the last time I was hunting in my twenties. But I also understood that some Egyptologists believed only 30 per cent of ancient Egypt had been officially discovered and therefore looting was still highly lucrative. I remembered an article I read that stated that when the Arab Spring protests of 2011 unseated president Hosni Mubarak from power after thirty years of dictatorial rule, the police state crumbled too. Hundreds of antiquities sites from the Pharaonic, Coptic and Islamic eras were left largely unguarded, and raiders swooped in to sell the antiquities on the black market. The treasures were passed to the black market through Egypt's international ports and porous borders.

Perhaps not much had changed.

I had started forward to take a closer look just as a strong grip closed on my wounded arm, yanking me back. A hand – no, a cloth – covered my nose and mouth. 'You shouldn't be here,' a voice hissed in my ear.

The cloth smelled sweet and made me dizzy.

I tried to fight. Those around me paid no attention, as if this were an entirely normal sight: a woman being seized against her will. My legs began to shake.

The world spun faster and faster until I didn't know where I was. There was no longer the murmur of voices from the secret auction. Had I left the suite? Two men were leading me away, supporting me by the arms.

'Where to?' said the man to my right.

'He wants to talk to her.'

The room spun as I closed my eyes.

Chapter Thirty-Nine

Carole

Carole watched the Halloween Ball extravaganza unfolding. She greatly approved of the nineties playlist, and the passengers drunk-dancing seemed to enjoy it too. She was in her element, and it was quite some time before she noticed that Freya hadn't come back.

Carole's anxiety began to mount when Freya didn't answer her text message.

Where is she? Is she with Phil?

She searched the ballroom a second time, but Freya wasn't there. Before panicking, she decided to order herself another vodka, lime and soda. If she hadn't seen Freya by midnight . . .

'There you are!' She turned back to see a familiar figure waving to her.

Carole bustled though the dancing passengers to meet Patricia, who was standing by the main door to the ballroom.

'We need to go. Freya's in trouble,' she said. 'She needs you.'

Carole's pulse raced and she scanned the room for Phil.

'Freya needs you right *now*.' Patricia took her arm.

'Is she all right?'

'We'll find out soon enough, but she's got herself into some difficulty.' Patricia patted her arm. 'No time to lose,' she said again.

It didn't occur to Carole until later to ask how Patricia knew Freya was in trouble, and by then it was far too late.

Chapter Forty

Bella

Bella knew enough traders in The Collector's world to get an invite to the auction. She was happily sipping her champagne, waiting for the fun to begin, when she saw Freya being drugged. It was deeply annoying. The only question was, did Freya's kidnappers know that she wasn't Laura?

Anger would have creased her forehead if it wasn't for her Botox. *I might have to help her and miss all the fun.* She scanned the room again, looking for Chris. She knew he'd boarded the ship after it docked in Egypt. Bella didn't want to leave the room until she got to see his world come crumbing down – but she also wouldn't stand for seeing a woman drugged.

There you are. I've got a surprise for you. No one ghosts me.

The magnetism that had first pulled them together was still as strong as ever, but Bella's sense of her own particular justice was stronger, just.

* * *

'What do you know about shipwreck ceramics?' Arthur was standing at a makeshift bar in a castle in the Scottish Highlands. It was Hogmanay.

'Happy New Year to you too.' Bella tipped her champagne flute towards him. 'And you know I'm more into rubies and sapphires.' She brought the glass to her lips and took a gulp, the bubbles tingling down her throat. She scanned the room for her overbearing boyfriend, Giles Metcalf.

'And diamonds?' Arthur's eyes twinkled and he motioned to her necklace.

'I saw a documentary about diamonds recently, about them all being man-made now and no one being able to tell the difference. Well, I still prefer old-mine ones.' Her fingers traced the necklace. 'I don't think they knew how to manufacture diamonds in Victorian times, did they?'

Arthur shrugged. 'I need to tell you about a museum on the Suffolk coast. I have a feeling you might enjoy a visit there.' It wasn't the first time the old man had brought up the topic of the remote Suffolk museum, but Bella had bigger things in mind.

She zoned out his ramblings and watched a tall, handsome man in his mid to late forties, heading straight for them. He had blue eyes over high cheekbones and close-cropped fair hair and wore expensive casual clothing like he had walked out of a Ralph Lauren perfume ad – he smelled like that too. As he approached, he reached out to shake Arthur's hand. The old man hesitated for a moment, she noticed, but shook the stranger's hand.

'I didn't know you'd be here,' Arthur said. 'What can I do for you, Chris?'

Chris leaned in close and whispered something. Arthur began shaking his head. 'Not now, dear sir, the timing isn't right. Why could you possibly need . . . ?'

Chris said something else, and Arthur's eyes widened.

'Interesting.' He turned his attention to Bella. 'Have you two met? Chris Prince, I'd like you to meet my . . . friend.'

'I'm Bella.' She gave her most dazzling smile.

'It's a pleasure.'

* * *

That man, who had become her lover after Giles's departure from the scene, was now on board the MVGoldstar and standing right in front of her. She had genuinely believed him dead until seeing him in the Egyptian museum. She had mourned his disappearance from her life, but now she knew he had chosen to leave her behind because he didn't like splitting the spoils. She clenched her fists in rage. She didn't like being played for a fool. Wouldn't tolerate it. Bella was on board to look for Chris's killer, only to have found out he was alive and well . . . so now she was going to take everything he had ever wanted away from him, just as he had done to her when he left.

Bitter realization pinched her frozen heart and she vowed to never let anyone get close again. But settling the score had to wait a few moments.

Bella followed the men taking Freya away. She took a second to watch over her shoulder as the black-market Egyptian relic reached the centre of the room and was wheeled in a circle so that potential buyers could get a good look. She knew now that the mummy's arrival on the scene meant a new candidate for the position of Collector was pitching their hat into the ring. There had been rumours for years that The Collector was stepping aside, and then Bella overheard Chris talking on the phone a few weeks before he left. He was livid when he learned that one of the contenders for the new Collector was bringing an 'impressive piece' to the auction. Chris was not to be outdone. Hence his renewed hunt for the vase.

In the Egyptian museum, Chris had told her that someone tried to kill him in the Lowestoft Museum and that he was being 'outmanoeuvred', whatever that meant. He wasn't giving up a chance to be the new Collector without a fight.

But Bella knew a few of Chris's secrets and who to tell them to. She sent a text to Phil with what was happening to Freya, in the hope that he would deal with it and she wouldn't have to do any more.

'I'll be back,' she said to the guard at the door.

'Once out there's no coming in again,' he replied, and checked out the spy hole before opening the door.

'Are you serious? Why?' *I'm going to kill Freya myself for this.* The man shrugged. 'Rules.'

Once in the corridor, Bella saw Freya being steered into a stateroom down the corridor from the auction, where they had seen the antiques stored.

Her phone pinged and she saw a message from Phil: *I'm in room 822.* Bella reluctantly messaged back – she didn't like being on good terms with the FBI. *I'll meet you there.*

She'd known he would come running. What she hadn't expected to see was Carole hurrying around the corner with Patricia by her side.

God, those women can't keep out of anything!

They were moving at such a pace Bella didn't have time to intercept Carole, who was being guided into the same state-room Freya had just entered. Dread prickled Bella's skin – she knew all too well how these things played out. Get one prisoner to control the other. It's what she would've done.

264

She knew most of the rooms along this deck. Passing herself off as a crew member whenever she needed to come and go had been child's play for her. Bella only knocked once, very lightly, when Phil opened the door to his stateroom on the opposite side of the corridor.

'Where is she?' he asked in a low voice.

Bella pointed, keeping her own voice as quiet as possible. 'She's five doors down from here. I've just seen Carole being led down the corridor to join her. By Patricia. They're in deep now.'

Phil nodded. No matter how uncomfortable working with an FBI agent might be, Bella mirrored him. The night had taken a very dark turn, and they needed to work together if they were to come up with a plan to save Freya and Carole.

Chapter Forty-One

Freya

Had I passed out? I wasn't sure, but my head was pounding behind my eyes and my tongue stuck to my teeth like I'd been on an all-night bender. My bleary eyes tried to take in my surroundings – I was sitting in an armchair very like the one in my stateroom. I lifted my hand to rub my eyes, but my wrists and ankles were tied.

I heard a mumble of voices and focused on two men, dressed in identical black suits, standing next to the door talking in hushed tones.

'Hello?' I coughed. Whatever was on the cloth they'd put over my mouth had ravaged my throat.

The tall man closest to me ignored the interruption.

'What do you want?' My voice had turned deep and husky like Carole's.

'You know how this goes.' He rolled his eyes at his accomplice.

But I really didn't.

'Don't bother calling for help.' He nodded towards the corridor. 'The passengers out there know to mind their own business.'

They were as relaxed as anyone on holiday, and as they

leaned back against the stateroom walls my heart hammered in my ears. I closed my eyes to quiet my stomach and decided to save my strength and study the room – find an escape route. The silver gaffer tape binding my ankles and wrists was so tight it would need to be cut . . . or maybe my teeth would do.

When the tall one's phone rang and he walked into the bathroom to answer it, I bent down to try and rip at the binding with my teeth.

'What are you doing?' murmured the shorter one. 'It's not like you're getting out of this.'

'My . . . nose itches.' To make it look realistic, I tried to rub a finger over my nose, but I poked myself in the eye instead – *smooth* – it stung, then blurred, and tears streamed down my face. And I couldn't wipe them away.

'He's on his way,' said the tall one, smirking. 'This one might not even need torturing. She's a liability to herself.'

The shorter one shook his head in disbelief. 'You can make sure she doesn't try and do herself any more harm. I'll wait outside.'

I pulled at my restraints. I tried to look annoyed at being the butt of their jokes but was inwardly pleased. People don't expect a clueless woman to be able to fight for her freedom.

Slouching back as far as I could, I rested my head on the back of the chair. I needed to focus. But as soon as I took in a deep breath, nausea crept up my throat.

From the other side of the door, I could hear Carole's voice. 'Where is she? I must talk to the doctor at once.' The words were a knife twisting inside me.

'Carole?' I shouted. This was the last thing I'd wanted to happen – my aunt coming to find me and stepping into danger.

The stateroom door opened, and Carole hurried in dressed in her long black fishtail-skirted Morticia outfit. The dress had been spattered with fake blood down one side.

Carole stilled when she saw me.

'What's going on here?' Her voice was low and full of anger. She tried to run to me, but one of the men grabbed her arm and held her.

Patricia Henderson entered with them. She tutted and took her reading glasses from on top of her grey head. I thought for a second she was there to help, but she was scanning the room coldly. 'Where's Tony?'

'Patricia? Why are you here?' I asked her. The memory of her helping me up when I had fallen over outside the restaurant and her kind eyes then were a stark contrast to her steely tone now.

Patricia focused her eyes on mine. 'I'm . . .' She paused as if getting her story straight. 'Are you really so uninformed? Did Arthur tell you so little? He was running auctions for us, and dealing in the black market. We therefore assumed you would introduce yourself when you showed up. But you didn't. You didn't follow any protocol at all, and that confused everyone. My husband, who was actually quite a softy at heart, God rest his soul, would have thrown you overboard straightaway. But we wanted to see what you did. There are rumours that Arthur kept journals, so . . . time was needed.'

'Your husband was The Collector?' I asked, trying to put it all together.

Patricia smiled. 'My husband was very well liked in the antique trade, and he had a great eye for collecting things. We were such a good team. But the job in the oil company was demanding so, in the end, I ran the antiques business. I met lots of very interesting people on the international art and antiques scene. They showed me a whole new way of trading.'

I tried to keep the surprise out of my voice. 'An illegal way . . . on the black market . . .'

Patricia is The Collector?

'You're a smart woman. I do like strong, intelligent women. Good for you. My husband and I made a great team, and boy did we have some fun.' She placed her glasses on the tip of her nose, looked down at me and hummed, as if that were an answer. 'Now, you don't look well. What happened to your eye?'

Another man entered the room. He looked familiar and I struggled to remember where I'd seen him before. He was tall with olive skin and dark brown eyes, and he wore a black suit and tie . . . not a costume. He checked his watch, an expensive Patek Philippe. Within a second it fit into place. He was the maître d' at the Seafood and Steak restaurant, but that's not the only place I had seen him. I had spotted him early one morning waiting tables in the cafe, and then again, dressed as a tourist, talking to Mark as they boarded the coach to the Egyptian museum.

'Tony, I'm so glad you're here.' Patricia reached out and patted his arm.

Tony pointed to my eye.

'Not my work!' said the short one. 'She did that to herself, sneezing.'

'Come here,' Tony barked and motioned to Carole. When she didn't move, he reached out and grabbed her arm.

'Will you get off me, you brute!' Carole struggled under his grip.

'Tony, dear, this lady is my friend. Carole, this is my nephew.

I'm so glad I could introduce you – perhaps the circumstances could have been better, but it is what it is.' She tapped Tony's arm. 'I would appreciate it if we could be well-mannered while still getting the information that we need.' She smiled sweetly. Tony met her eye, gritted his teeth and nodded.

It was clear who was in charge.

'*Friend!*' Carole's eyes widened. 'This isn't how you treat friends, darling!'

'If you would sit?' Tony's tone was cold and measured. Carole reluctantly sat down on the bed.

'Right to business, as this is not the best timing.' He checked his watch again and then, in one smooth motion, slipped off his jacket and hung it on the back of the dressing-table chair.

'Let's get to the point. You worked with Arthur Crockleford,' he said to me. 'With your aunt Carole, you inherited his shop. Now tell me about the journals.'

Phil's warning came rushing back to me: 'If *he's* here and he knows you and Arthur worked together . . .' Except now I knew The Collector was actually a little old lady with a lot of employees, including this scary one standing before me.

When I didn't answer, Tony said, 'We want Arthur's journals. They tell the location of a grey vase my aunt is keen to recover. What would it take to convince you to tell us where it is? Carole told Aunt Patricia that you know everything Arthur did and more.' He reached my aunt in a couple of strides and pulled her to her feet.

'I did not!' But the flush in her cheeks told me she might have. She looked at her false friend with despair. 'Patricia, please. This isn't necessary. I thought we were . . .' She couldn't say the word 'friend' again. The pain of betrayal filled her eyes with tears.

Fury blazed inside me and I surged forward, forgetting that my hands and feet were bound. 'Get off her,' I shouted. I went crashing face-first to the floor. Carole shrieked as I hit the carpet. All the air left my lungs.

I couldn't breathe.

I couldn't . . . breathe . . .

Pain shot through my arm and the wound reopened, sending droplets of blood to the carpet.

Carole's beaded fishtail skirt came swishing into my sight line and she sank down at my side, lifting my head into her lap. 'Help her,' she pleaded with Tony. 'She's bleeding.'

Tony had grabbed my aunt's arm and was yanking her back. 'Sit down,' he ordered. I was left struggling on the floor.

Patricia bent down, her face close enough to mine for her perfume to make my head swim. 'That was a silly move, wasn't it? Even very small amounts of chloroform can have an effect. Headaches and nausea. Arthur would've talked his way out of this by now.' She tsked and pointed to Carole. 'And she never came to any harm when he was around.' Patricia lifted her gaze. 'Better get her upright, Tony, then you can begin.'

When I was upright, my eyes met Carole's and I cleared my head of all the other ideas running through it. Like how to get proof that Patricia's late husband – and then Patricia herself – was The Collector, and who she was about to hand over the role to. Was Tony to be the next Collector? It would be keeping it in the family, wouldn't it? But now my chief mission was to get Carole out of there safely.

'Last year, I started to hear whispers that Arthur Crockleford had saved the vase and had hidden it. But it wasn't his to hide!' Patricia's fists clenched and her knuckles whitened. 'That vase was to be an anniversary gift from me to my husband, and Arthur kept it from me.'

'Why that particular vase?' My voice was small and gravelly, but she heard it.

'My husband grew up in Athens. He used to go to the museum and stare at it. It was one of the pieces that got him interested in antiques. He loved it and I wanted him to be able to have it. To look at it as a symbol of how far we had come and what we had achieved. I thought that it was lost at the bottom of the sea, until we started hearing those rumours about Arthur. We knew you were estranged from him. We'd never seen you at any of the meetings or events. And then you turned up here.'

Tony said, 'My aunt believed that you were here to fill Arthur's spot as an expert, to give a few talks, so we left you alone. But then you went to the museum to meet with Chris Prince. That changed everything.'

'But I didn't . . .' Tony raised a hand to silence my protest. He had no intention of hearing me out.

'And tonight you ended up in the auction. Now it's clear you know far, far too much.'

I shook my head and my eyes locked with Carole's. 'But we don't . . .'

Tony leaned into my ear and whispered. 'You see, I believe if Arthur knew where the vase is, then you do too. It wasn't hard to get all the information we needed on you and the shop. You like Sky, don't you – you're so very trusting.' He tutted. 'And now Aaron will . . . Well, Aaron will be Aaron if we don't get what we want.'

I glared at him and pulled at my binding no matter how much my arm screamed in pain. 'You leave Sky alone. She doesn't know anything.'

He straightened. 'She'll talk.'

Patricia leaned in close again. 'Tony tells me that Sky went to a most interesting place – an art gallery in Burnham Market – and started asking the artist who owns it about a commission Arthur had given her. Of course, after some . . . persuasion, we got the same information as Sky did – the painting in the Gallery and the photograph of a trunk. What is so special about the trunk?'

Arthur hid something inside it.

'We have no idea why Sky was in Norfolk,' my aunt lied, her lips pursed and her brow furrowed. She was furious.

'If we tell you what we know, then you need to let us go?' I asked.

Patricia gave a short nod. 'Let's hear it first.'

Carole met my eye, and I knew we were in for one of her very long stories. She rambled on about Betty in the museum in Lowestoft, where the painting was stolen from. That it was just Arthur's joke. That we really just wanted a holiday and to see the museum. We never went to meet some man. Carole was a great actress, but I wasn't sure they believed her.

'I suppose we really don't know anything,' I added.

Patricia stood very still, studying me.

I shook my head. 'My aunt doesn't need to be here. Arthur always kept her out of his business, and I insist you keep her out of it now.' I tilted my chin defiantly.

Is that enough to get her out of here?

Patricia shrugged. 'Let me be clear on what I want and what

will keep you both alive. I want Arthur's journals showing where the vase is. I want the Ming Dynasty grey vase itself or direct information of its location.'

'I don't know—'

Tony grabbed Carole's arm. 'If I keep twisting, it might break or pop out of its socket.'

Tears sprang up in Carole's eyes.

'No!' I shouted, rage pumping through me and my heart threatening to crash out of my chest.

'Or we flip the situation.' Tony pulled out a knife and headed in my direction. 'I'm sure your aunt knows far more than she lets on.' He smiled at Carole. 'Your niece is stubborn. You wouldn't want to see how much pain she can endure, would you?'

I needed some time to work out what to do. 'I think the painting stolen from the Lowestoft Museum and now in the Gallery is a clue to where Arthur hid the vase, but I've never been able to get close enough to study it. He didn't *write* anything down. He had it painted.'

Patricia looked at me with interest. She motioned for me to continue.

'We can go to the Gallery, and I'll show you what I mean. But only if you leave my aunt out of it.'

I prayed that Bella or Phil was somewhere nearby.

'You're playing a dangerous game, my dear,' said Patricia.

'Tony, take Freya on this goose chase and bring that painting back here. I'll wait with Carole. We won't have any problems, will we, Carole?'

'I wouldn't dream of it,' she replied as her shoulders relaxed a little bit. Our eyes locked and a silent message passed between us. *Go, I'll deal with her.*

Chapter Forty-Two

Tony grabbed my arm as we stepped out into the narrow corridor. 'Move.'

I took the opportunity to look feeble and stumbled forward. Tony caught me before I fell to the ground. 'How did Arthur let you anywhere near priceless antiques, when you're so accident prone?' His steely grip dug into me near the wound and I winced.

The corridor was quiet and made me think that the auction had finished as we passed the door where it had been held. While trying to walk as slowly as I could, a few doors down I saw something move behind the spy hole in the door to my right . . . Phil's stateroom. It was all I could do to not scream, but I bit my lip and said loudly, 'You can't just leave my aunt in that room with that old crazy woman!' I prayed Phil had heard me and trusted that meant he'd rescue Carole from Patricia's clutches.

Tony's eyes narrowed. 'Talk again and the knife I'm carrying will come out.'

Next, I noticed a pink hairband that had been flung over the room service tray outside a stateroom just before we turned to the lift.

By the time we had reached the shopping parade, there were

very few passengers around, but as we approached the Gallery, I saw someone I knew. Mark's tall, bulky frame was now out of costume and dressed in black T-shirt and trousers. Picking up my step, I tried to catch his eye. But when he saw Tony, he adjusted the large portfolio he was carrying on his shoulder and picked up his pace.

When we arrived at the Gallery, I knew something was wrong. The shutters were up and the lights were on, but the Gallery was deserted.

Where's Laura's body? I hurried over to where she had been, expecting to see some evidence of her murder, but there was nothing but a freshly mopped floor and a gap on the wall.

Panic flooded me, but I forced myself to keep Tony distracted. I didn't want him to see that the painting of the burning ship wasn't on the wall anymore, and I needed to give Phil as much time as possible to get Carole out of that room. 'This void under the cabinet here. Was that where you stored things that were going to be in the auction?'

Tony laughed. 'This isn't question time.' His eyes scanned the room and came to rest on the empty space on the wall. 'What's—'

I stepped closer, interrupting him. 'How did Laura get involved in all this?'

His brow creased, but I couldn't be sure if it was guilt or sorrow. 'Laura was all right, but she shouldn't have tried to get into stuff she knew to keep her nose out of.'

'You didn't kill her?'

'No, I didn't.' He walked towards the gap in the wall. 'The painting was here.'

'I'm not sure . . .' My eyes betrayed me and flickered to the empty space where the painting once hung.

'It's not here.' Tony's voice was dead calm.

I remembered that Mark had been here moments before carrying a case large enough to hold the painting. But why did he want it? Was he trying to find the vase too?

'It's been stolen.' *Tony didn't see what Mark was carrying?*

Phil rushed into the Gallery.

Our eyes met and relief rushed through me. 'Is Carole . . . ?'

'Bella is on it. I followed you.'

'The FBI has no power here.' Tony pulled out his knife and his phone.

They knew who Phil was all along.

Phil put his hands up to calm the situation and adrenalin turned my stomach. 'No one said anything about the FBI,' he said, stepping towards Tony. 'How about you put the phone down? We need to talk.' He took another step.

'Who are you calling?' I panicked.

'Who I was told to call.'

I stepped towards Phil out of pure instinct and our eyes met for a brief second. Phil read the panic on my face.

'Go.' He hurtled forward and swept his leg behind Tony's knees. They went crashing down together.

Phil's voice cracked with pain. 'Go!' He blocked Tony's knife with his arm, and the knife went skittering away. Phil grabbed for the phone.

Tony hammered his fist towards Phil's head, but he ducked out of the way and rolled sideways.

I hesitated, not knowing if I could leave Phil in this mess. But he saw me. 'Go. Now.'

Desperately hoping that he would be all right, I ran as fast as I could back to Deck Eight. The door to our former prison had been kept from closing by a discarded towel wedged between the door and the frame. I quickly looked around the room and found Carole's phone on the floor by the bed but nothing else. Driven by blind panic, I ran down the flight of stairs and hurtled into my stateroom, which had a connecting door to Carole's room.

There was no sign of her.

Chapter Forty-Three

I stood in the middle of my room. My eyes stung and I scrubbed at the corner of one – but my emotions had to be kept under strict control. The only hunt that mattered now was for Carole.

I considered alerting the ship's crew or trying to find the captain, but Patricia and Tony's status on board was clear. To get all those antiques on the ship, they had to have Head Office in their pocket. And they had to have a lot of money or power to get everyone to turn a blind eye to a live black-market auction.

Who was I kidding? Why did I ever think that I could do this? The Collector – Patricia and her husband, and now Tony and all the people they worked with – were far too powerful for one person to take down. They were too powerful for all the international agencies together. It was why they had never been touched before. Their tentacles reached everywhere.

I rubbed my hands over my face and hardened my resolve. *Find Carole*, I told myself over and over. *Don't stop until you find Carole.*

I changed out of my costume and into the crew polo shirt Bella had given me, and I went out again in search of Carole.

By 2 a.m., deep dark images had taken over my senses and I had searched every place I could think of.

When my phone died, I was forced back to my room to charge it. I had just pulled back the curtains to Carole's balcony – in the vain hope she might be out there – when I heard my door open and close.

My impulse to run and see if it was Carole was frozen by the rumbling of male voices.

'She's not here,' one man said.

'Let's wake one of the officers to track her key card. It will be easier than all this running around.' It was Tony's voice.

'Do it. I'll just check in there before we go.'

There was nowhere to hide in a stateroom, where everything was bolted to the floor. In a moment of panic, I swept behind the curtain, which covered the length of the balcony, to get as far away as possible from the connecting door Tony's friend was about to walk through. I crept along between the curtain and the window until I got to the very far corner.

The lights were switched on and I flattened myself against the balcony window. A phone buzzed.

Was that my phone?

'Shit! My aunt's messaging me. I gotta go. She hasn't seen you, has she?' asked Tony. 'This message sounds like she knows something.'

A pause. 'No sign of those Lockwood women. I'll call Aaron again and use their assistant to get them to play ball.'

'That didn't answer my question, Chris. Tell me she hasn't seen you on this ship!' The panic in Tony's voice caught in his throat.

'Calm down. I only took a quick look around the auction when she wasn't there. I'm pissed that mummy was sold.'

'If I hadn't spotted that woman pretending to be Laura and told my aunt, you would've been seen – and it's bloody rash, even for you,' hissed Tony. 'And if you'd gotten the vase like we planned, it might have softened the blow of our new arrangement.'

'It wasn't rash. I thought I'd left enough clues on Ben's body for Bella to think I was dead, but now she's here.' The wardrobe doors snapped shut. 'Room's clear. They wouldn't be stupid enough to come back here.'

I was! I gripped the curtain and tried not to breathe.

'Bella's deadly as a black widow when she's mad. And she's mad as hell at me. Oh yeah, go ahead and laugh about it. I dare you!'

'That's on you. You should never have let it get that far with her.' There was a scuffle. 'Get. Your. Hands. Off. Me. You won't get anywhere without . . .'

Choking gasps filled the room. Horror at what I was hearing made my fists clench, ready to – I didn't even know what. Suddenly, the sounds of violence stopped.

'OK. OK,' Tony rasped. 'I'll find the Lockwood women and your ex. They'll all be dealt with.'

Chris huffed. 'We could take out the board of directors too . . .'

'No. My aunt's powerful – far more than you give her credit for. And she has a lot of influence. They *all* have connections that would be helpful.'

'She shouldn't have sent Ben after me.'

Tony tsked. 'Nope. She just always overestimated Ben's

abilities. We need her to be there to make the announcement and give them all a chance to decide . . . If it doesn't go our way, then we'll do what we've been planning since school. Right?'

Chris sighed. 'Perhaps we should just do that anyway.'

They walked away, still talking, then the light was switched off and the stateroom door slammed shut. I stayed where I was a few moments longer.

It sounded like Chris and Tony were working together without Patricia's knowledge. And that Ben Wells, the missing expert, was the dead man behind the Lowestoft Museum.

Once I had hauled the curtains aside and tentatively checked both rooms, I slumped down on Carole's bed. I had never felt so alone in my life, and hope was beginning to leave me. I impatiently watched the phone light up with charge and knew I had to give it a few minutes before I could go out again. The throbbing of my arm was blurring my vision, and I staggered to the bathroom to take more painkillers.

I should never have left Carole.

From what I had just overheard, The Collector's/Patricia's dealings were structured like a company – with a board of directors. Who would they be? And what was going to happen in Petra?

Bella said Chris was at the museum to 'bribe' people. Sally Bright, Mark Rushwell, Archie and Jenny had been at the museum with him. Were they on the board and being bribed to accept or vote for a new Collector? The more I looked at the bigger picture, the more it reminded me of the small snuff bottle in the antiques shop back in Suffolk. The one that I had to polish to see the picture behind the dust . . . the one with the small chip. I needed to look for the small chip in The

Collector's operation, the place where somebody had made a mistake or shown their hand.

At least now I had a focus . . . a direction. I let my mind sift through all I had learned so far and hoped my latent brain would come up with something.

We must have sailed closer to shore as the signal on my phone came back on. I dialled Crockleford Antiques in the faint hope that Sky would be awake so that I could warn her about what I had just overheard.

'Freya?' Sky's voice was low and urgent.

'Are you OK?'

'Sky isn't available,' a male voice answered, one I didn't know. 'This is Aaron, her business associate.'

But I knew better than that.

'You're a nasty piece of work, that's what you are. Put Sky back on the line. She doesn't work for you, she's *our* shop assistant.'

There was a rumble of laughter. 'No. She's not. She's a hacker sent to spy on you. Not very good at it though. And she tried to get out of it because she *liked* you.'

A hacker and a spy?

I buried the questions and focused on a solution. Because whoever she really was didn't matter right now. I needed to keep her safe. 'I'll call the police.'

'No police – all you need to do is tell me where Arthur's journals and the vase are hidden.'

'Please, Freya, no police!' called Sky.

Think!

'I'm on a cruise ship! You need to give me time. It's the middle of the night and nothing is kept in the shop.' *Think!*

'The shop will need to open as normal or . . . the village will worry about Sky. You might not want the police there, but you certainly don't want the village at the door,' I said, hoping that I sounded self-assured and in control even as the phone shook in my hand.

Aaron scoffed. 'What are a lot of old people going to do?'

There was a pause. I honestly had no idea. 'I need time,' I said again.

There was a distant muttering and then Aaron was back on the phone with me. 'I'm told you and your aunt have until six a.m. Jordanian time, so that's four a.m. in the UK, to report to the ship's Library with the location of the journals and the vase. Or you won't see Sky again.'

This had to be a trap set by Chris and Tony, but what else could I say?

'Fine, we'll be there.' But first I had to find a way to keep Sky safe and track down Carole.

Chapter Forty-Four

I watched my phone slowly charge and placed the heels of my palms over my eyes.

Think!

How could I help Sky when I was so far away? And if she really was a hacker, then it was clear why she didn't want the police involved. There had to be another way.

The Library meeting was in four hours' time. Precisely the time passengers had been told to depart for the tour of Petra. Was the timing deliberate to keep us away from the Petra meeting?

And what had Aaron said about the villagers? He clearly hadn't met anyone in Little Meddington – and at that very moment I knew exactly what I had to do. I reached for my phone.

'Agatha?' There was a rustling of covers.

'Freya, is that you? It's midnight here, you know?'

'I have an emergency. And someone might need to get into the shop – do you have the keys for the back door?'

'Of course I do!'

'Great, and I need you to activate the Little Meddington Call Tree.'

'What?' I knew Agatha had sat straight up in bed without having to see it. Activating the Call Tree – which started with the Parish Council – was only done in a large-scale emergency. 'Why? What's going on?'

'Sky's life depends on everyone following my instructions to the letter.'

'I'll get a pen and paper. We won't let you or Sky down. No one messes with our villagers.'

My pulse skipped. 'Agatha, we need to keep this within the village boundary until I can get back there. Do I have your word?'

'You do.' I could hear the excitement in her voice. 'Is this to do with all the Indiana Jones adventures you and Arthur used to get up to? You're getting up to it again?'

I tried to keep the laughter from my voice as I replied, 'It's top secret, Agatha, so can I trust you'll keep quiet?'

'Absolutely. My pen is at the ready.'

* * *

I was starting to put together Sky's mention of stateroom 825 and what Tony had said about tracking a key card. If Sky was really a hacker, then she could have broken into the ship's system and found a way to track key cards as well. But the question remained – what did she believe I needed to see in 825? I hid my key card in a plant pot near the lift on our deck and used the adrenalin pumping through me to pick up my pace. It was the only thing keeping exhaustion at bay.

Deck Eight was empty now the auction and the Halloween Ball were over. Most of the passengers would have headed back to their staterooms.

I stood outside room 825 and looked down at the room service tray. The one with the pink headband on it.

Someone's been living out of their room.

I recognized the pink headband. Bella had been wearing one.

I pressed the doorbell and placed my foot by the door, ready to barge my way in if necessary. 'Room service,' I called lightly.

There was no answer.

I pressed the buzzer three times.

The corridor was quiet, but there was no comfort in it. I rubbed my sweaty palms down my jeans.

Please open. I pressed the buzzer again, letting my finger linger on the button. 'Bella?' I whispered.

I stepped back from the door.

Why did Sky send me here?

My heart dropped to my stomach, and I'd turned to leave when the door swung open and a hand grabbed me, pulling me into the dim stateroom. A desk light was switched on and I relaxed when I saw who had seized me.

'Now you!' Luke said, with a curl of his lip. 'I've had enough of this. It's not Piccadilly Circus. It's the middle of the night and we're trying to sleep.' He flung his hand around the room.

Luke wasn't who I'd expected to be standing before me. 'You? You were taken away to hospital.' Suddenly I remembered Sky's half-written email about Luke. She had sent me here to find *him*.

Luke pointed at the sofa. 'I suppose you're here for those two?'

I turned. 'Carole and Bella?' The wave of relief was so strong that it brought tears to my eyes.

Carole sprang towards me and pulled me into a bear hug. 'I've been so worried, but Bella wouldn't hear of me leaving. Said that if you had half the intelligence she does, you would work out where we were. I tried to be mad at her, darling, but she did stage a *marvellous* rescue attempt.'

Bella pulled herself up to a seated position on the sofa bed, her hand gripping her ribs.

'Are you hurt?' I asked.

'I'm fine.' She winced as she lowered herself down.

Even though Bella wasn't the hugging type, I wanted to grab her and try to tell her how grateful I was. 'Thank you for saving my aunt. Where did Patricia go?'

'Scurried away pretty quickly, but you shouldn't make the mistake of thinking that she isn't a formidable enemy. She's as ruthless as they come. Arthur was always on guard around her and the others. Anyway, I sent Phil after you. Thought I'd make him into your knight in shining armour. You old people like that shit.'

I felt my cheeks grow hot. 'He's not . . .'

She flicked her hand, dismissing any more talk of Phil. 'I need to sleep. Tomorrow I'm going to kill my ex.'

I opened my mouth to protest, but Carole linked her arm through mine. 'I've tried to convince her not to, but we need to give her a reason. She's mighty mad at being dumped and cut out of whatever money he promised her.'

Bella opened her eyes. 'Ghosted – it's far worse than dumped – and betrayed.' And then closed her eyes.

'You're all right!' Carole's voice cracked with gratitude.

I interrupted. 'Before you tell me what happened, I need you to give me the key card for your room.'

'Why?'

'No time to explain, but I have to get rid of it.' She handed it over, and I pulled open the balcony doors to the sea salt-laced darkness. I flung the key card under the gap in the balcony partition so that it ended up a few staterooms down. That ensured that if Tony tracked Carole's card it would lead him to the wrong stateroom.

I retreated inside.

Carole had settled on the sofa bed and I took a seat next to her. 'Tell me everything.'

Carole took a deep breath. 'After Tony dragged you out of there, Bella knocked on the door and Patricia just let her in.' She lowered her voice. 'I have a feeling that Bella and Patricia have had some dealings in the past. But Bella was so calm and confident . . . gave her a telling off about holding Arthur's friend hostage! She said Patricia should've retired years ago instead of letting Tony get his feet under the table. But when Bella told her about Chris being on board, Patricia turned white, and actually shook with rage. She's not a fan of Chris Prince. When Bella promised to kill him, Patricia let her take me with her. Darling, it was very dramatic.'

'And why are you both in *Luke's* room?'

I had almost forgotten that Luke was still standing watching us by the door. 'Because Bella has dirt on everyone and likes a bit of blackmail in return for a sofa bed.'

What dirt did Bella have on Luke? The fact that he wasn't in a hospital in Cairo? Bella looked like she was sleeping, but I was quite sure she was listening to every word.

In the far corner of the room, I noticed the portfolio case that Mark had carried earlier. The only way Mark could have entered the Gallery was with help. Luke always looked very interested in the painting. He must have given Mark the alarm codes.

I looked closer at Luke. 'I didn't take you for an art thief.'

Luke had large dark bags under his eyes and his shoulders slumped. 'You have no idea.' He turned on his heel and went back to his bed on the other side of the suite. 'I want everyone out of here at first light.' His bed was rumpled, almost as if someone was already in it with the covers pulled over their head. Who was it?

'Like I said, we're not going anywhere,' said Bella, her eyes still closed. 'Safest place to hide is right in the middle of the fox's den – Luke has been working with Patricia for years. She won't look here.'

So, Luke was The Collector's onboard curator. I sat next to Carole on the edge of the sofa bed, our fingers entwined, trying to make sense of the alliances. I had considered at one point, as had Phil, that Luke could be The Collector, but that assumption was proving false.

'What happened in the theatre?' I asked him.

'Laura happened. Handed me some water and . . . well, you were there for the rest.'

'Why?'

'Laura worked for Chris Prince, helping traffic black-market antiquities. I think that she also had some side hustle; she really wanted me out of the way. She wanted to get something from the Gallery, but whatever it was, someone got to her first.'

'Do you know that Tony and Chris are working together?' I asked.

Luke's brow furrowed. 'I didn't. But it means we're right to get out of it all.' His gaze swept down to the large person curled up in his bed.

Who's that?

292

'And now they think I'm off the ship and too ill for them to worry about – Laura did me a good turn with that doping stunt of hers. It was easy to ham it up after she spiked me, get off the ship for a little bit to make some arrangements for my retirement and then slip back on when everyone was enjoying the museum excursion.'

A deep voice came from Luke's bed. Instantly recognizable as Mark Rushwell's. 'Chris Prince slipped back on board in Cairo too. And he's all set to take control. The mummy sold for a huge sum, financing his reign. And since Tony already has most of the board on-side, who is going to oppose them? God only knows the havoc those two will cause together.'

Luke caught me staring at Mark Rushwell's form and glared at me. 'Why are you really here?'

I didn't answer him. I didn't know what to say. My head was racing with thoughts. We needed to catch Chris and Tony before they took over the position as Collector, and I still needed proof of wrongdoing. I whispered to Bella next to me on the sofa bed, 'What's the plan? We only have tomorrow. Do you know where to find Phil?'

She chuckled. 'I'll message lover boy for you, but get some sleep before we dock. Tomorrow is going to be interesting.'

I snuggled into Aunt Carole on my other side, and she snuggled me right back.

* * *

It was 5.15 a.m. and I had just checked in with Agatha to make sure everything was in place. There was a soft tap on the door and I checked the spy hole.

Phil stood on the other side, eyes heavy with sleep, fixed on the door as if he could see me standing there. I pulled it open and stepped back.

'Is everyone all right?' he murmured, closing the door quietly behind himself and striding into the room. 'I looked for you but . . .' Our eyes met.

'We're fine.'

He was dressed in a baseball cap and an old T-shirt, both from some American university, and grey tracksuit bottoms, like he had just been pulled from bed. There was a gash above his eyebrow and his cheek looked swollen.

'Are you hurt?' I reached out to touch his face, then stopped.

'It's nothing.' He traced his fingertips over the broken skin, checking that the bleeding had stopped. 'Why did I get a message from Bella saying to meet my lover in Luke's room at five a.m.?'

I swept around to glare at Bella, but her head was under a blanket.

'Quiet. Some of us want to sleep,' groaned Luke from the bed. 'This isn't a brothel, for God's sake. You all owe me for this.'

'Luke is back on the ship?'

'And fine, it seems.'

Phil hummed and his brow creased. 'Do you want to tell me what everyone is doing here?' His eyes shone as they caught the soft light of dawn seeping through a crack in the curtains.

'We can't talk here.' I opened the door of the bathroom and realized that it was too small in there for both of us. Phil was as impressive in height as he was in breadth and would take up all the space. Instead, I motioned towards the balcony, hoping the sea air would cool the growing warmth in my body.

I yanked at the handle of the balcony door and the freezing night air swept in. Bella moaned and pulled the blanket tighter over her head. I stepped outside. 'We need to talk through some new developments and what we should do about them.'

Phil listened while I told him all I had learned about Tony and Chris, that I believed Patricia's husband was The Collector and that she'd been in charge since his death. Then I told him about the trouble Sky was in.

Once I finished, I shivered with exhaustion and uncertainty.

'You're freezing,' Phil whispered.

'I'm fine.'

But he had already slipped back inside, returning a few seconds later with one of the unused dressing gowns from the back of the bathroom door. He placed it over my shoulders, his hands resting there for a second too long. 'Thanks.' I pulled my arms through the sleeves and tightened the cord around the dressing gown as tight as it would go.

I gripped the ice-cold railing and focused on the lapping waves. 'I believe that the trip to Petra has been designed by Chris and Tony to talk to the board members, but I also think that something else might be afoot.'

'I have agents and local law enforcement standing by to monitor that trip,' Phil said. He moved closer to me, our hands nearly touching on the railing. 'And there is no way you're going to the Library at six a.m. Why would they even ask that?'

'I think it's probably to keep us away from Petra and whatever is going to happen there.'

'He's going to bring it all down,' he said to himself.

'Chris or Tony? That would sort of be doing your job for you, wouldn't it?' I half joked.

Phil turned to face me, concern etched into the crinkles of his eyes. His hand reached for my arm. 'I'm trying to stop all this without anyone else getting hurt.'

He was so serious I felt bad for joking. 'I do know that. Let me help you.'

'Are you sure I can't talk you out of getting involved?' His gaze met mine and lingered.

'This is my life now. Danger or not, I'm in,' I replied. 'Let's do this together.'

'When this is all over, we'll need to talk and get some things straight, set some boundaries if you're really going to take over Arthur's hunting,' said Phil. 'This . . . recklessness can't go on.'

'Sure.' I kept my face as neutral as possible. There was no point arguing on the balcony. But no man was going to tell me what I could and couldn't do ever again – I hadn't been married for a long time.

'Thanks to you, we now know who we are dealing with – Patricia, Tony and Chris. Now we need the evidence to take them down. If there's going to be a meeting in Petra, we need to be there.'

I checked my watch. 'Let's hope the villagers of Little Meddington are as fearsome as I know they can be. If I don't get word that Sky is safe, I'll go to the Library and see what awaits me there.'

Phil pulled off his baseball cap and raked his hand through his hair. 'So much like Arthur.' But it didn't sound like a criticism.

Chapter Forty-Five

Agatha

It was 3.45 a.m. in Little Meddington and Agatha Craven, owner of the Teapot Tearoom, was a woman on a mission. When Freya called from her holiday explaining what was needed, there was no hesitation . . . if someone was in trouble, then the village was mobilized. It was the Suffolk way.

Agatha had her husband, Simon, at her side – which wasn't as comforting as it sounded – standing outside the back door to the shop with keys in her pocket and a flashlight in her hand.

'You're terrifying enough on your own. You didn't need to get the whole village involved,' Simon grumbled.

'You hush now, or you'll be sorry.'

'That's what I mean.' He wiggled a finger at her and smirked. 'Let's get this done. No bullies in this village.'

'No bullies.' They nodded at each other.

One by one the villagers of Little Meddington gathered – about fifty in all – half around the back and the other half out front.

'You lads around the front with Simon, and make sure you're all in position at exactly three fifty-five a.m.'

He saluted. 'Yes, sir.' And casually sidestepped her playful slap.

Under the cover of the alleyway's shadows, two of the local gamekeepers and one farmhand huddled around Agatha with their rifle bags slung over their shoulders – they all went to the shooting range together. She had known them all since birth, knew all their mothers and understood none of them had a bad bone in their body. There would be no cartridges in those rifles, but the bad man in the shop with Sky didn't need to know that.

'Right, boys,' she whispered. 'Let's get ready and wait for Owen.'

When one of them didn't answer, his mother coughed from behind him. He snapped to attention.

Agatha smiled. *Well-brought-up young men, each and every one of them.*

As moonlight broke through the clouds and lit the high street, Owen, the village mechanic, arrived, and Agatha pointed out Sky's old Ford.

'Get the alarm to go off, will you? We need a reason to get Sky out of there.'

She clasped her hands so no one could see them shake. The thought of what Sky had been through all night made her hold firm.

'And when she gets out of there,' Owen said, 'I'm going to take matters into my own hands with that piece of shit for doing this to her.' His fists clenched and Agatha reached out for him.

'Let's get her out and you get her far away from here. How about that?' She saw the concern in his eyes. 'Sky has had quite a bit of car trouble over the past few weeks, hasn't she?'

Owen shrugged, but Agatha had been around a long time and recognized an attraction when she saw it.

'Get over to that car, and when I give the signal . . .'

She checked her watch, then mouthed, 'One. Two. Three.' And pointed to the car.

Owen bounced the hood of the car, which made Agatha understand that she hadn't needed a mechanic to put the car alarm part of the plan into action. He wanted to be here.

Agatha waited a moment and then put her spare key into the lock and twisted. She looked over her shoulder at the three rifles now trained at her back, ready to stand against what was coming – all the barrels shook in the boys' hands.

'Sky, are you here? I think my car just tapped yours and the alarm is going off. Can you come and turn it off?'

Silence.

'Sky?'

'Um . . . yes, I'm here.' There was a muttering of voices from upstairs in the flat.

Agatha's heart thumped so hard she wondered if this would bring on a heart attack. But this was her village, and no one treated a woman that way, not on her watch. Freya's plan was a good one and Agatha was going to make sure it worked.

'As it's waking up the whole village, I'm concerned some-one in the Neighbourhood Watch scheme might call Officer Blake's direct number,' she called. It was a lie but all for a good cause.

'No! It's fine, I'm coming.' Sky ran down the stairs, a tall man on her heels. She lifted her car key and the alarm went off.

A moment later it started again. *Well done, Owen.*

'I think you might have to go out there. And as I said, I might have dinged it, so I'll need your insurance details. I'm so very sorry. I can go and get Officer—'

'No! No, I'm coming.' Sky glared at the man behind her, and he let go of her arm as she said something to him.

Agatha checked her watch. They had two minutes until Freya was meant to meet at the Library, so they didn't have any time.

'I can call him if you like?'

'I'll come.' She looked back a few times, but as soon as she reached the back door Agatha pulled her out and slammed the door behind her. Locking it.

The man roared as he ran to the door, but he was met by a crowd of villagers and a number of rifles.

Owen had his arm around Sky and was leading her away down the cobbled courtyard and towards his vintage truck. But she turned back and met Agatha's eye. 'Thank you,' she said.

Agatha smiled and turned back to the man. 'I don't know who you are, but we do not tolerate this kind of thing in our village. The only reason that you are not surrounded by police is that Freya had asked us not to call them. But see here.' She pointed to the butcher's son. 'He's recording everything. Now, you turn around and go out the front of the shop. My husband is waiting to escort you to your car.'

She pointed towards the shop front. 'Simon has opened the door. Never come back.'

Agatha pulled out her phone and typed: *Sky is safe with Owen. Bully is gone.*

Chapter Forty-Six

Freya

Before the break of dawn, Phil had escorted Carole and me back to our staterooms, leaving us to shower, dress and pack. I had relieved Mark and Luke of the painting stolen from the Lowestoft Maritime Museum, which they said they had taken thinking it would pay some sort of insurance policy. That, and the sword Luke had swiped for Mark.

I suspected that the painting was a clue that led to Carole's trunk back home, where I hoped the vase was hidden, but for now it was time to find a way to stop the succession of the new Collector.

I constantly checked my watch and prayed that Agatha and the villagers of Little Meddington would get to the shop and keep Sky safe. It was a slow, dripping torture trusting others to do a job, but I couldn't be in two places at once.

Relying on other people was not something that I was used to, but this case seemed to demand that of me at every turn.

It was 5.58 a.m. and I hadn't heard from Agatha – Carole and I were going to have to get to the Library and hand ourselves over to Chris and Tony.

Then my phone pinged. Relief had me sinking back against the walls.

'They did it!' I called to Carole.

Carole crossed the room in a few strides and pulled me into one of her glorious hugs. 'Sky's safe?' I nodded. 'That village is unstoppable. It's the Suffolk way.'

'Now, let's get ourselves to this meeting at Petra and stop this succession once and for all.'

* * *

The Aqaba port was encircled by new five-star hotels. A huge flagpole flew the Jordanian flag. Pictures of King Abdullah II ibn Al Hussein and his sons, Prince Hussein and Prince Hashem, hung before us in the immigration room. There was a quite sleepy hush among the passengers, but Carole and I were wide awake.

Once we were out, staff directed us to more waiting coaches. Carole nudged me as Patricia boarded one of the last coaches along with Mark, Sally, Tony, Jenny and Archie.

'Should we try and get on there?' Carole asked.

'They're leaving. Let's get on the coach behind them. We can keep an eye on them.'

We had a two-hour drive through the Jordanian desert and into the mountains. As I looked out the window, I noticed that Aqaba was very different from the sleepy fishing village of twenty years ago. Nostalgia twisted in my heart as if a cobra had coiled around it. The twenty-one year-old woman I was, the one that last walked on Jordanian sand, was so different from who I was now. I was older and bore more cracks and scars, but my determination to uncover the truth was the same. My sense of justice was still as strong. There was a comfort in the possibility I would come full circle and at last retrieve the vase that Arthur and I had hunted so long ago.

* * *

Both Carole and I had fallen asleep almost as soon as we settled in our seats, but I woke as we turned off the Kings Highway towards our destination. The route to Petra had taken us through the never-ending Wadi Musa desert and we were now entering the barren, rust-coloured mountains. As the coach climbed higher, sweeping views stretched out beyond my window – the natural hues of sandstone and earth pitted against dazzling bright blue sky with wisps of clouds. The slim roads twisted and turned until at last we descended into the remote valley where the ancient site had been created in the narrow sandstone gorge.

It was said to be one of the places where Moses struck a rock and water gushed forth. Later the Nabataeans, an Arab tribe, made it their capital, known as a wealthy and legendary trading centre especially for spices. The Nabataeans carved into the sandstone, creating homes, temples and tombs that changed colour with the shifting sun. An aqueduct system chiselled into the rock walls brought water through the city and enabled beautiful gardens and bountiful farming land. But time changes all things. Trade routes were rerouted. Earthquakes and tremors hit around 363 CE and again in 551. People drifted away. Perhaps they believed that the land was angry in some way.

The coach parked behind the shiny modern building block that held the Petra Museum, and we walked towards a crescent-shaped market that appeared to be the entrance. I scanned the hundreds of passengers around us. Chris was nowhere to be seen.

'This doesn't feel right,' I whispered to Carole, but she was watching Sally and Mark, who were holding up folded umbrellas and calling names. Next to them were twenty or so local guides taking other groups.

'Do we split up?'

'No, I have a feeling that their groups will be sticking together.'

Sally was chatting with Jenny and Archie, and I saw that Tony was on the outer edge of the group with a swollen lip. I ducked my head, but I doubted he could do much to me with so many onlookers.

I couldn't see Phil among the passengers. He had said he was going to meet with the Jordanians and some of his team on the ground when the ship docked, but that he would be here . . . watching.

Sally noticed us approaching and took a few steps away from her group. 'Keep your lanyards on at all times. They hold your tickets. Take a left and start walking down the slope to have your tickets checked and enter the main site,' she called to her group as she hurried towards us. 'You're both with Mark.'

Carole leaned in. 'But we'd prefer to be with the real expert.'

'That's not possible.' Keeping her eyes on us, she called, 'Mark, these two are yours.'

Mark tried not to roll his eyes and motioned us over to join him. He sighed. 'Don't bring trouble to my door.'

Carole beamed at him. 'I've never been trouble. What a thing to say.'

'Walk in with me and then you can go where you like.'

We nodded again, both keeping our eyes on Sally's group as they had their tickets checked and entered the site. Patricia had now joined them and was joking with Jenny. I noticed a wistful look on Carole's face.

'You really liked Patricia, didn't you?'

'I did. But after your kidnapping . . .' She sighed. 'I have to hand it to the woman. She's done exceptionally well for being from a generation of women who were told to stay home and look after the kids. She's defied convention and thrived in a man's world. She's been on the wrong side of the law a long time, but damn, did she take equality of the sexes to heart.'

'You still admire her? Even now we know who she is?'

'A feminist and a criminal?' Carole smiled. 'One of the things I love about you is your strong moral compass, and although I don't condone what Patricia has done, I can admire a woman who has thrived in exceptional circumstances.' She linked her arm through mine and squeezed. 'Doesn't mean we won't take this all down, but . . .'

'The world's not always black and white?' It was what she used to tell me as a child.

'Not all women had the opportunities your generation did, nor that of my firecracker of a grandniece.'

Archie was the last to have his ticket checked. He looked back up the slope. Scanning the passengers, he nodded to himself as if something pleased him. He passed through the gate and disappeared from sight. Carole met my eye, and we knew that we weren't going to wait for the six or so of Mark's group to come back from the bathroom.

We slipped away and hurried after Sally's group.

Chapter Forty-Seven

The walk to the famous Treasury and the larger site beyond was a long one. Locals with horses met us as soon as we walked through the ticket barrier. Sally's group of eight or nine had filled all the golf carts and were speeding away.

To our left, down a few steps, was a separate footpath with donkeys and mules tethered along one wall.

'We take you to the entrance, then you walk,' called a man.

'Very fast horse – fast like Ferrari.'

'Has built-in air-con,' shouted another. 'Save your legs for the long walk.'

'Yes! You. You.' I turned to see that Carole had stopped to talk to one of them. She beamed at me and I knew we were about to go for a ride.

'Really?' I mouthed, jogging over to her.

'They're getting away, darling!' She pointed at the golf carts. 'We'll take the sports car ones!'

Sally's group was almost out of sight, and the large crowd of cruise passengers behind them would slow our pace.

But my main question still remained . . .

Where is Chris Prince?

I checked my phone. No signal, but I had an email from Sky that I couldn't open. Dread came crashing over me – we had no way of contacting anyone. Phil said they had lookout posts around the site, but it felt like we were very much on our own.

Carole was already on a small horse and chatting away to the Jordanian holding the guide rope. I was about to climb on a horse that looked nothing like a race car with air-conditioning when I saw Mark directing his group down the path.

I ran to him. 'Mark, I have one last question.'

He tutted. 'Make it quick.'

'Why Petra? I know there is meant to be a meeting here, but why *here*?' I flung my arm towards the sandstone hills and boulders around us. 'Why not meet at a nice five-star hotel overlooking the Red Sea at sunset?'

'This is a bucket list item for many people. The cruise was planned accordingly.' He waved at an elderly couple helping each other over uneven ground. 'Take your time. Sunrise doesn't hit the Treasury until eight thirty. Watch your step.'

'Laura organized all this,' I said to myself as a thin thread of concern – one so thin that it could easily be ignored – tugged at my consciousness. *I'm missing something . . .*

'Laura?' Mark dipped his head and shook it. 'It should never have come to that . . . I liked the girl.' He swallowed. 'But it wasn't right, playing both sides without paying the consequences. Talking to Arthur Crockleford was the first mistake of many.' He stepped away and called to a woman in his group, 'I'll see you there.' His eyes slid to mine. 'I need to go. Have a look at this marvellous site and then go home. Don't get involved . . .'

My mind was spinning. 'Laura planned all the specialist antiques events on board. The museum expedition. This.'

Mark started to walk away as Carole trotted off down the separate trail for horses.

'Come on,' she called to me.

'Why exactly was Laura killed? You must know . . . have suspicions.' I reached out and grabbed Mark before he could leave. 'Why?' When he didn't answer, I said, 'Before I tell Patricia that Luke stole the sword from her.'

He tilted his head at me, considering what I'd just said. He almost looked confused. 'The sword was mine and it was time to take it home to the family seat. It was never here to be sold at the auction. You seem to have a lot of things muddled up. You would be wise to walk away now before the truth gets you killed. Like Laura, if you know too much and try to sell that information, it won't end well. As you have found out, Chris is trigger-happy and volatile.' He sighed. 'There hasn't been a new Collector in decades, so the scramble for succession has been fraught. The promise of power does crazy things to people.' A couple of passengers waved to him. 'I have to go.'

Mark believes Chris Prince killed Laura for double-crossing him in some way. Laura said in the note she left me that she had an arrangement with Arthur. Did they know that and kill her for it?

It was the word 'muddled' that stuck with me, as it implied that I had come to the wrong conclusion about something I'd said. 'What have I got "muddled"?'

'Listen, Arthur was a valued member of the community, and out of respect for him you have remained unharmed. But you're pushing your luck with all your questions.' Mark snatched his arm back and strode away.

'Apart from Patricia and her nephew abducting us!'

He shook his head.

My mind was whirling. Chris Prince was the type of man that used women. He used Bella, and Laura and I hated him for it more than I hated him for shooting at me. He killed Phil's friend Ed, and he likely killed Ben Wells and Laura and God knows how many other people over the years who stood in his way.

The thought of running into Chris Prince again filled me with dread.

I had remembered one thing about Petra . . . Most of the huge sandstone carvings were tombs. Was it here that Chris planned to make sure that Patricia retired? The sort of send-off that no one came back from?

'I need one of your fastest horses,' I called to the men.

* * *

Dawn was almost breaking as we hurried through the towering sandstone gorge – at times it felt as if the walls above me were closing in. The crisp morning air stung my lungs and urged me forward. Where would this meeting happen? There were so many witnesses.

I headed towards the light, and my eyes lifted at the sight of the Treasury – its ornate classical-style facade with towering columns and false windows and the one entry point carved into the sandstone cliff. Sally's group was huddled in one corner, chatting away.

I nudged Carole. She turned to me and breathed, 'Oh, isn't it just the most beautiful thing that you've ever seen?'

It really was, and as I paused for a moment to take in the sight, a lump formed in my throat – there are very few places in the world that hold so tight onto their magic even when overrun with tourists. I understood why someone would want to see this before retiring.

'We need to know what they're talking about.' I nodded towards the group.

I felt a presence behind me. 'I think I can help with that,' Phil murmured in my ear, his chest close to my shoulder. My stomach flipped.

I smiled a hello and looked up into his hazel eyes as he placed an earbud in my palm. 'Chris Prince isn't here, as far as we can see. I'm worried we are missing something. My colleague Sloane said she just saw Bella arriving in a taxi. Any idea what she's doing here?'

'With Bella it's anyone's guess, but I'm going to have to go with revenge.' I gave him a level look.

'I've hidden a listening device in Sally's umbrella.'

I placed the earbud in my ear and heard Sally talking to her group.

'We'll follow the gorge together until we get to the Street of Facades, and then you'll have time to explore on your own for an hour or two before lunch. You can go off to see the Obelisk and the Royal Tombs. Local guides will be with you for that part of the tour.'

Sally broke away and started talking to Patricia, but the listening device was filled with static so I couldn't hear what they were saying.

'They found the ones we had planted on them. So now we're using other devices that are less reliable,' Phil whispered.

As Sally spoke, Patricia was scanning the faces of everyone in the crowd. As her gaze reached where we were standing, I swept Carole and me around so that our backs were to her. I risked a look back over my shoulder and detected a softness in her jaw and hope in her eyes . . . There was a longing in her demeanour.

'Who's she looking for?'

The sun began to stretch down the long gorge, and an orange glow lit the sandstone. I took out the earbud and tapped Phil on the arm. 'They're about to split up. We need to follow Patricia.'

'Agreed,' said Phil. 'They know they're being watched, so I'm unsure if we're actually going to get anything from here.'

'Laura planned this trip while working for Chris. But I think that Chris isn't playing the same game anymore. He's changing everything up. Coming here was about a once-in-a-lifetime trip for Patricia – perhaps she feels like it's the last time she will ever get the chance.'

'Have you seen Tony?' asked Carole.

Phil turned and talked into his chest and then waited. 'He's walked farther down the gorge.' He paused. 'There is a small restaurant and snack shop near the Street of Facades. Tony is talking to the owners.'

'Then we are going to need to split up too. Carole, can you keep an eye on Patricia? I'll keep walking to see what Tony is up to.'

Phil reached out for me. 'If they see you . . .'

'It's a chance I have to take. This is our last shot.'

I hurried through the gorge, promising myself I would come back one day and see every inch of the amazing site. But right now, I needed to find out if the meeting Arthur had told Phil about was at last going to happen.

Chapter Forty-Eight

For the past three-and-a-half hours I had followed Tony up a torturous climb to the Obelisk, the Jordanian sun pounding my back and sandstone grit scratching my eyes. Phil had joined Sally's group on a tour around the Royal Tombs. Carole had kept close to Patricia, who was heading for the Byzantine Church.

If Tony knew I was following him, he didn't seem to care. While huddling close to one of the cruise's tour groups, I spotted him break away from them and join another man with his back to me.

I stepped around the group and recognized Archie. He and Tony were facing the Obelisk like casual tourists. Archie shook his head – whatever Tony was saying, he didn't like it. There was no sign of Jenny – wouldn't a husband and wife want to see the site together?

Confusion itched in the corner of my mind.

It was noon by the time I descended the never-ending steps back into the gorge. The three or so hundred cruise passengers were gathered to hear about the nearby restaurants, or the stairs up to the top of the gorge and the Monastery for the more adventurous.

I overheard Sally explaining to the group that she was

handing over the rest of the visit to the local guides. With the hundreds of cruise passengers milling around, it became hard to keep sight of Tony, and the only thing I could focus on was finding Carole in her red shirt.

'Something is up,' whispered Carole as she grabbed my elbow through the throng of passengers. 'I've had a wonderful time seeing the sights but . . . I'm quite sure Patricia saw me following and couldn't care less.'

'I had the same feeling with Tony. Like we're no longer a threat – what's changed?'

More passengers flowed around us and one bumped into Carole, so I linked my arm through hers and led her out of the crowd to stand next to the wall of the gorge.

'I've no idea, but it makes me uneasy,' she said. 'And where's Bella? If Patricia is handing the reins to Tony – why is all this necessary?' She flicked her hand at the sandstone tomb towering in front of us. 'They're just being tourists.'

But when I looked around, I couldn't see any of them.

'Where are they?' I asked Carole, panic pitching my gut. In the moments we had been overwhelmed with tourists, our targets had merged into the crowds and vanished. 'Mark said that I had it all muddled. So what are we missing?'

'Do you see Sally or Mark?' asked Phil as he strode over to us.

'No!' Carole and I said in unison.

Fear twisted in my chest. 'We've lost them . . .' *And this was our last chance . . .*

'All of them, Patricia, Tony, Mark . . . Sally, Archie.' As Phil spoke, his eyes scanned the area and every face in it.

'*How?*' asked Carole. 'They were all just here with their groups.'

'You're right,' I said. *Think! Where could they have all gone?* 'The only time any of them were separated from the passengers was when I followed Tony to the restaurant this morning, but he was just buying a soft drink and chatting to the local behind the till . . .'

Carole met my eye and nodded.

* * *

Just past the Theatre – which looked very much like a small sandstone Roman amphitheatre – was a low, flimsily built building covered head to toe in traditional black-and-red fabric in varying stages of deterioration. It was the only restaurant in the middle of the canyon. Attached to the outside were faded soft drink signs and pictures of ice cream, but there was no way to see inside as the fabric covered all the openings. It looked closed.

'I'll go around the back,' I said.

Phil nodded and headed around the other side. However, Carole must not have gotten the memo explaining we were going to have a look quietly. She went right up to the entrance and pulled back the curtain.

'Carole!' I whisper-shouted.

But it was too late. Mark stepped in front of her and scowled. 'Restaurant's closed,' he said.

'Then why are you inside?' she asked, trying to angle her head to see what was going on behind him.

Mark sidestepped to allow Carole to pass. 'You lot just don't give up, do you? Come on in, he's expecting you.'

He?

315

Carole gave me a little wave and then ducked her head around the fabric door as she entered the restaurant.

I had no choice but to follow her; I wasn't going to let her go inside alone. Someone coughed behind me, and I turned around to face Chris Prince with gun in hand. Phil stood in front of him with his palms up.

'Guess we're all going inside,' said Phil.

'Just move,' said Chris, and shoved Phil forward.

This is not the day I die! I repeated in my mind. 'Gonna shoot me again?' I asked. I wasn't going to show him any fear, no matter how much my heart pounded.

'Move. Now. Both of you. And I'll happily shoot anyone who gets in the way. Didn't it hurt enough last time?' He prodded my shoulder and blazing pain shuddered down my arm. Phil placed his body between Chris and me.

'Try and keep a low profile in there,' he muttered.

'Is my ex-witch with you?' Chris looked over his shoulder, but there was no one around who looked like Bella.

Which was a good question. Where was Bella? I raised an eyebrow at Phil, asking the silent question, and he shrugged.

Inside, it took a moment for my eyes to adjust to the darkness and I hesitated, but Chris pushed my shoulder and I stumbled forward. The interior of the restaurant was separated into two parts – one side was a gift shop with all the normal tourist bric-a-brac, towers of local fabric, wooden camels and donkeys with 'Jordan' written on them, while the other side had a long table down the middle.

Patricia was at one end with Tony to her right, then Sally, Mark, Jenny, Archie . . . and Luke sat at the opposite head of the table.

'I've been expecting you three,' said Luke. 'Why don't we pull up some chairs and you can all get settled? Unless you have more FBI agents or Jordanian police joining us?'

Phil grunted and his jaw clenched.

Is Luke The Collector, not Patricia?

'Really, it doesn't matter.' Luke took a sip of water from the glass in front of him. 'You have nothing on any of us – even if they come storming in, no one has enough evidence to hold me. We are just a group of old friends catching up for a coffee. Patricia was just telling us about her nephews and how very accomplished they are. I think that you have met Tony?' He threw his glance towards Tony and then raised an eyebrow at me, but my throat was too dry to reply. 'No? How about her other nephew, Ben Wells?' My surprise must have been written all over my face, as Luke replied, 'I see you do know of him . . . Well, I was just about to inform Patricia that Ben isn't going to be able to make it today.'

So, Ben Wells, the missing antiques expert, was Patricia's nephew . . . and I believed Ben Wells was the murdered man behind the Lowestoft Museum. Patricia's brow was etched in confusion. *She doesn't know . . .* I swallowed hard and closed my eyes. *Oh God, she doesn't know . . .*

Patricia glared at Luke. 'What does that mean?'

Luke didn't acknowledge Patricia's question. Instead, he studied me. 'I have invited you here to get some things straight. For starters, what did Arthur tell you about all this? Perhaps Ben wanted to modernize this operation, and Tony here is a simple soul who just wants lots more money? Ben's ideas were . . . interesting, but I preferred Chris's vision . . . Who would Arthur have backed?'

I didn't answer – because it seemed I was getting more information by being silent.

'My curiosity gets the better of me. On to the second reason you're here.' Luke reached into his leather satchel, which was hanging from the back of his chair, and pulled out a letter-sized file. He tapped it with his index finger.

'Patricia and her husband have been loyal to the company for decades. Patricia's acumen for business is exceptional – moving money between layers of private shell companies in tax havens is her specialty. But then she started thinking above her station, encouraging her nephews to be more than they should be . . . were capable of being. Tony, your recent actions have saddened me – you have no loyalty, not even to your own brother.' His eyes bored into Tony and then fixed on Chris, who was still standing behind us with his gun pointed at Phil's rigid back. 'I knew that when I announced my retirement all the knives would come out . . . especially from those seated around this table.' Luke wiped his brow.

'We haven't done anything. We didn't . . . Tell him, Chris . . .' Tony stuttered to a stop.

Mark shook his head and turned to Patricia. 'You think after being *friends* for all this time we wouldn't know what you were up to, Patricia? Preparing your nephews to take over. Sending Ben to kill Chris to get him out of the running. Except it didn't work out that way.'

Archie smirked, and Jenny batted his arm with the back of her hand. 'Not now,' she mouthed.

Sally tutted but didn't move an inch.

Luke stood and picked up the folder and walked over to Phil, dropping the file in his lap. 'A gift for you. I'm sure you have many files on who and what you think I am and do. But you will never get close to the truth of all The Collector is. So I'm doing a small part of your job for you. Here is some incriminating information about Tony, Ben and Patricia.' He swung around to Patricia. 'It's all over now. You shouldn't have gotten involved with the bid for succession.'

'And who will you choose? Your protégé?' Patricia jabbed a finger at Chris. 'And I think you're forgetting that I know where all the money is hidden.'

'The money from the recent auction has gone to an account you have no access to. It's more than enough for me to retire on. Hence the reason I had Chris smuggle my mummy and a large part of my collection on board the cruise. It is money that cannot be traced. And I'm sure Chris can persuade you to hand over all the details of the old companies – he's very good at getting what he wants out of people.'

Tony shook his head and said to Luke, 'Chris has been playing you.'

Luke scoffed. 'Your need for wealth and power took over your senses years ago. You care more about it than your own brother. You sold him out just like we expected you would. Chris hasn't been playing me – he's been working for me all along.'

Patricia's pale face went ghost white. 'Where's Ben?' Her voice was barely audible. 'You told me that plans had changed. He was going to meet us here.'

'He's dead. He came to kill me, and I killed him,' said Chris Prince, his voice cold and flat, his gun rising above Phil's head to aim at Tony.

Even with a fan in each corner, the air was stifling. A bead of sweat ran down my spine.

'We were to run this together. That was the deal . . .'

'Deal's off,' replied Chris.

'Dead . . .' Patricia was shaking her head as the truth set in. A tear escaped the corner of her eye. She stared at Luke. 'I understand having Chris get rid of Laura when she was telling Arthur, and probably the FBI, everything she knew. I'd suspected there was something up with Arthur. He was always asking questions . . . I told you so . . . but Ben . . . he was loyal to you, Luke . . . he didn't . . .' She bit her clenched fist to try and stop her sobs from escaping, before composing herself and pointing at us. 'And why did you allow *them* in here?'

'Arthur was valuable to me, and they were valuable to him . . . I wanted to see why,' said Luke.

I took a lungful of air for courage and said, 'Can you let Carole go? She doesn't need to be here. Arthur never would have wanted her to be involved in all of this.'

'Nonsense, I'm staying,' Carole replied and glared at me for even suggesting it.

Phil tried to stand, as if he too sensed that the atmosphere was turning sour. Tony looked like he was about to explode. 'Sit. Down,' said Chris and shoved Phil by his shoulder. 'We need to let him have his little goodbye speech so this can be over.'

'You killed them . . . all.' Phil twisted so his eyes met Chris's. Rage tightened his lips, but he remained seated.

'Enough!' barked Luke. 'All of you.' He pointed at Tony. 'Sit. I haven't finished telling Freya and Carole the full and truthful story of their lately departed friend. Arthur knew the organization he was up against, and I want these women to know it as well. It will stop them meddling in the future if they understand that their new Lockwood Agency needs to look the other way when it comes to The Collector's dealings. Then Chris won't have to come for you. Last spring, Arthur asked for Freya to be an expert on the cruise as a favour to him, and I agreed. He asked that she be given time to get her feet under the table, as it were, and I agreed. I am a man of my word . . . so here we all are.'

So, we were brought here to be given a warning . . .

'You see, at the beginning, Arthur started out trying to take the black market down. Always trying to rescue stolen items,' he sneered, 'when he should've just let the insurance companies pay out and concentrate on running his little antiques shop. But, back then, Arthur Crockleford was very moral, and on more than one occasion he had recovered an item we had taken . . . That was, of course, decades ago . . .'

Luke smiled at me as if I were a child being told a bedtime story.

'When Arthur started working for the Metcalfs back in the early 2000s, it became clear that he had turned over a new leaf . . . he had entered the black-market side of things. Patricia had a chat with him, and she offered him the position of auctioneer on these trips. Perhaps he believed Patricia was The Collector and that I worked for her, or vice versa, but he never pressed me on it. Misdirection is the best magician's trick, isn't it?

'Arthur was a damn good verifier and auctioneer, and so, when his heirs boarded this cruise, I showed them some respect and honoured my word to him; wondering if Freya would approach one of us and offer to take his place. Disappointingly, that didn't happen, and then this rabble' – his index finger pointed at Phil and Carole – 'showed up last night in my state-room. I realized then that they knew nothing whatsoever.'

'Rabble!' Carole fumed. Her chair screeched as she rose and was standing in front of Luke before Chris could grab her. 'We are professionals! My niece is—'

Chris hauled her back to her seat and Carole huffed as she sat back down.

I turned to her. 'What are you doing?' I mouthed.

She made the smallest motion with her chin indicating that I should look to the very far corner where a crack of sunlight entered the room, a face barely visible. Someone was watching us, and Carole was making sure that she was seen.

Chapter Forty-Nine

The air inside the restaurant crackled with electricity. There was a strangled silence as Tony and Chris glared at each other. Luke was studying Carole and me.

It was a good thing nobody had a tinderbox, as a single spark could have detonated the whole situation.

Patricia spoke first. She straightened and scrubbed her face of tears. 'You're wrong about those women. They know far too much – I believe that they have Arthur's journals. But I did as you asked and let them be until I saw Freya in the auction and I knew Arthur must have told her everything. Arthur put her here to bring down the whole operation, *not* to join it.' There was poison in Patricia's words even as another tear rolled down her cheek. 'Arthur got his information from him.' She pointed at Chris. 'And you want to make him the new Collector!'

'Stop your lies,' said Chris between gritted teeth. 'Arthur worked for The Collector.'

He was trying to cover his tracks, but from what Phil had told me, Chris had been Arthur's informant long before Arthur started working on the cruise's auctions. His web of deceit was coming undone.

'You're wrong, my dear. Chris proved his loyalty long ago.'

Luke smiled at Patricia, but it didn't meet his eyes. 'Back when you called and asked for my help to arrange the theft of the Greek museum vase as a gift for your husband, I suggested Chris could transport it. If it wasn't for Chris, you and your husband would've been arrested by the FBI, who had followed you there.'

Luke must have seen me frown. 'We had had a particularly fruitful year, and it was to be the Hendersons' bonus. Always best to keep the board of directors happy, don't you think?' I nodded, not really knowing what to say or why he was telling me all this. 'However, it came to my attention that the FBI was closing in.'

His eyes flicked to Chris, making me think that it was Chris who'd told him – because Chris was playing both sides. Feeding information to Phil's partner, Ed, to Arthur . . . all without Luke's knowledge. Luke continued, 'Chris had an interesting solution: blowing up a boat to put an end to the surveillance, taking out the main FBI agent, who he had arranged to be on board, and convincing Arthur – who then operated all above board – to get the vase out of the country and hide it for him. It was a bold move. I wanted to see if Chris could pull it off, to convince someone like Arthur to hide the vase rather than hand it over. So I agreed. If Arthur returned the vase, it wasn't a great loss to me.'

'But the plan worked just as Chris said it would, and Chris rose considerably in my estimation.' Luke's eyes shone with pride.

Now was my chance. I caught Phil's gaze and mouthed, 'Go with it.'

He frowned, not understanding, but I had no other option,

and I prayed the confusion I was about to rain down on the tent would give him time to get out of harm's way.

'But Patricia is right,' I said. 'Chris was an FBI informant. He also gave Arthur information on the movement of the vase and other stolen items long before Arthur started working for the black market.' Time for a small lie. 'Arthur told me at the time, and it's why Phil is here . . . because Chris is his informant.'

Phil's lips parted and his eyes widened in shock at my lie. I gave him a pleading look, hoping he would go along with it, and he regained his composure, understanding what was needed to create mistrust between the group. 'It's true,' he said. 'Chris was my partner's informant and then became mine.'

Phil's a convincing liar!

'What?' spat Chris. 'I never was.' His gun pressed into the back of Phil's head and Carole gripped my arm, her eyes wild with fear. *Had we pushed too far?*

Mark pulled out his own gun. 'Have you been an informant all this time?'

'Let's all stay calm,' said Luke, but there was a shadow spreading over his face as he studied Chris. *He's considering what we said.*

'Look.' There was an edge of panic in Chris's tone as he raised his gun and pointed it around the table. 'I only ever talked to Arthur *after* I set the bomb on the catamaran. You know that . . . the only reason I spoke to Arthur again was because you told me that I had to retrieve the vase from him.' He was trying to remain calm, but there was a slight shake to the gun, which gave away his anxiety. 'I am the best candidate to run the company . . . to be The Collector. I have proven myself over and over. They are trying to bring it down.'

Luke sat statue still. 'What an interesting development. Sometimes one must put another to the test. See where their loyalty resides . . . see what comes out of the woodwork, as it were. I have always played the long game. When I decided to retire, I thought it was time for another test. I gave you and Ben the same one – see who could outwit the infamous Arthur Crockleford first and find what he had hidden.' Luke took another sip of water. 'In the end, the strongest always survive.'

'It's time for you to retire,' said Chris. 'You promised me . . .'

I looked towards the crack in the fabric. Whoever was watching us was gone. In the seconds I looked away Tony had gotten to his feet again, lunging over the table towards Chris. 'You double-crossing . . . I told you where Ben would be. But you were working with the FBI all along . . .'

The flimsy table caved under Tony's weight, and Sally, Jenny and Archie jumped backwards. Carole fell sideways off her chair and I reached to help her up, my heart threatening to break out of my ribcage. We needed to run.

It was clear that the lies Phil and I had told were the spark . . . and the restaurant had erupted into chaos.

Tony scrambled across the broken table, fists flailing. Chris dodged the first volley and landed a punch to the ribs. 'You wanted your brother dead. What did you think would happen when you told me Patricia was having him follow me to that museum?' He punched him again in the kidneys and Tony crumpled with a grunt.

Phil was on his feet diving towards Chris, revenge hardening his clenched fists. He disarmed Chris in one swift movement, but that didn't stop Chris from landing a blow to Phil's cheek.

I gripped Carole's arm. 'Keep walking backwards.' From outside the tent, boots pounded on the barren ground.

Phil landed a punch to Chris's ribs.

Luke stepped away and brushed dust from his jacket. 'Time to go,' he said to Mark.

'Stop!' shouted Patricia, tears tracking down her cheeks. 'I can't bear this. Tony . . . why did you tell Chris about Ben?' Tony was trying to stand. 'Why did you choose Chris over family?'

When I looked around, Jenny, Archie and Sally were slipping out the back.

Phil's eyes flashed to mine. 'Go!'

Phil looked between Luke – about to leave the restaurant – and Chris, who was on the floor under him. It was never really a decision. Chris had been directly responsible for the deaths of Ed and Laura and many more. 'You're not going anywhere,' Phil said to Chris between gritted teeth.

Luke pulled at the fabric at the back of the building, and bright Jordanian sun lit the side of the room. His gaze met mine. 'I gave Arthur my word and you have not been harmed, but the next time you get in the way of The Collector's business, things will be different.' Behind him I could see a pack of men in uniform running towards the restaurant.

Tony was struggling to stand with the help of Patricia. 'He . . . he can't be The Collector.'

Patricia glared at Luke. 'You know he can't . . . We would have voted against it.' Then the understanding dawned on her. 'We were never called here to vote, were we? You were always going to use them' – she pointed at Carole and me – 'to get us all out of the way.'

'Times are changing, my dear. That's the whole point of succession – out with the old and in with the new. It is the way the position of The Collector has been kept alive for so very long. When Chris told me how he wanted it to go, I upheld his wish . . .'

It was all a set-up. Luke planned Chris as his successor all along, and the meeting was to get rid of the old board to enable Chris to set up a new one or go it alone. Given his treatment of Bella and Tony, it didn't seem he was eager to share.

Phil reached for Chris's gun and held it up. Everyone paused for a brief second before light flooded the tent from the main entrance. Bella strode in, dressed as an old lady with grey hair and a walking stick.

'Seems like I'm just in time.' She looked behind her and smiled as the Jordanian police, twenty or thirty of them, surrounded the restaurant with their weapons out. 'I'm sorry I'm late. It took me a while to get everyone together.'

As Luke, Mark and Sally were already standing by the back opening, they were the first arrested.

'You were the one watching us?' I asked, relief crashing over me. 'You brought the police.'

Bella strode towards Carole and checked her over. 'It's a good thing that I can always spot Carole in a crowd, and I knew Phil must have made arrangements with the local authorities. Might have told them I was working with him.'

Phil scoffed in disbelief, but Carole pulled Bella into a quick hug.

'Darling, you never cease to amaze me.' Carole looked a little shaken, but she was brushing dirt off her red shirt and flicked her hair from her eyes. 'Thank you for coming to our aid. What a team we all make.'

Bella gave me a wink, and then her face darkened as she saw Chris, who was being held by Phil. 'Enjoy Jordanian jail,' she said as the police entered the tent behind her.

* * *

It took four hours for Phil to explain to his counterparts in the Jordanian police that Bella, Carole and I weren't involved in any wrongdoing. Bella shoved Chris at an armed policeman as they stormed in . . . It made me think that if Luke had really wanted a worthy successor, he should have interviewed Bella for the role.

Everyone around the table that afternoon was arrested and taken to Amman.

Patricia and Tony had huge amounts of information on Luke's business operations – private shell company after shell company specializing in logistics. I asked the policeman assigned to us to check the email Sky had sent as we entered Petra. It contained a photograph of a photograph, but when we zoomed in it was clear we had even more information on the UK operation of The Collector's business – and it all led back to Chris. Patricia made a deal after being reminded that the death of her nephew Ben Wells was a direct consequence of Luke's test and Chris's need to sway the odds in his favour.

In the wake of the new information from Patricia and Tony, Interpol and the FBI set up a new investigation into each and every case on file relating to The Collector. And Sloane Clarke – the agent who had dared to mention the existence of The Collector all those months ago – was assigned to the case. She started with compiling the case against Chris for

Laura's murder and had her remains sent back to her family in Australia. Her first success was getting Chris to give up the location of Luke's home in Oxfordshire. The Scotland Yard Art and Antiques Unit, along with other international agencies, raided the house and recovered, among many items, the First Folio of Shakespeare's plays that Phil and Sloane suspected The Collector of stealing in New York.

Phil took some well-earned holiday, and Bella . . . well, Bella, I had no doubt, would show up at some point and demand to see the third journal.

Chapter Fifty

One week later, Crockleford Antiques Shop

An ice-cold November breeze seeped in through the cracks in the shop window. We all had our coats on while the central heating struggled against the winter chill. Carole had supervised Phil as he gathered armchairs and placed them in a semicircle around the table in the arched front window. Two were currently occupied by Carole and Sky. Carole poured the tea.

I stood in front of the painting of the burning ship, which was on an easel by Arthur's old desk. Phil came to stand next to me. 'Betty wanted it to stay with us until the Lowestoft Maritime Museum reopened in the spring,' I said. She was now under the impression that because it was the only item stolen, it had to be the most valuable piece in the museum's collection. It couldn't be left in the museum over winter, and it should be guarded around the clock. I was happy to oblige. I liked having the painting with us – it made me feel like Arthur was with us still.

Without taking my eyes from the painting I said to Phil, 'Arthur wrote under a photo of this painting, "What fire does not destroy, it hardens." It's from *The Picture of Dorian Gray*. Do you think he was trying to tell us something?'

He shrugged. 'Maybe he always knew your strength, even when you didn't see it yourself.'

I looked up at him. 'Fire has marked both our pasts, and Arthur used that to send us a message. You have justice for your partner now . . .'

'I do. And you have successfully solved your very first case.' I sensed he wanted to say more, but it didn't come.

We stared at the painting in silence.

Thank you, Arthur.

'If Arthur could see us all now, he would be utterly thrilled.' Carole walked over and linked her arms through both of ours, and she studied the painting. 'I'm so very proud of you. He would be so proud of you both, although I'm still a little confused as to why Arthur stored a priceless vase in my old trunk.'

When we had arrived home, I headed straight for Carole's trunk in the spare room. Inside was the Ming Dynasty vase. Next to it was the file Arthur and I had received from the insurance company over twenty years ago with all the details they had on the vase stolen from the Greek museum. It was all we needed to make sure that it was returned to the right people.

'And Betty was thrilled when you called to say we had the painting.'

Phil looked over at me, and I said, 'This painting was a clue, but it only led to the painter and the photo of the trunk. Perhaps Arthur had stored the vase in the museum for the past twenty years, but when he realized Chris might find it there, I think he moved it and left the clue in the museum.'

Carole led us to the chairs by the window and we all settled down.

Phil picked up the second journal and placed it on his lap. I had no idea if Arthur would have approved of me sharing the information inside. But I saw now that legacy had to be what we made it and not what we thought it *should* be. I didn't want to carry Arthur's legacy on my own . . . it was too great a weight. Others needed to be trusted with the truth if I was ever going to find every item Arthur had catalogued.

Only time would tell if I was right.

Beyond the window, a woman battled against the wind, the pompom on her bobble hat bouncing as she ran. The shop door crashed open and Bella closed it behind her.

I beamed at seeing her again.

'Celebrating without me. That's charming, isn't it?' She studied the table. 'Is tea the best you can do?' She pulled out a bottle of champagne from her bag. 'This is more like it.'

'You vanished after we were released. We wanted celebratory cocktails. But . . .'

'Didn't want to stay around in case the police changed their minds.' Her eyes fixed on the journal in Phil's lap. 'I think you'll find that's mine.' She glared at me. 'We had a deal, and you gave it to lover boy?'

I couldn't help the laugh that burst out of me as Phil reddened. 'Bella, you know he's not that, and that's not the journal you wanted.'

Bella shrugged. 'How many are there?'

I didn't answer her – I was dealing in selective truths now. The third journal sat on Arthur's old partners desk. Bella didn't need to know about the other three that were well hidden in the shop.

I rose and collected the third journal.

'She shouldn't have that,' said Phil.

'Well, *she* does have it.' Bella glared at him and then returned her gaze to the journal. 'There's a list here of antiques and antiquities stashed in Scotland somewhere. Arthur doesn't identify it, but the clues he's included point to one of four locations. I need to find out which it is.'

'We,' I reminded her.

'Fine, *we*. Let's drink.'

I'd taken a few steps towards the kitchen to get some glasses when I turned back and saw it. The smiles they shared, the sense of common purpose. By trusting Phil, Bella and Sky with the secret of Arthur's journals, I had gained so much. Our combined knowledge and skills would take the Lockwood Agency to a whole new level.

This wasn't what I had expected before the cruise. Then, I had wanted to do it all on my own, to prove myself. But I didn't want that anymore, and I hoped Arthur wouldn't have wanted it for me either. Working undercover for so long, he'd had no choice but to keep most people at bay, so as to protect them. But I had a chance to do it differently . . . to set up a new agency in a new way.

I opened the cabinet and reached for the glass flutes. Phil followed me and stood leaning against the door frame. 'Shall we have that talk now?'

I met his gaze. 'What's there to talk about?'

'I would like you . . . your agency to become a consultant for the FBI.' It wasn't what I'd expected.

'A paid consultant?'

He hummed. 'We don't normally ask consultants to work for free . . . but if you're offering . . .'

'No! I mean yes, I would love to be a consultant, of course I would!'

'Then I'll start the paperwork.' He leaned forward. 'I'll need to see *all* the journals.'

'What other ones?'

Phil left the kitchen, shaking his head, but his face was lit by a smile.

We spent the rest of the afternoon passing the journal between us, mulling over possibilities. Listening to Carole's stories about happy times spent with Arthur in one or two Scottish castles back in the day. And going into great depth about a laird she'd dated in the eighties. It was then, right at that moment, surrounded by these people I had trusted with the truth about the journals, that I knew I was on the brink of something life-changing. All I had to do was stop doubting myself, have faith in my own instincts, and go wherever they led me.

The antiques underworld had no idea what was coming to take it down.

Acknowledgements

This book was written in an emotional whirlwind of a year. The utter joy watching my debut fly into the world, meeting readers at events and making so many new bookish friends online and in real life has all been a dream come true, but I've also had to deal with the devastation of losing my mother. I had always expected to write these books with her by my side and it has been hard to come to terms with the alternative. Those two extremes made this book a struggle to write, and it would not be in your hands today without the help and encouragement of people mentioned below.

To my editors Francesca Pathak at Pan Macmillan, Kaitlin Olson at Atria and Adrienne Kerr at Simon and Schuster Canada thank you ever so much for everything over the past year. It is always said that it takes a village to publish a book, but this book would not be here without your exceptional editorial skills, and I have so appreciated all your hard work to get this book over the line on time.

Over the past year I've had the pleasure of working with some brilliant publishing teams who have helped my book fly. Thanks to Lucy Hale, Christine Jones, Stuart Dwyer, Claire Evans, Leanne Williams, Alex Coward, Becca Souster, Laura Marlow, Becky Lushey, Josie Turner, Laura Sherlock, Grace

Rhodes, Emma Harrow, James Annal – for yet another brilliant cover design – Emily Sumner and the wider team at Pan Macmillan. And thanks to Gena Lanzi, Dayna Johnson, Morgan Pager and Ifeoma Anyoku at Atria. Mackenzie Croft and Cayley Pimental at Simon and Schuster Canada.

As always, I'm hugely grateful to my agent, Hannah Todd – she was the very first to believe in me and this series and it wouldn't have seen the success it has without her guidance, also Elinor Davies and Valentina Paulmichl at Madeleine Milburn Literary Agency, and the wider team at the agency.

The writing journey can be a lonely one and therefore finding your writing team is some of the best advice I can give to pre-published writers. Here are some of those that I have befriended along the way and I'm so grateful for their support, encouragement and sage advice . . . Ali Clack, Tania Tay, Annette Caseley, K. C. Collinson, Catherine Whitmore, Kate Poels, Annaliese Avery, Karen Ball, Karen Minto, Alison Penny, Lui Sit and the Totleigh Bees writing group, Tricia Gilby, Katy Hays, Jessa Maxwell, Veronica Henry, Sophia Bennett, Katy Watson, Ellory Lloyd, Eve Chase, Lucie Whitehouse, Celeste Connally, Hannah Brennan, Jessica Bull, Kristin Perrin, Orlando Murrin, Alex Hay.

To my husband, Billy, and my children, Aria and Leo, thank you for your everlasting belief in me and my writing. I could never have done any of this without you. To Clare Flaxen, Katy Hayward, Kat Taylor, Liz Kurr and my siblings, Samantha, Tanya, Tasha, Kirsty and Tom, and my stepfather, John Wainwright, and Frances Howard-Brown for making all your friends buy the book!

To Olga Cree who has painted the best watercolours of both of my books which have turned into bookmarks and posters – thank you for all your creative magic.

To the book bloggers and book influencers who have supported my book. Please know that I have loved chatting to you all online and at events and thank you so much for all your encouragement. My book would not have found its way into the hands of so many readers without you all.

A special thanks to the librarians, booksellers and book festivals in East Anglia who have gone above and beyond to support this local author. Andrew at Dial Lane Books in Ipswich, Kate at Harris and Harris, Jo at Red Lion and all my local Waterstones booksellers – especially Grace in Sudbury, Jem in Ipswich, Alison in Lowestoft and Clive in Colchester, who have all been so very welcoming and supportive with events and signings. I'm ever so grateful to you all.

And of course, to you, dear reader, thank you for reading.

You can find out more about me and the books at www.clmiller author.com.

Cara x

Get ready to join Freya and Aunt Carole
as they embark on a race against time in the
haunting Scottish countryside . . .

THE ANTIQUE HUNTER'S:
MURDER IN THE CASTLE

Coming 2026